The Great Grave Robbery

BOOKS BY JOHN MINAHAN

A Sudden Silence
The Passing Strange
The Dream Collector
Jeremy
Sorcerer
Nine/Thirty/Fifty-five
Almost Summer
Nunzio
Complete American Graffiti
Eyewitness
The Great Hotel Robbery
The Great Diamond Robbery
Mask
The Face Behind the Mask
The Great Pyramid Robbery
The Great Harvard Robbery
The Great Grave Robbery

TRANSLATION
The Fabulous Onassis

The
Great
Grave
Robbery

John Minahan

W·W·Norton & Company
New York·London

The text of this book is composed in Times Roman, with display type set in Trump
Bold. Composition and manufacturing by The Haddon Craftsmen, Inc.

First Edition

Grateful acknowledgement is made to *People Weekly* for permission to reprint the
article "A Clinically Doggone Beagle, Medical Miracle Miles Is a Former Chilly
Dog Back from the Beyond" (issue of April 20, 1987), copyright © 1987 by Time
Inc.

Library of Congress Cataloging-in-Publication Data
Minahan, John.
The great grave robbery / John Minahan.
p. cm.
I. Title.
PS3563.I4616G685 1989
813'.54—dc19   89-3188

ISBN 0-393-02721-X

W. W. Norton & Company, Inc., 500 Fifth Avenue, New York, N. Y. 10110
W. W. Norton & Company Ltd., 37 Great Russell Street, London WC1B 3NU

1 2 3 4 5 6 7 8 9 0

Acknowledgments

I want to express my appreciation for the
technical advice of Robert M. Cavallo, John F.
Adams, Dr. Stephen A. Samson, Pan American
World Airways, the Trinidad & Tobago Tourist
Board, the New York Police Department, and
the Port-of-Spain Police Department. A special
note of gratitude goes to my longtime friend
R. C. W. Ettinger, founder of the cryonics
movement and president of the Cryonics
Institute and the Immortalist Society, both
headquartered in Oak Park, Michigan, who read
the galleys, enjoyed the story, but wants to assure
the general public that although some of the
background is based on fact, most of it, including
the cryonics history and present organizations,
has been fictionalized.

J.M.

The greatest minds are capable of the greatest vices as well as of the greatest virtues.

RENÉ DESCARTES
1596–1650

The Great Grave Robbery

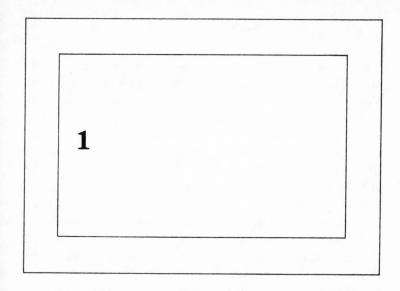

1

BEFORE THE MEETING, Tuesday morning, January 12, 1988, I'm sitting at the conference table in Chief Vadney's office when he slides a thick paperback copy of the *Guinness Book of World Records* toward me, tells me to turn to page 391. I flip to that page, it's a listing of the greatest robberies of all time under various categories. Now he tells me to read the one under the heading "Industrial Espionage."

The greatest robbery on record attributed to industrial espionage occurred on August 26, 1966, when the International Cryogenics Corporation, NYC, reported the theft of classified documents and 36 vials of microorganisms representing 12 years of research and development and valued at $24-million. No one was ever arrested for the crime and none of the documents or vials were ever recovered.

I look up, Chief leans across the conference table, swipes at the cowlick over his forehead. Visualize John Wayne in his late fifties playing a hard-boiled old coot who's just had some good news. Flattens his forehead, knits one brow, arches the other, ears jut back just an instant before he gives in to an all-out left-sided molar-shower. Got that? Okay, now you got Vadney nailed, that's him, boom, case closed. I mean, it's spooky but true, that's why we call him the Duke. Plus, he's built like Duke Wayne was, six-three, about 175, bowlegged, raw-boned, neck like a bull, collar always open, tie yanked down at an angle, sleeves rolled to the elbows. So, if you were a John Wayne fan like I was, it's a pleasure doing business with this geek, brings back memories of childhood, Saturday afternoon movies, sucking on one of those long black licorice sticks they used to sell for a nickel, remember those? Sitting there, wide-eyed, not a worry in the world, you knew the good guys from the bad guys and you knew the good guys would beat the living crap out of the bad guys in the end, what's to worry? That's the feeling you get working with Vadney. Forty years have passed, the world's gone completely wacko-sicko, the bad guys are beating the living crap out of the good guys, but he doesn't know it yet. Refreshing change of pace, sometimes it's hard to keep a straight face, the man's Looney Tunes all the way, but he's not just an empty suit, he gives you your money's worth, you take one look at him, it's like sucking a licorice stick. Me, I love every minute, but what do I know?

"August, nineteen-sixty-six," he says. "Remember that case, Little John?"

"Remember reading about it."

"Remember where you were when it happened?"

"Where? Yeah. Brooklyn South, Robbery Squad."

"Brooklyn South. How old were you back then?"

"How old? Let's see. Thirty-three."

"Just a kid. How old're you now?"

"Now? Fifty-four."

"Fifty-four. How many years on the job?"

"Thirty-two."

"Thirty-two. How many times you work with me?"

"You? Five times."

He nods, sits back, glances off into space. "That's right. And I remember 'em all, buddy-boy, remember 'em clearly. The big hotel case, the diamond case, the rape-murder case, the pyramid case over in Egypt, then that weird Gutenberg Bible caper up at Harvard in 'eighty-six. Know why I remember 'em so clearly?"

"No, sir."

"Sam."

"Oh?"

"Sam. My wife, Samantha."

"Ah."

"You met her in Cambridge two years ago."

"Yes, sir. Lovely lady."

"Looks like a bloodhound, but she's smart as hell."

Silence. I elect not to touch that line.

Chief keeps staring off into space, smiles, glances at me. "I used to think all women were dogs, but I was wrong."

"Yeah?"

"Yeah. They're not that *loyal*!" Forehead flattens, ears jerk back, left-side molars spew sneeze-like sputters of spray.

Me, I'm laughing too. Not at the joke.

"They're not that—*haaaah*!" He can't get it out. "*Ya*! Ya-ha! *Ya*!-ha-ha! *Ya*!-ha-ha-ha!" Sounds to that effect, but at least the showers have stopped. Now his eyes are watering, he wipes 'em with his big mitts. "Sorry, Little John, just heard that one yesterday. Totaled me, knocked me out. Now, where was I?"

"I'm not—really sure."

"Oh, yeah, those five cases. Why I remember those five cases so clearly, they were all biggies, of course, they all got a ton of publicity, so Sam, she ups and starts a *scrapbook*. Yeah. When I cracked the big hotel robbery in 'eighty-one, Champs-Elysées Hotel, three-point-four million, first she grabs all the New York papers, then she trots down to Hotaling's—Hotaling News down on West Forty-second—y'know, that out-of-city, out-of-country newspaper place? She scoots down there, she thumbs through every major newspaper in the country, Boston to Los Angeles, Chicago to Miami, plus all the news-magazines and that, she comes home with a Macy's shopping bag crammed with all this stuff. Next, she goes and buys a scrapbook, okay?, not a conventional paste-in scrapbook, but an expensive Hallmark photo album, fifteen bucks. Y'know, with these big pages that you peel back the plastic sheet, seals everything airtight? So, with that one case alone, she fills up thirty-two pages, front and back side, she has to get packets of refill pages and all. Plus, that's not all. Plus, starting the night I cracked that case, she starts a VHS library, she tapes every news show she can find, local and national, regular and cable. Including—months later, of course—including that fifteen-minute segment on 'Sixty Minutes' with Mike Wallace. Re-member that, buddy? Remember how Mike interviewed me right in the car and all, driving to the hotel to collar the perp there, the murderess, what was her name again?"

"Nancy Kramer."

"That's right. Looked like Elizabeth Taylor, remember that?"

"How could I forget? Talk of the department."

"I know. We hit the mass-media jackpot on that one. So, to make a long story short, Sam does the same deal on the other four cases. Now we got *five* full photo albums of clippings, five thick Hallmark albums, all neat and clean, the logo of each paper over each story, a total of—I think it's a total of a hun-dred and sixty-two pages now, counting the front and back sides. Takes hours to read 'em all. Plus five VHS tapes, not all filled up, of course, but there must be twelve, fifteen news segments on each tape, including interviews, parts of press conferences, all like that. I mean, we're talking a full night's entertainment here, right in the privacy of our own living room, not that we watch 'em all that often. So, anyhow, to answer your question, that's how come I remember all five cases so clearly."

"Good way to do it."

"Your wife do anything like that? What's her name again?"

"Cindy. No, but my name was never mentioned in connection with any of those cases."

"Oh, that's right, I forgot that. You worked undercover on those operations, we had to keep you out of sight. But make no mistake, Little John, I know the key role you played in all of 'em. Matter of fact, the truth is, I doubt if I could've cracked any of 'em without you, without your undercover expertise."

"I appreciate your saying so, Chief, but—"

"Not at all."

"—in fairness, I think it was always a team effort."

"A team effort?"

"More or less, yeah."

"Bullshit."

"No, that's—how about Louie Diaz in 'eighty-six?"

"Who?"

"Lieutenant Louis Diaz."

"Name sounds familiar."

"Commanding officer of the forensic unit."

"Oh, yeah, Diaz."

"He had a lot to do with the Harvard thing, he actually came up with a positive ID on the guy."

Chief sits forward, clears his throat. "That's true, he did. I forgot that. Well, but he wasn't up there, he was working in New York. Don't be so modest, Little John, ya gotta learn to accept credit when credit is due. Now, let's get down to business here, let's call a spade a spade here, buddy, cards on the table. You ever so much as *dream* of working a case that's so big it actually made the *Guinness Book of World Records*?"

"No, sir."

"Twenty-four million dollars back in nineteen-sixty-six,

that's probably worth—at least four times that amount today, maybe more. So we're talking in the neighborhood of one hundred million dollars here. Ever dream of working a case *that* big?"

"No, sir. Is that what this meeting's—?"

"That's what this meeting's gonna be about."

"Holy shit."

"You're on special assignment, effective immediately, relieved of all precinct duty. I'll call Lieutenant Barnett after the meeting, tell him what's happening." He swivels around, opens a drawer in his teakwood cabinet, pulls out a fat file folder, swivels back, flips it open. Conference table is actually his "desk"; he sits at one end.

I take out my notebook and pen. Tell you what, I'm tickled to be on special assignment, always get a kick out of this kind of duty. Also, it gets me away from the shithole of a temporary precinct we're in up on East Ninety-fourth. Real dump. Nineteenth Precinct's historic old station house, 153 East Sixty-seventh, that's being gutted and renovated, won't be finished until sometime next year.

Chief's all serious now, studying the file. "Let me get you up to speed here before the others arrive. Naturally, I was involved in the initial investigation, I'd been chief since 'sixty-two, so I was very heavily involved for the better part of a year. We came up empty, but the case was never closed. Here's a fast rundown. Take notes. First, there was never a question—according to Dr. Stegmueller, that's Carl S-t-e-g-m-u-e-l-l-e-r, he's president of ICC, International Cryogenics Corporation, he'll be at the meeting—according to him, there was never any question about who stole the classified documents and vials of microorganisms, because only one scientist had the level of security clearance necessary for simultaneous access to all the material. That man was Dr. James Mailer, M-a-i-l-e-r, head of the company's Chemical Research Division. He joined the firm in nineteen-forty-nine, was appointed supervisor of the division in nineteen-fifty-four, and directed the top-secret project from beginning to end, twelve years of research and development. Okay, now, when Mailer was writing the final report in the summer of nineteen-sixty-six, he disappeared with all the critical documents and vials. Now, here's one of the strange things about all this, Little John, listen up. Our initial investigation concluded that it was a case of industrial espionage, okay? A realistic assumption at the time. But twenty-two years have passed. And, to the best of anyone's knowledge—no, I mean to the best of Dr. Stegmueller's knowledge, because he's the only one who would know this—to the best of his knowledge, no firm in the industry, here or abroad, has ever made *use* of the stolen secrets. Okay, am I going—am I talking too fast for you?"

"No, sir. That's interesting. So why were they stolen?"

"That's a good—"

Chief's telephone console buzzes. Voice of Doris Banks, his Tiffany-type administrative assistant: "Dr. Stegmueller and his group from BCI have arrived."

"Show 'em in, please."

"So why were they stolen?" I ask again.

"Good question, Little John." He gets up, buttons his collar, pulls his tie up, goes to the door. "Ask Stegmueller himself."

Door swings open, Doris appears, blond hair in a stylish coif, size six figure poured luxuriously into a banker's-gray designer outfit. "Dr. Stegmueller and his associates."

Chief shakes hands all around, Stegmueller first, then the four men and two women, apparently he knows them all. Now he ushers them over, introduces me, I shake hands. Okay, I got to be honest about this right from the beginning, I can't fake it. Dr. Stegmueller, he's a tall, distinguished, white-haired old gent, mid-seventies, but you look at his face, the first impression you get, this guy's got the hawklike eyes and beak of Vincent Price. Yeah. This is straight, this is no shit. Even sounds like him, rich resonance, perfect diction, slight British accent on certain words: "Detective Rawlings, what a pleasure to meet you, sir, we've all heard a great deal about your accomplishments." Hawk eyes sparkle, thin lips smile warmly, gives me a two-hand shake. Vincent Price in *The House of Wax*. Remember that? Swear to God, that's him, that's a wrap on this guy. Sends a jagged icicle up my asshole.

Ladies and gentlemen from BCI seem like a clean-cut group, early to mid-fifties, strong handshakes, soft voices: Ed Young, Ann Blackall, Dick Gorman, Barbara Pakenham, Dave Essex, Frank Vadney. Frank Vadney? That's what the man said. Now, BCI, all I know about BCI, it stands for Bethlehem Central Investigations, private agency headquartered upstate, specialists in industrial espionage. That's their bag, that's all they do; they've been working this case, on and off, for twenty-one years now.

We all take seats around the conference table; seats twelve, we got nine. Stegmueller's at the far end facing the Chief, I'm in the middle, flanked by Barbara Pakenham and Dick Gorman; across the table, left to right, Dave Essex, Ann Blackall, Ed Young, Frank Vadney. Take a closer look at Frank Vadney. Vague resemblance to the Chief, but the glasses make him look a lot brighter. Distant relative? Could be, it's not that common a name. Have to check it out. They've all got fat file folders like the Chief's, they flip them open now.

Chief clears his throat, clasps his hands on the table. "I briefed Rawlings here on the basics. Carl, you want to lead it off?"

Dr. Stegmueller nods, smiles warmly. "Thank you, Walter. Detective Rawlings, sir, may I take it that you're familiar with the specialist operations of BCI?"

"Yes, sir."

"It's a relatively small but well-established firm, headquartered in Delmar, New York—that's a suburb of Albany—with offices in Boston, New York, Detroit, and Los Angeles. And, of course, it's one of the very few investigative agencies in the country that deal exclusively with industrial theft. They've been in the business for some thirty-five years now. Those facts, coupled with the firm's reputation for never closing the books on a case until it's solved, are why I selected them initially and why we've continued to work with them for such a long time. Now, Walter indicated that he'd briefed you on the basics of the case. May I take it that you understand the specific scientific nature of what was stolen?"

I hesitate, shrug. "No, sir. Just that it was classified intelligence dealing with twelve years of research and development, plus thirty-six vials of microorganisms."

"Do you understand cryogenics?"

"No, sir. Just that it has something to do with freezing."

"That's correct," he says. "It's the branch of physics that relates to the production and effects of very low temperatures. Naturally, it's important that you learn more about it—and about ICC—so we'll have some homework for you. But for the present, I'll let Ed Young explain what his firm discovered—quite recently, in fact. Ed is president of BCI. Ed, please."

Ed Young, I'd guess him to be about fifty-two, full head of dark hair graying at the temples, strong chin, athletic build, he looks me straight in the eye, doesn't even glance at his file. "Within the past two weeks we've acquired new intelligence that might possibly lead to the whereabouts of Dr. Mailer. An investigator in our Boston office learned that Mailer began suffering from coronary heart disease in nineteen-sixty-five, at age fifty-three, and started confidential treatment with a Boston cardiologist that year. According to our investigator, Mailer traveled from Boston to Oak Park, Michigan, in the summer of nineteen-sixty-six to visit an old friend, Professor Robert Erickson, a longtime consultant to ICC." He removes a slim hardcover book from his file folder, slides it across the table to me. "Erickson is the author of this book, published in nineteen-sixty-four, that's generally credited with launching the so-called cryonics movement in this country and abroad. Have you heard of it?"

I pick up the book, glance at the title: *The Prospect of Life Extension.* To the right of the title is an almost obscured young face seen behind a white sheet of ice crystals. "No, sir, I can't say I've heard of it."

"I'm not surprised," Young says. "But when it was published, it caused a minor sensation in the scientific community and was the genesis for the formation of the Cryonics Societies of America, as well as the societies of England, France, Germany, Japan, and others. Most of those organizations are gone now, but the basic premise of the book is still quite valid. Ann, you want to explain it—briefly? Ann's husband is a physician, he's made an independent study of the subject."

Ann Blackall, she's a slim, attractive lady, short brunette hair, easy smile. "Well, in layman's terms, it's easy to understand. The essence of Erickson's central thesis merely joins one scientific fact to one logical assumption. Fact: At liquid nitrogen temperature, three hundred twenty degrees below zero Fahrenheit, practically all molecular activity ceases, so that it's possible to preserve the clinically dead right now, today, with virtually no deterioration, indefinitely. Assumption: Based on the scientific revolution of just the past thirty years, it's logical, even quite predictable, that medical science should eventually—stress *eventually*—be able to cure almost any disease that's incurable today and repair almost any damage to the human body, including freezing damage and senile debility or other cause of death. In other words, no matter what kills you, disease, heart failure, old age, whatever, and even if freezing techniques are still relatively crude when you die, the probability is extremely high that at some time in the future scientists will have discovered methods of reviving and curing you."

"Unless you're flattened by a steamroller," the Chief adds.

Blackall smiles briefly. "Yes. Whatever condition the body is in at death, it remains unchanged indefinitely in liquid nitrogen. There's almost no cellular deterioration whatsoever."

Frank Vadney takes over now, big, strong, healthy-looking guy, trim hair graying at the temples, tortoiseshell glasses, deep voice, doesn't waste any words: "Detective Rawlings, less than three years after that book was published, the first human being was placed in cryonic suspension." He pulls a paper from his file, slides it over to me. "Here's the actual press release. It's short, take a minute to read it, it's important."

Press release is typed, double-spaced, written under the letterhead of the Cryonics Society of California. It's obviously a copy of a copy, dated January 13, 1967, legible, but I have to squint:

The first reported freezing of a human at death, under controlled conditions, occurred Thursday, January 12, 1967, in Los Angeles. A patient was frozen immediately after his death from cancer in the hope of eventual revival and rejuvenation by future techniques. The next of kin concurred in the patient's wishes.

Special freezing procedures were applied by Dr. Thomas J. Rice, a local physician, Dr. Erich C. Weber, Scientific Advisor to the Cryonics Society of California, and Dr. Dan R. Davis, President of the Cryonics Society of California. In consultation were Robert Erickson, author of The Prospect of Life Extension, the book that proposed the current LTA (low-temperature anabiosis) program, William Miller, attorney and President of the Cryonics Society of New York, and other members of the Cryonics Societies, coordinated by Dr. Davis.

When clinical death occurred, Dr. Rice was present and at once began artificial respiration and external heart massage, to keep the brain alive while cooling the patient with ice. Heparin was injected to prevent coagulation of the blood.

Later, the team of Dr. Weber, Dr. Davis, and William Miller perfused the body with a protective solution of DMSO (dimethyl sulfoxide), using a Westinghouse iron heart sent by the Cryonics Society of Michigan.

The patient is now frozen with dry ice, $-79°C.$, and will soon be stored in liquid nitrogen, $-196°C.$, when a Cryocapsule is supplied by Cryonics Equipment Corporation of Phoenix, Arizona. He will be kept frozen indefinitely until such time as medical science may be able to cure cancer, any freezing damage that may have occurred, and perhaps old age as well.

The patient's family has requested complete privacy; consequently, no personal questions will be answered.

All of those involved in the effort hope that this will lead to a massive biomedical effort on research into the prolongation of life.

Dick Gorman, sitting to my right, waits until I've finished reading, then clears his throat and turns to me. The lower halves of his glasses are rimless, giving him a scholarly, almost severe look, reminds me of a math teacher I had in high school, a guy I happened to like. "Now, let me try to put all this in perspective for you. During the last decade—and I'll go slowly, John, because this gets a bit complicated, but it's important that you understand exactly what was stolen. So please interrupt me if you have any questions. Okay, during the last decade or so, the cryonics movement in this country and abroad has virtually collapsed for a variety of reasons, most of which are not germane to this discussion. However, one of the major arguments against cryonics that's been advanced by the scientific community runs along these lines: Revival of people cryonically suspended with today's perfusates is *improbable.* Possible, granted, they're guarded about that, but improbable. They say—the scientists say—face the realities: All freezing techniques today result in the formation of ice crystals, and a certain amount of water to form the ice is drawn from *inside* the cells. When that water freezes, its dissolved *salts* are expelled, so the permeability of the cell membranes is altered. Therefore, the capillaries have to be damaged and many enzyme systems have to be ruined. If the long chains of electrically polarized blocks of molecules are allowed to *fold,* they will undoubtedly stick together and die after being revived. The idea of unfolding literally billions of these chains is just improbable. That's essentially the argument. Now, if a way could be found to *repair* that inevitable freezing damage, it would represent a scientific breakthrough of absolutely enormous significance. Do you follow me so far?"

I nod. "And I assume that a way was found."

"Exactly," Gorman says. "When Dr. Mailer became supervisor of ICC's large Chemical Research Division, his top priority was an extensive research project involving advanced experiments in low-temperature anabiosis and in creating artificially constructed *virus* particles to *repair* cells damaged by freezing techniques. The project required twelve years and cost ICC approximately twenty-four million dollars to complete."

I'm taking notes, of course, so the room falls silent for a while until I finish and glance up.

Next, Dave Essex decides it's his turn, tallest guy in the

group, lean, blond-gray hair receding. "Okay, now, here's the bottom line, John. There are two key elements in the theft, both virtually priceless today. One, Mailer's detailed documentation of the viability of the artificially constructed virus particles. Two, the actual virus samples themselves, contained in thirty-six vials, believed to be of a quantity more than sufficient to repair damaged cells in at least three cryonically suspended human beings."

I finish writing, then: "How many people have been frozen—cryonically suspended—since that first one in 'sixty-seven?"

"Barb?" Dave asks.

Barbara Pakenham leans forward, adjusts her glasses, she's on my immediate left. Bright-looking lady, penetrating eyes, dark hair slightly windblown over her forehead. "The most recent statistics we have are through last year, December, 'eighty-seven, for this country alone: Twenty documented cases of cryonically suspended individuals in the United States." She removes her glasses slowly, blinks several times, looks in my eyes. "Obviously, if the stolen documents and vials were recovered and used to successfully revive a single individual, it would constitute one of the greatest scientific discoveries of all time."

Dr. Stegmueller lets that statement sink in, nods his thanks to Pakenham, flicks his hawklike eyes to me. "Any questions?"

"Just a clarification," I say. "I'm sure the statute of limitations has long since expired. We can't arrest the man. Are you simply after restitution of the stolen property?"

"Exactly," Frank Vadney says. "The New York State statute of limitations for this type of grand larceny, called a Class C felony, is just five years. It's defined under article thirty-point-ten of the Criminal Procedure Law. Restitution can be demanded in a civil action. That's what we're after. If we can find the man."

"Detective Rawlings," Dr. Stegmueller says, "as I'm sure you can imagine only too well, over the past twenty-two years, a great number of people from BCI, as well as from your own department, have been directly involved in this investigation. Involved to such an extent, I might add, that they are known, and known personally, by virtually all of the leaders of the cryonics movement—or what's left of it—from coast to coast. Therefore, in order to pursue the new intelligence we've acquired about Dr. Mailer, BCI's recommendation to me, and to my board of directors, was quite simple and logical, and I've asked for Chief Vadney's cooperation. Specifically, we need an investigator who has had absolutely no connection with this case whatsoever, and an individual with extensive experience and expertise in undercover work. The consensus opinion favors an older individual to infiltrate the cryonics movement under the guise of wanting to make arrangements to purchase the equipment, insurance, and maintenance necessary for his personal cryonic suspension."

"And that's you, Little John," Chief says. "I volunteered your services. You're the perfect oddball to work with these wackos. As they say in the movement, 'Many are cold, but few are frozen!' "

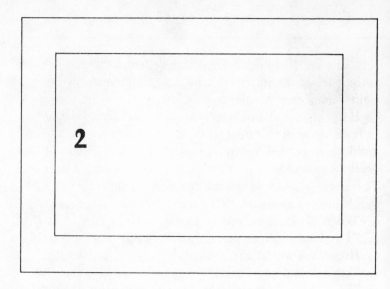

2

D E T R O I T   I S   R E C O V E R I N G from a heavy snowstorm when I arrive on Wednesday, January 27, and the early afternoon is like white dusk. Professor Erickson is supposed to meet me in the gate area at the airport, but I have trouble finding him in the big crowd. I thought I'd recognize him easily after seeing so many photographs over the past two weeks, doing research, but most of the men around the gate wear topcoats and hats, so it's difficult. After five minutes of looking at faces, I'm not even sure I can remember what he looks like. I'm about to check for messages when I hear my name paged. Off I go to the American Airlines ticket counter and Erickson's there, walking toward me tentatively, smiling, limping slightly, and wearing a heavy left shoe. He's taller than I expected, hatless, a bald semicircle making his forehead seem higher, thick black-rimmed glasses distorting his eyes. Although I'd read almost everything by and about him that BCI had given me, and our two letters had been long and at times quite personal, I have a feeling of anxiety as he approaches, looking scholarly, severe, despite the smile. He's retired now, professor *emeritus* of physics, but he's still quite active in the cryonics movement, particularly in the Immortalist Society and the Cryonics Institute.

He drives me to Stouffer's Northland Inn in Oak Park, only a few minutes from his home. It's still snowing lightly, and cold, and we try to keep a conversation going over the sound of the heater fan.

"You've got to leave tomorrow?" he asks.

"Right. Ed Cerabino's expecting me."

"Well, I envy you. Wish I could get away."

"They had snow in Flagstaff yesterday."

He nods. "Phoenix will be hot and dry."

"I just want to see the facilities."

"Well, I think you have to. I think you've got to get down there and see for yourself."

"And we have to work out the finances."

"Yes, right, get it all settled."

Stouffer's Northland Inn is a small, modern hotel, not very crowded this evening. I check in and go upstairs to clean up, and Bob waits for me in the lobby. The snow has just about stopped when we drive to his home, but the car is very cold again. Heater doesn't start to warm up until we're almost there.

The Ericksons live in a modest ranch-type house in Oak Park, with a carport and small front lawn. Bob introduces me to his wife, Mae, an attractive woman with short white hair and glasses; seems very warm and personable. I know from my research that she's also active in the movement, editor of *The Immortalist,* a monthly publication that's been going to members for nineteen years now. Must say, I enjoyed this month's issue; Mae's got a good sense of humor.

We have drinks in the living room and exchange small talk for a while. I want to make a good impression, so I lead off by asking Bob about the Scientific Advisory Council, the new group I'd been reading about.

He clears his throat softly, a habit he has before speaking

about anything of a serious nature—not a smoker's cough, he doesn't smoke—then sits back and crosses his left leg, revealing the high and heavy black shoe. "Well, we hope to have it operative by the time the next national conference gets going in April. A number of cryobiologists seem ready for it. If we could effect a significant split in their ranks, it might well be a giant step forward."

"What's its actual function?" I ask.

"It's complicated, but basically the Scientific Advisory Council could do this. It could be a link. It could make possible a closer association between the scientific community, especially cryobiologists, and the American Cryonics Society. And it could benefit both groups, greatly benefit both, as well as the general public. In the past, as everyone knows, there's been some reluctance on both sides. To put it mildly. Many cryobiologists misunderstood the premises and aims of cryonics. They had exaggerated fears of embarrassment. And I think—rather, I know—that some proponents of cryonics had insufficiently appreciated the urgency of accelerated research and the importance of academic ties. The situation is changing. Attitudes are changing. It's a gradual thing, I never had any illusions it wouldn't be. Several organizations stemming from the cryonics program have begun financial contributions to research in cryobiology."

"It's slow, but it's happening," Mae says softly in the pause. "Trans Time, a service arm of the American Cryonics Society, now has several physicians as active members. Part of the reason is improved communication, correct information, accurate. The confused ideas many people had are being corrected. But I think the most important reason, in my opinion anyway, is the increased number of freezings, twenty-one verified freezings."

"Twenty-one?" I ask. "I thought it was twenty."

"Twenty-one verified freezings as of this month," Bob says.

"The current literature hasn't mentioned that number."

"I know," he says. "I realize that. But let me clarify. When I say 'freezings,' I mean that twenty-one people have been perfused, placed in dry ice, and transferred to the capsules of liquid nitrogen they purchased. Two others were perfused and placed in dry ice, recently, while their families try to raise the necessary funds to purchase the permanent storage units, the capsules. Or at least raise the required downpayment and make arrangements to finance the balance. As you know, right now it's an expensive proposition if a person isn't covered by the life insurance plan suggested. What's your situation now with finances—any change?"

"I think there's a good possibility I can finance it through my bank. What does Ed Cerabino actually charge now, same thing?"

"I believe it's one-third down, still, but I understand he's working on a plan to reduce the entire cost. He's starting to get a little competition now, finally, which is a healthy thing."

"But he still has the best facilities?"

"As of now, yes, no question," Bob says. "The capsules themselves I'm talking about. Ed's firm is the first continuously active firm to manufacture cryonic suspension equipment since the inception of the idea. They've spent more time and money developing equipment; they were the first to place a human being in cryonic suspension. To my knowledge, Cryocapsules are still the only *available* permanent storage units."

Mae sips her drink, smiles. "But that's something else that's encouraging. The new companies, the new facilities coming along. They're getting the answers they needed. Last year the attorney general of Wisconsin issued the first formal statement of its kind on the subject. I don't know whether you read about it, he—"

"Yes," I say.

"—stated that nothing in—oh, you saw it—that nothing in Wisconsin law prohibits cryonic suspension, either expressly or by implication. It came about because the state health officer requested a formal statement; he'd received inquiries from attorneys representing Joe Kelleher, the man there who's making arrangements to be frozen."

"He's established a legal precedent," Bob says. "The Wisconsin facility is virtually complete now on a thirty-acre plot of rural area just north of Appleton."

"Isn't the Life Extension Society building one also?" I ask. "Near Washington, D.C.?"

He nods, anticipating. "Yes. Coming along quite well, too; they've had money problems, of course. It's been constructed little by little, quietly, over the years, whenever they've had some money. At the national conference of the American Cryonics Society—it's being held in San Francisco this year—there'll be papers presented on several new permanent storage facilities, including a large one near Los Angeles, a multiple storage facility. Of course, Ed's firm is still the largest—Cerabino has eighteen people in cryonic suspension now—but his firm is also the oldest and best known. Trans Time is second, with small storage facilities in a converted warehouse in Oakland. They have two men stored there now in a single capsule. Plus—I hesitate to mention this, but you probably know it already—plus two heads and one brain in another single capsule. It's a process called 'neuro-preservation,' and the general idea is that at some future time scientists will find a way to clone bodies for them. Personally, I don't count the two heads and one brain in the number I mentioned—twenty-one verified freezings."

"Are they all nonprofit companies?" I ask.

"Yes, except Ed's firm. There's still a kind of chicken-and-egg situation, the old cycle. Many firms who could provide cryonic services still aren't convinced that a large enough demand exists, but in the absence of a supply, prospective buyers have no adequate way to demonstrate demand. Also, the older cryogenics firms and the morticians and cemeterians are reluctant, predictably, to go ahead and take the initiative, to stick their necks out, without the formal blessing of a substantial number of scientists and physicians. But the point I was getting at is that despite all the new permanent storage facilities, buildings ready or under construction, Ed Cerabino still has the only available cryonic suspension *units* on the market, units that you can buy right now, today. That's the point. That's why I recommended you go down there and make arrangements."

"I understand."

He sips his drink, stares at the carpet. "We're very fortunate in your case, John. You've got a distinguished physician on your side, a specialist in chronic myelocytic leukemia. It's an ideal situation. Keep it that way. Cover yourself from every conceivable angle. You'll need to. Did your attorney complete the documents yet?"

I take the copies from my inside coat pocket, hand them to him. "They're based on the general forms suggested by the Cryonics Institute."

He glances at the Body Authorization. "I'd like to read these through after dinner."

"You've got about forty-five minutes," Mae tells him. "Why not show John the basement now instead of after dinner?"

He nods, stands up. "Well, if that's all right with you, John. This shouldn't take longer than half an hour, I'll show you my equipment, the essentials, anyway."

I follow him through the kitchen and down a narrow wooden stairway to the basement. In the largest area is a long table holding what looks like a man wrapped in a white sheet to the neck and wearing an oxygen mask. The table is surrounded by equipment. Bob switches on a set of strong lights directly above the table. The figure is a life-sized dummy and the table is white porcelain supported by a single thick leg. The dummy's head is in a circular pan filled with empty plastic bags and the pan has a semilunar notch for the neck. A dry-pump machine is near the head. But the machine that holds my attention most is a heart-lung apparatus with a piston arm resting on the dummy's chest. I follow Bob as he limps to that machine, squinting in the sudden brightness.

"This is a Westinghouse iron heart," he says softly. "It's less expensive than some on the market, but it does the job well. Actually, this is the one used in the first perfusion, Professor Bradley's. I sent it to the Cryonics Society of California, out to Dan Davis in Los Angeles. About a week before Professor Bradley died."

It's white, modern-looking, clamped to the table and holding a green oxygen tank upright. One tube extends from the tank to the trunk of the mask, another from the tank to the white double-bar piston arm reaching out over the dummy's chest; the arm holds a vertical cylinder with its rubber end touching the sheet over the dummy's heart area.

"Now, interrupt me if you have questions of any kind," Bob says. "Ideally, as soon as possible before clinical death is pronounced, the medical team fills the container around the head, this pan, with packs of crushed ice, just regular ice, to lower the brain temperature. The iron heart should be set up and ready to work at the instant of clinical death. It's a completely mobilized unit that can be operated by one person." He draws back the sheet by the dummy's upper arm. "It's mounted on a metal base about fourteen inches square which is placed under the back, you can see the edge of it here. This places the piston directly over the sternum, the breastbone. The piston is lowered onto the sternum so that it rests firmly, not tightly. You can secure it with the locking device, this. The piston is powered by compressed oxygen and provides automatic cardiac compression, no electricity is required. It presses down on the sternum for about a third of a second, one stroke per second, depressing the base of the sternum about an inch and a half to two inches. It has a force adjustable from twenty to about one hundred eighty pounds. What it's doing, it's squeezing the heart, squeezing it sixty times a minute, to keep oxygenated blood circulating. At the same time, oxygen is recovered by this tube"—he shows me—"and pumped to the lungs with this"—he holds up the other tube—"to feed the oxygen mask."

He turns on the machine. The big arm of the piston moves up and down, a fraction slower than I expected, its rubber end pushing back into the cylinder slightly as it hits, making a rhythmic hissing of air and hollow punching sounds against the dummy's chest.

"How long do you keep it up?" I ask.

"That depends. The purpose is to maintain circulation of oxygenated blood while you keep lowering the body temperature."

"By packing with ice."

"Right."

"Over the whole body now?"

"Yes, right, you're just a step ahead of me, John. As the body temperature decreases, the cells' demand for oxygen decreases. Protection of the brain is the major consideration. At this point I'd pack ice over the entire head and face, leaving room only at the neck for the incisions. At normal body temperature, the brain can be deprived of oxygen for only three to five minutes, usually. As you lower that temperature, the brain needs proportionately less and less oxygen. So as soon as possible we bring the body to a temperature of twelve degrees centigrade, at which time the brain no longer requires blood circulation. At fifteen degrees centigrade, human blood circulation has been completely stopped for as long as forty-five minutes, the amount of time necessary for heart surgery. And, despite this, heart patients rarely suffer any loss of memory upon revival. Basically, that completes the process before perfusion. Now there are two possibilities. You can move the patient to a mortuary for perfusion with an embalmer's pump or you can perfuse right at the place of death, providing you have the facilities. We have everything here we need."

He turns off the iron heart and steps over to the small green dry-pump machine near the dummy's head. It's on a rectangular metal platform and has three connected sections—a dynamo-shaped motor, a box-like speed control unit, and a cylindrical open-faced peristaltic pump with three rubber rollers. A clear plastic tube goes through the rollers and down into a container on the floor; its other end is connected to a yellow catheter taped to the right side of the dummy's neck. A second yellow catheter is taped to the left side of the neck and reaches up to an inverted bottle hanging from a slender pole near the table. Last, a clear plastic tube extends from the inverted bottle down to the machine.

"This is an Amtec dry pump with zero-max speed control," he says. "It's merely a peristaltic pump in which the fluid being pumped doesn't contact any part of the pump itself." He points to the tube set in the rollers. "A squeezing action is exerted by this set of rollers, causing the fluids to flow through without touching the mechanism. It has a capacity of up to five gallons per minute. The pump action is soft and eliminates fluid shear. In the perfusion process, the whole area has to be disinfected, naturally, the table has to be saturated, even the machine housing. It's a surgical operation, the medical team scrubs, wears scrubsuits and surgical gloves. And, of course, the instruments must be absolutely sterile."

"Do you have the instruments here?"

"Yes." He turns, walks out of the bright light to a table against the near wall, carries over a small aluminum instrument sterilizer, places it near the pump, and opens it. A paper with typewritten lists is on top of the instruments. He hands it to me. "I've sent a copy to your physician."

It's a list of the instruments and chemicals. I glance at it as he talks.

"The perfusion solution has to be isotonic to avoid damage

to the red blood cells. 'Isotonic' means, simply, that the solution must have the same osmotic pressure as the liquid inside. Salt and other chemicals in solution determine an osmotic pressure due to their ability to capture water. If the concentration, the percentage, of salt inside the red blood cells is higher than outside, the cells absorb water until they burst. So to avoid this, the liquid outside the cells must be isotonic. Otherwise, if the liquid outside is hypertonic—has too much salt—the cells lose water and wrinkle. Cells other than red blood cells have a more resistant membrane. So, in the case of open-circuit, it's preferable to inject hypertonic liquids. The cells will lose water and this will facilitate the penetration of the cryoprotective agents inside the cells. Incidentally, we'd been recommending a fifteen percent solution of dimethyl sulfoxide—DMSO—as the best available perfusate, but we've gone back to glycerol now because of the success of the Suda experiments in Japan."

"So you inject the isotonic solution first?"

"Yes. First the body is perfused with ice-chilled sterile Ringer's lactate solution to which sixty-four milligrams of heparin has been added for every liter used. Six liters of heparin–Ringer's lactate solution is used for every thirty pounds of body weight. So, a man about your weight, say about a hundred and thirty-five pounds, would be perfused with twenty-five liters of solution. You introduce the Ringer's solution into the right carotid artery, here, with the probe pointed toward the head, first. A drain tube from the right jugular vein, about here, allows for the withdrawal of the blood. The probe is then reversed, pointed toward the body. During all this time, of course, the iron heart is still functioning, permitting—through blood circulation—the transfer of heat from the core of the body to the skin. Both the pump and the iron heart are now working simultaneously. When the drainage flow from the vein changes color, it's the first sign of a completed cycle, the circulation of the solution."

"I know you're simplifying," I tell him, "but let me see if I understand. The physician has opened the right carotid artery and the right jugular vein. He pumps the perfusate into the artery, toward the brain first, then reverses the direction, toward the body. Blood is being drawn off through the vein. The perfusate is pushing the blood through and finally draining it off, replacing it."

"Correct," he says. "Next, the body is perfused in exactly the same way with a cooled solution of twenty percent *glycerol* in Ringer's lactate solution. First toward the head, then toward the body. For a person weighing, say, a hundred and fifty pounds, eight liters of Ringer's solution and two liters of glycerol would be used. Massaging and flexing of the extremities will help in the distribution of the perfusate and drainage. After that, the pump is turned off, the arterial and femoral tubes are withdrawn, and clamps are placed on both sides of the vascular incisions. Cotton pledgets saturated with the solution are placed directly into the incised areas. With me so far?"

I hesitate. "What about the lungs, the stomach—"

"You're ahead of me again," he says, smiling. He removes the dummy's oxygen mask, picks up a carotid injection tube, and places it near the neck. "Now, the iron heart is turned off. Both machines are off. The lungs and gastrointestinal tract must now be filled with the same second solution, the glycerol in Ringer's lactate. The arterial tube is inserted into the trachea and the pump is placed on steady flow at two to six pounds of pressure per square inch. After five minutes or less, a backwash will appear from the mouth, indicating the flooding of the lungs and respective organs. Last, the arterial tube is inserted into the mouth and the pump placed on steady flow again to fill up the stomach and intestines. The body is then enclosed in a plastic sheet with crushed ice—and again, remember that this is ordinary ice, nothing special about it—in contact with the skin. To facilitate crystallization. This will reduce the body temperature to twenty degrees below zero centigrade. Twenty-four hours should be sufficient to permit a slow formation of ice crystals—outside the cells, of course. Now, if you'll come over here . . ."

I follow him to a corner near the stairs. He leans over to open the lid of what looks like a simple, light-colored walnut casket with brass handles. Inside is a fitted top layer of thick pink insulation, which he removes, revealing the lid of a steel container, separated from the outside casket by walls of the same thick insulation. He removes the steel lid. The container is empty except for a quantity of carefully folded plastic and a long roll of some type of silvery film.

"This is the last step before permanent storage," he says. "After the twenty-four-hour period to allow for the ice crystal formation, the cryonics team removes the ice and plastic sheeting and encloses the patient first in this plastic covering." He hands it to me. "They zip him into it, then wrap him carefully in layers of aluminized Mylar polyester film." He picks up the roll, pulls out a few inches, holds it out for me to feel. "As you can see, it's extremely thin and strong, easily able to withstand liquid nitrogen temperature. So, as I say, the patient is wrapped carefully, then transferred to a cold storage shipping unit like this one. He's packed in dry ice inside the steel unit, reducing the body temperature to minus seventy-nine degrees centigrade. It's called a Ziegler case, just the standard mortuary transporting case, insulated against the wooden case by a four-inch layer of fiberglass on all sides. To minimize temperature change during transportation."

"And you ship immediately?"

"Just as soon as possible, yes." He walks a few steps to a small wooden bin built into the wall opposite the stairs. It looks something like a coal bin and it's filled almost to the top with thick brown bags of dry ice. The walls of the bin are insulated with white Styrofoam.

"Dry ice is quite cheap," he says. "It's merely solid carbon dioxide, costs about twenty-five cents a pound in quantities of fifty pounds or more. I keep two hundred pounds on hand. With insulation, I only need a replacement of about fifty pounds a week, often less. It offers no hazard of any kind if you handle it with gloves."

"So the next step is liquid nitrogen?"

"Yes, shipment to the permanent storage facility and transfer to the capsule of liquid nitrogen, which maintains the body at a constant temperature of minus one hundred ninety-six degrees centigrade. Ed will show you everything he has."

"What about the shipping requirements?"

He scrapes his shoe along the cement, squints down at it. "Yes, good question. Ordinarily, you're required to have the body embalmed before shipping and the coffin has to be hermetically sealed. But now there's an exception—in this country anyway—when you show proof that the body is being transported as a specimen for scientific research. Check that with Ed, make sure. And I'd suggest you confirm the requirements through the specific airline also. The Body Authorization should provide proof of scientific research intent."

I glance across the room at the dummy on the table, surrounded by equipment in the white light. It looks like an operating table. But there's no antiseptic hospital smell, just the peculiar odor of carbon dioxide from the bin.

"It's strange, you know," Bob says very quietly, leaning back against the bin. He gazes steadily at the table, adjusts his glasses. "Twenty years ago, there were solemn warnings about cryonics. From every side. It would lead to panic buying of freezers and wholesale swindles of the gullible. I recall how the press kept stressing this sort of nonsense. The rationale was deceptively simple: Self-preservation is the most powerful instinct in mankind, therefore the ill or elderly would grasp at any straw. But this kind of thinking is predictable from men who understand neither society nor themselves. Twenty years have passed and of course only twenty-one people have been frozen. The reasons are obvious to anyone who's taken even elementary psychology. The so-called survival instinct, when it involves foresight, is largely a myth in modern society. People will *not* go to any length to protect their lives—until the danger has some degree of immediacy. They just can't be bothered. They'd just rather not think about it. The forces that really motivate the average person are more basic and direct than the abstract eventuality of his or her own death. But if you cut through to the subconscious guts of the matter, the indefinite extension of human life frightens most people. The idea terrifies them."

I wait, then: "Why?"

He walks slowly to the switch near the table, turns off the bright overhead lights, then looks at the dummy, his back to me. The only light comes from the single bare bulb at the foot of the stairs. In the pause, we can hear Mae walking around in the kitchen.

"It's a complicated question, John," he says finally, very quietly. "There are no easy answers. Part of the reason may be that although we're largely the intellectual heirs of the Greeks, our moral heritage is Judeo-Christian, and in this tradition death is the fulfillment of life; death is the means of immortality, the final orientation. Any new idea to the contrary unsettles people, makes them nervous, even angry, because it disturbs the established order. It raises serious questions and demands serious introspection. We're a death-oriented society. We've got to become life-oriented. That will take a long time, obviously, but I believe it will happen. Cryonics is merely a stopgap measure, of course; the real key is in gerontology, in arresting and even reversing the aging process. And that will happen; there are experiments going on in gerontology today that already indicate a significant breakthrough. And when aging is arrested and reversed, it will require a psychological transition that will make today's transition to cryonics seem laughable. The reward will be on a scale so colossal as to stun the imagination. In the meantime, we struggle along with what we have. In a very real sense, we're just emerging from the scientific and technological dark ages. With all the usual people fighting it all the way for all the wrong reasons. The transition will be made in time. But today we have primitive realities to face. And so long as cryonic suspension is administered on a part-time, occasional basis, the method will continue to be primitive and the cost will be high."

"You think the method's that primitive?"

He turns to face me. "Quite primitive. Considering what's possible by today's technological standards. We're years behind where we could be if we had massive support."

"But you've made a beginning."

"Yes, we have. We've tried. We've taken the first difficult steps. We've listened to all the laughter, the ridicule and anger and insults that people seem so eager to offer us, and we've gone ahead. Maybe they're right, maybe it's a pipe dream. But we're going to dream the dream. Maybe we're fighting with weapons still far too crude to hope for such a victory. But we've *tried*. We've tried and we'll keep on trying, and others will try, and the world will never be the same."

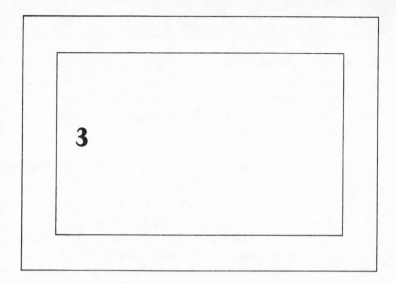

3

HALF-PAST NOON, Phoenix time, the flat geometrical patterns of farmland below look bleached and dead and the city sprawls bone-white and glaring. Temperature at Sky Harbor Airport is ninety-three. You aren't supposed to feel it so much because of the famous low humidity, but I feel it after Detroit. I rent a car, head north toward Scottsdale, and the sun throws a glaze ahead like water that keeps moving away. Palm fronds hang dry and limp and my tires whine on the straightaway and then squeal at turns like I'm speeding. But nobody's speeding and few people are out at this time of day unless they have to be.

I check into Mountain Shadows in Scottsdale about one-thirty, call Ed Cerabino right away, and within an hour I drive in to see him. He lives on West Indian School Road, a small one-story wooden frame house next to one of his wig shops. He's got a chain of shops like this in Phoenix, Tucson, and Kansas City, and, according to the research provided by BCI, he's been something of a pioneer in modern wigmaking. It's his major interest and he's been commissioned by the government to teach wigmaking to the Indians.

I pull into the dirt driveway between the shop and the house, wait for the dust to settle, then go to the screen door and knock.

"It's open."

In I go, takes a while for my eyes to adjust. Entire house seems to be just a large room without partitions. Small kitchen to the left, two long and cluttered desks placed at right angles in the center of the room. Big four-poster bed against the far wall. Cerabino, he's on his knees by a window, working on the air conditioner, a short, chunky guy, late forties. His neck seems too muscular for his face, bulging into the work shirt without much of a pause.

He glances at me, nods. "Be right with you, John, sit down."

"Troubles?"

Nods again, ear close to the air vent. Sound is changing gradually from a quiet flow to a strain. He switches the bottom knob now, listens. Same thing. "I'll be a son of a bitch."

"Tried kicking it?"

He smiles, shows the palms of his hands. "I'd shake hands with you, but . . ."

"Take your time."

"You checked in and all?"

"Right."

"I'll just be a minute."

"Anything I can do?"

"No." He unscrews the plastic front, removes it, studies the inside, switches the top knob, listens. His face is sweating. "I'm expecting a guy from CBC."

I squat near him. "What's CBC?"

"Canadian TV."

"Yeah?"

"Science show."

"Today?"

"Yeah. They won't bother you."

"What're they filming?"

"Just the facilities. You know."

"You going to be interviewed?"

"I don't know. I don't go in for that stuff, I'd rather they talked to the engineers. They got a front man supposed to be here this afternoon. The crew arrives tonight. They shoot tomorrow. Nothing to do with you. They won't bother you." He turns the knob to "air" and then to "cool," listens.

"I saw Bob Erickson on the way down."

"Yeah, you mentioned you would." He pulls the wire-mesh filter from the plastic front and holds it up to the light. It's thick with dust. Now he stands, takes it into the kitchen, runs the faucet hard. "Want a beer?"

"Love it."

A car pulls into the driveway; its door slams, then a second door. Screen door opens, slams, bounces, and a small blond woman walks in, attractive, mid-thirties, wearing a colorful print dress and sandals. She's German and has a slight accent. "Hello. I am Rita Cerabino."

"Oh, Mrs. Cerabino—I'm John Rawlings."

She shakes my hand. "Oh, you are from—? We had the letters from you."

"From Bellmore, Long Island."

"Yes, Bellmore. Where is that, Bellmore?"

Ed sticks his head out of the kitchen. "This is my wife, Rita. John Rawlings, honey."

"Yes, from Bellmore, I remember."

Telephone rings. As Rita goes to answer it, I notice a man standing in the dark hall near the door. Apparently, he came in behind her. He stands absolutely still, hands by his sides.

Rita puts the phone down. "Eddie—a Mr. D'Arcy."

"I'll take it." Ed walks out, hands me a can of Bud Light.

Rita immediately takes the can from me, then motions to

the man in the hall. "Mr. Bentley, come in please and sit. He'll be with you in only a minute." She takes my can into the kitchen.

Bentley walks into the room reluctantly, grinning, eyes averted, not knowing what to do with his hands. He's about Ed's age, wears a blue work shirt and overalls.

Ed hangs up. "Guy from CBC. On his way over."

"Frank Bentley," the man says.

"Yeah, right, let's see how it looks."

Bentley walks over slowly, touching his new hairpiece.

Ed adjusts it, whips out a stainless-steel comb, works on the part, then the front, turns the man around, combs the back, turns him around again. "Match couldn't be better, Frank. All we need now is to get you down to Charley Singer. How's it feel?"

"All right. Takes some getting used to."

Rita comes back with three glasses of beer on a tray.

"You want to come along?" Ed asks me.

"Where to?"

"Barbershop. We can talk on the way. Rita, stick those on ice, huh? We'll be about a half hour—tell D'Arcy, he'll be here any minute."

Rita shrugs, smiles at us, holding the tray.

Ed darts into the kitchen, comes back with the washed filter, replaces it in the plastic front, screws the front on the air conditioner. "Honey, call the service guy. Get him over here this afternoon, Watkins, I think, it's in the book. Tell him it's the motor again. Haven't shut the thing off in Christ knows." Telephone rings again. "I'm out. Get the name."

Singer's Barbershop is just a short drive west on Indian School Road, a small and narrow shop in a relatively large and modern shopping center. It's empty when we go in, just one barber on duty, which I assume to be Charley Singer, and Ed gives him instructions. Bentley sits in the chair nearest the window, barber's apron tucked around his neck, glancing at himself in the mirror, serious, uncomfortable. Singer trims the hairpiece slowly, carefully. Ed stands next to him, watching every move. Me, I'm having a ball, reading *Sports Illustrated*. August issue.

When we get back to the house, Jacques D'Arcy is waiting, a tall young French-Canadian, looking almost skinny in a double-breasted gray suit, holding a briefcase on his lap. Ed makes with the introductions and Rita goes for the beer. We sit around Ed's desk, littered with papers, coffee cups, plates, you name it.

Jacques takes off his rimless glasses and wipes his forehead with a handkerchief. "I am not used to such hot weather."

"Our air conditioner is on the fritz," Ed tells him.

"No, I mean outside."

"You guys don't know what hot is," Ed says. "In the summer here, we go to a hundred fifteen, twenty. It's always over a hundred in summer."

"How do you stand it?" Jacques asks.

Ed shrugs. "When's your crew arrive?"

"The seven-forty flight tonight."

"I've got your model on call for tomorrow."

"Oh, you hired the model."

"Right, professional model."

"What does he charge?"

"Her. She'll do it for union scale."

"We have a very limited budget, as you know."

"Well, AFTRA scale is two-fifty a day minimum."

"Yes, I know this."

"That's their minimum."

"We might have to use her for two days."

"Yeah, well, she'll only do it for scale, Jacques."

"You understand I'm just a liaison man for Mr. Dellacourt, the producer, he arrives tonight with the crew. He's the man you had the correspondence with. He hopes to be able to shoot tomorrow and possibly the next day, if needed. Is that possible?"

"Well, the deal is, we got the mortuary embalming room from nine to noon tomorrow, that's what I set up. I arranged for two of the morticians to work on camera with the model. Y'know, to go through the perfusion deal. They'll play the part of the doctors. We're renting the room there, Dellacourt knows about that. A hundred and fifty dollars for three hours. *Not* including the morticians, they get fifty bucks each on top of that. Which is dirt cheap."

"Yes, he explained this."

Rita comes back with the same three glasses of beer on the tray and passes them around. There's no head left, but it's nice and cold, goes down easy.

"After that," Ed continues, "the crew can go from there to the Cryotorium out in Tempe. That's just the temporary place I've got, they can shoot the exterior of the original Cryotorium on Washington Street. As I told him, I rented that to a machine-tool outfit just temporarily because we didn't have enough business to make it worthwhile. Then I sold it to them outright. I'm building a new one out near the airport. It'll look like the one on Washington, the outside will. So then they can shoot interiors with the capsules and all out in Tempe. I'll have my two engineers out there ready to be interviewed and all."

"Could we film there the following day if necessary?"

"Well, we agreed on a figure for the single afternoon."

"Yes, but I mean could we have your facilities for the extra day if necessary? We could arrange something extra, I'm certain."

"Oh, yeah, no problem then."

"Could we film Professor Bradley's capsule?"

"Certainly. We got eighteen of them out there now, as I told him. But they can't be moved around much. Plus we got the one brand-new demo, that's open and all, he wants to use the model in that one."

"Yes, right. So you have a total of eighteen in storage now?"

"Yeah, I told him. We got the other two late last year."

"I didn't realize that."

Ed jumps up, walks to the air conditioner, leans over, listens. "Rita? You call that service outfit?"

She leans out of the kitchen. "They did not answer. I'll try them again now."

"No, no, I'll do it." He goes to the phone book on the desk, looks up the number, dials.

"Are you just visiting?" Jacques asks me.

"Yes. I'm from New York."

"Have you seen the Grand Canyon?"

"No. First trip to Arizona. You have a series on CBC?"

"Yes, a science documentary series called 'Atome et Galaxies.' We have a half hour every week. At present we are doing a study dealing with man in the twenty-first century. Twelve programs."

"The possibilities?"

"Yes. Well, in the sense of reporting what is being done now, what is possible now, what is probable in the next twelve years or so, you see. The ideas that may be realities in the year two-thousand. So far we have examined the idea of creation of life in a laboratory, kidney and heart transplants, grafts of artificial organs, the artificial eye. On Sunday we leave for Houston—we are doing a program on the doctor who designed the heart pump?"

"Oh, yes, the artificial heart."

"Yes, that is next on the shooting schedule." He pauses, takes a long swallow of beer. "Here, our general theme is the new frontiers of death, clinical death and real death. The congelation of the human body. We hope to combine this with the discoveries now being made in gerontology, you know, the study of the aging process. So that we could perhaps approach the questions: Is death an absolute, is aging a biological necessity?"

"Sounds very exciting."

"But tell me, what do you think of this cryonics movement?"

"Very intriguing."

"Knowing Mr. Cerabino, you must be familiar with it."

"I'm learning."

"Have you seen the facilities in Tempe?"

"No."

Ed overhears that question as he hangs up. He motions to me behind Jacque's back, comes around the desk, glancing at his watch. "Well, look, I've held you two up long enough, I'll get you going now. Jacques, you all set, you checked in and all?"

"Yes, I'm in the Towne House."

"You got wheels?"

Jacques laughs. "Yes, I have wheels."

"Well, look, how about I'll meet you over there for a drink when your crew gets in? What time they due again?"

"The flight is due at seven-forty."

"Check, I'll come over there—what time would be good?"

"Oh, I don't know. Eight-thirty?"

"In the bar at the Towne House. You get a table."

"Splendid."

"Sorry to rush, but I've got to get John here going."

"No, no, I understand."

We say goodbye to Jacques and Ed drives me first to the building on East Washington Street that he'd constructed in 1965 and intended as a permanent storage facility. It's a long, low, rectangular structure of blending brick, no windows in the conventional sense, but three tall, arched, plate-glass doors in the center. It's handsomely landscaped.

"The new one will look something like this," he tells me. "Only a little smaller. Out near the airport."

He takes I-10 southeast past the airport, enters Tempe at Forty-eighth Street. Area here is still fairly open and industries are just moving in. We drive past long stretches of flat land broken now and again by small factories and homes. He turns right at Priest Road and left at Twenty-third Street into an isolated row of single-story connected office units called Palo Verde Complex 2. The units are low and identical, about twenty-five in all, looking something like a long warehouse of tan brick, each with individual roofed entrance platforms, and brick facades holding the company names.

Ed stops at the one reading CRYONICS EQUIPMENT CORP., about three-quarters of the way down the row. We get out and he opens the steel door, number sixteen, and switches on the lights. We walk into a small walnut-paneled room, simply furnished with a desk, a bookcase, and several chairs.

He turns on the air conditioner. "This is the office, the big room's over here." His footsteps sound hollow as he goes into the next room and turns on the lights.

It's a very large and clean area, white walls, cement floor, a long brown garage door at the far end. Most of the floor space is occupied by the eighteen capsules, six rows of three, all white, each one about nine feet long and three feet high, most of them resembling boilers on wheels, a vacuum pump and three gauges attached to the end of each. The pumps make soft whirring and clicking sounds.

Off to the right, separated from the others, is a white capsule that's more streamlined in design, obviously the newest model. The vessel itself is essentially the same size as the others, but has a steel cowl extending out in a clean continuous line from its end to house three gauges, shielding their mechanisms behind a semicircular pastel blue instrument panel.

"It's a quarter to five right now," Ed says. "I asked Tom and Ralph to be here after work. Shouldn't be too long, they're with an engineering outfit right at the airport. They're through at five."

"Your partners."

"Right. Ralph Richter and Tom Collier." He leans back against one of the capsules, folds his arms. "Just to give you a little background while we have time, they're both directors of the corporation. They handle the technical end of it, the scientific work, that's their part. I handle the financing, contacts, publicity, sales, all like that. That's the way it works out. They designed the capsules and supervised the construction, we've made twenty so far, tested and refined them. They handle the liquid nitrogen freezings right from the time the bodies arrive, straight through. I don't normally have much to do with that. I buy the materials, hire the welders, and so on. Ralph is a mechanical engineer, a graduate of MIT and RPI. He's working now as an aeronautical engineer. Tommy got both his degrees at MIT, he's a mechanical engineer with a cryogenic background. He's with the same firm here, he's an aeronautical engineer on his regular job. They're both relatively young men, both in their early forties. Up till now they haven't allowed their names to be used in the press, they wanted to stay in the background. Y'know? They didn't want their firm's name to be associated with any controversial publicity. They can't risk that, they both have families here. Tomorrow's an exception, it's a Canadian TV deal, it won't be shown in the States."

I can't keep my eyes off the capsules. "Could you tell me something about these people? I know about Professor Bradley, but not much about the others."

He walks around to the first capsule in the first row. "Okay, this is Professor Bradley's, he was frozen in nineteen-sixty-seven, as you know. That was done under ideal conditions all the way. Now, a lot of people make the mistake of thinking he was the first human being to be frozen. Actually, he was the second, you might not know that. We had a woman frozen here first, no publicity at all, the family insisted on that. But from the beginning it was a messed-up deal. They waited several days before they perfused her, she was actually embalmed first, then the family changed their minds again and decided to honor her wishes and have her frozen. It was what I call a 'cosmetic' freezing. In other words, just to preserve the body; there was never any hope of reanimation. You follow me? But then the family changed their minds again and wanted her buried, so we emptied the capsule and returned the body. In other words, Professor Bradley was the first *man* frozen—and the first human being to be perfused and frozen properly, under controlled conditions, with a chance of eventual reanimation."

I walk around the capsule, inspect it.

"I'll brief you on the construction when we go to the demo unit," he says. "Now, this next capsule, we froze another woman here, this was another case of a cosmetic freezing, the family requested it. It's a woman from L.A. Not the one got all that publicity, that one's still in dry ice, temporary storage, out on the Coast. This is just another woman from the same city, there was absolutely no publicity. The third capsule here, this is a man from Detroit, a member of the Cryonics Society of Michigan. Again, his family insisted on privacy. The perfusion was done under fairly good circumstances."

He goes on like that for another three or four capsules, to give me a general idea, then I follow him to the right side of the room, where there's an open cold storage shipping unit with a Ziegler case inside. Next to it is the new demonstrator capsule, its lid open, revealing the stainless-steel inner capsule, also open. Within the inner capsule is a sliding tray, pulled out about a quarter of its length, holding a white foam-rubber mattress. Between the two capsules are many layers of aluminized polyester film, wrapped tightly around the inner vessel to a thickness that almost fills the space between the two.

As Ed explains about the construction, I can't help remembering what Bob Erickson told me just last night: *"But let me clarify. When I say 'freezings,' I mean that twenty-one people have been perfused, placed in dry ice, and transferred to the capsules of liquid nitrogen they purchased. . . . Ed's firm is still the largest—Cerabino has eighteen people in cryonic suspension now—but his firm is also the oldest and best known. Trans Time is second, with small storage facilities in a converted warehouse in Oakland. They have two men stored there now in a single capsule.*"

I'm sure that's what he said. In fact, I'm positive.

But eighteen plus two equals twenty.

Ralph Richter, short but well built, dark-haired, wearing glasses, takes a pad of yellow paper from the desk drawer; his short-sleeved sport shirt reveals muscular arms. Tom Collier, standing nearby, looks older by a few years, over six feet and very lean, blond hair cut extremely close; from the back he almost seems bald. Ed picks up a coffee pot and leaves the office.

"Now, as you know," Ralph tells me, "the rate of biological deterioration is highly temperature dependent, becoming slower as the temperature is decreased. The actual rate of biochemical reaction can be approximated by this equation." He jots the equation on the pad and turns it to me.

$$\text{Rate} = K \exp - (\Delta E/RT)$$

"Delta E is the energy of activation," he says. "R is the gas constant and T is the absolute temperature. Using this equation, it can be shown that a biochemical reaction that takes one-millionth of a second to occur at room temperature would take three million years to complete at liquid nitrogen temperature."

I frown at the equation, try to look intelligent. "A biochemical reaction that takes less than a second to—"

"One-millionth of a second," Tom corrects.

"One-millionth of a second," I go on, "to occur at room temperature would take three million *years* to complete at liquid nitrogen temperature?"

"Approximately," Ralph says, straight-faced.

Ed comes back with the coffee pot, plugs it into the wall socket next to the desk, and sits down with us.

"Of course, the overall problem isn't that simple," Ralph says, turning the pad back to him. "The techniques used in freezing must minimize the damage that the freezing process *itself* can incur. As the body fluids are cooled, water freezes out, leaving behind a solution of increasing salinity. The saline content will eventually reach the point where permeability of the cell membranes is altered enough to lead to loss by leakage of essential metabolic compounds. In addition, structural damage may occur as the cells become trapped in a matrix of growing ice crystals. To counteract these freezing effects, as you know, a cryoprotective agent is injected into the body to replace much of the normal body fluid."

Tom leans forward, elbows on the desk, still standing; Ed took the last chair. "One of the most promising agents was a solution of blood plasma and dimethyl sulfoxide—DMSO. It seemed to have remarkable penetration characteristics that enabled it to pass through the cell walls. But Ralph and I feel now—and Erickson agrees—that glycerol should be used. Especially in view of Suda's good results. The introduction of this neutral solute limits ice formation until the temperature is low enough to reduce the rates of reactions—between the highly saline solutions and the cell components—to negligible levels. As the water is frozen out, the increased concentration of additive in the remaining solution may prevent further phase change. Because a vitreous substance has been formed."

Coffee pot begins to steam. Ed pulls the plug, takes off the lid. There's no coffee inside, just water. He goes to a small table against the wall and puts instant coffee into the two cups.

"Again, I don't want to repeat what you already know," Ralph says. "Basically, the Cryocapsule utilizes liquid nitrogen to achieve the required low temperature. Liquid nitrogen is ideal for our purposes because it's relatively inexpensive, inert to chemical reaction, and easily used. We've designed, tested, and modified the Cryocapsules to exacting specifications. This is a continuing thing. To provide progressively more reliable capsules with very low utilization of the refrigerant. For example, the Bradley capsule requires a liquid nitrogen refill every three or four months, but our new model can go as long as seven or eight months."

"Now we're redesigning for the nth time," Tom adds. "We're at the prototype stage this time with a one-fourth-scale working model. The objective is to get away from the conventional cryogenic vessel and into one specifically applicable to cryonic suspension. We're trading some holding time for greater reliability, simplified usage, and lower cost. If the test results verify the heat transfer analyses, we'll produce several of them and build a totally different marketing setup around them."

Ed brings over the two cups of instant coffee, sips from one, places the other in front of me. "We don't have any cream, but I've got some sugar over there if you want it."

"Thanks, Ed," I say. "Don't you guys want any?"

Ed smiles, shrugs. "That's all the cups we have."

Ralph and Tom talk for a while longer, then lead me into the large room to demonstrate. They decide the easiest way to explain the process would be to give me an idea of what happens from the time a body arrives in the shipping unit. Ralph takes a large sample of aluminized polyester film from one of the filing cabinets, ushers me over to the shipping unit next to the demo capsule, gets down on his haunches by the unit.

"All right," he says. "Say the body's just arrived."

Tom clears his throat. "The first thing we do is *panic*!"

Ralph laughs with us, nods. "That's true, that's true. No, but that reaction doesn't last long, simply because there's so much to do." He adjusts his glasses, pauses a moment, becomes quite serious. "First, we open the lid and remove some of the dry ice from around the head. We wear gloves and technician's aprons. Now, as you know, the body's already wrapped in layers of this aluminized polyester." He hands me the sample. "It's like—it's something like the commercial aluminum foil you buy in the stores, but much thinner and stronger. It's only five ten-thousandth of an inch thick, coated with vapor-deposited aluminum. Try pulling it apart."

I try several times, can't, hand it back.

"Tough stuff," Tom says. "They used the same basic material for the Echo satellites back in nineteen-sixty. Remember them? Before the Telstar project? And they're still up there, most of them."

"It's terrific insulation," Ralph says. "Anyway, the next step, we unwrap the head, quickly, just temporarily, for some photographs of the face."

"What's the body temperature then?" I ask.

"Minus seventy-nine centigrade," Tom says.

"There's no change during transportation?" I ask him.

"Possibly, yes, depending on the time involved. But you've got the thick fiberglass insulation and the entire body is packed in dry ice inside the steel Ziegler. I'd say the change is minimal."

"Depends on where it's shipped from also," Ralph says. "How long it's in transport." He stands now, moves to the demo capsule, pulls the tray out about halfway, slaps at the foam-rubber mattress. "Next, we remove the body from the Ziegler case, the dry-ice packing, and transfer it to the tray. What we do, actually, is take the tray completely out of the vessel, the inner vessel, and place it next to the Ziegler unit. To minimize lifting and carrying. Several straps are used to secure the body to the tray—we don't have them on the demo. Then we attach four temperature sensors to the body itself, copper-constantan thermocouples, attached to the head, the chest, one hand, and one foot, so we can test the temperature of those areas at any time. Next, we slide the tray into the inner vessel." He slides the tray all the way in, picks up the stainless-steel cutaway cover of the inner vessel, holds it in place. "The cover is then braced in place and welded shut, sealed. We have a professional welder on call for that."

"Last time," Ed says, "we got him out here to stand by at three in the morning."

"He absolutely *loved* us for that one," Tom says.

Ralph puts the cutaway cover back on the floor, pulls the inner vessel itself out just enough to give me a view of the heavy layers of aluminized film wrapped around it. "At this point, after the welding, dry nitrogen gas is pumped into the space between the inner and outer vessels and a small amount of liquid nitrogen is introduced into the sealed inner vessel to prevent undue warmup of the body. The purpose of the nitrogen gas is to prevent condensation and buildup of ice on the cold inner vessel. And, again, we use the same aluminized polyester film as insulation here around the vessel, as multiple radiation shields."

"Eighty-five layers," Tom says. "In the Bradley capsule and the one before that, the first one, we used sixty-five layers. Eighty-five is actually the ideal."

Ed pulls the inner vessel out more. "The layers go back to cover the entire vessel—can you see back in there? And they go over the cutaway cover after the welding and the leak test. We wrap the same eighty-five layers around the exposed cover, fold them back over the rounded end of it, and tape them. That's done after the leak test."

"Right, the leak test is next," Ralph says. "We slightly pressurize the inner vessel with helium and the welded area is scanned for leaks with a helium spectrometer. We have a new model, the Vecco." He points to his right, walks over to a large modern console about four feet high with complex gauges, valves, lights, and switches of different colors. There's a portable leak-scanner on top connected to the body of the console by a slender tube. "We test initially right after the vessel is constructed, before we cut off the front end. The final scan is essentially a test of the welded area."

"If the test checks out," Tom says, "the helium pressure is released and the exposed front end of the inner vessel is insulated, as Ed explained. Then the vacuum jacket—that's the outer vessel—the vacuum jacket is put in place and held with special fixtures for the initial evacuation. And the vacuum pump is started."

"Like the pumps on the working capsules," Ed explains.

Ralph indicates the gauge marked "Inner Vessel Pressure" on the cowl instrument panel of the new model. "When the pressure reaches approximately fifty microns, we feed more liquid nitrogen into the inner vessel." He taps his finger against the glass face of the gauge. "An important aspect of the first stages is that the liquid nitrogen is never allowed to rise to *body* level. Because temperature gradients may cause cracking. As you saw, the tray slides into the center of the inner vessel, so the body itself actually occupies the top half of the vessel, leaving plenty of room at the bottom. The vacuum pump is allowed to run for several days to permit all materials in the vacuum space to outgas, reaching a final pressure of zero-point-one micron. Then the long cool-down period begins. We maintain the liquid nitrogen level *below* the body for three weeks before filling the inner capsule completely. The new model, as I said, will require filling only once every seven or eight months. The capacity is one hundred fifty gallons of liquid nitrogen. When full, it weighs about twenty-two hundred pounds, depending on the weight of the body."

"So you fill only the inner vessel?" I ask.

"That's correct," he says, smiling. "And that's a common misunderstanding people have, they tend to think both capsules are filled. What we have is a double-walled cryonic vessel insulated with multiple radiation shields in a vacuum. The vacuum space is the space *between* the inner and outer vessels. The outer vessel door is sealed finally with an O-ring gasket. The door is held on by the differential pressure between the vacuum and the atmosphere. So the outer door acts as a safety pressure release. It opens only if the pressure in the vacuum jacket rises above atmospheric pressure. The inner vessel, containing the body, is filled very slowly for three weeks, as I said, to cool down the body. Then the inner vessel is completely filled."

"Of course, we run a series of checks constantly," Tom says. "For example, we take readings every day, seven days a week, on the critical functions of each capsule—the liquid level gauge, the inner vessel pressure gauge, the vacuum gauge, and the temperature of the four areas of the body provided by the sensors, the thermocouples. We check each function on each capsule seven days a week and make any adjustments indicated." He steps back and glances over at the vacuum pumps on the floor near the working capsules. "All the vacuum gauges indicated a need to outgas this week to keep the vessels within the allowable operating range. That's a constant maintenance job."

"What's the maintenance cost per year?" I ask.

"Today, it's included in the overall cost," Ed tells me. "Suspension, maintenance, and the establishment of a perpetual trust fund for each individual, so you get the advantages of compound interest over the years."

"Uh-huh. So what's the overall cost?"

"Including the capsule itself?"

"Yeah."

"Whole package comes to one-twenty-seven-five."

There's a pause after he says it. I stand there with my hands in my pockets, looking down and away toward the spinning wheel of one of the vacuum pumps. All eighteen pumps continue their steady soft rhythm, whirring and clicking.

But eighteen plus two equals twenty.

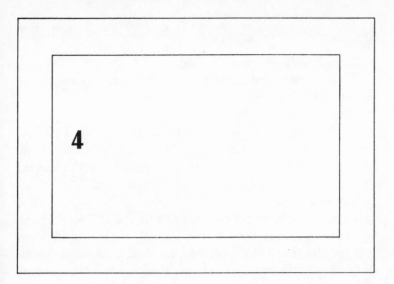

4

WEIRD STUFF going on here, I know, I hear you, but that's the way it is, what can I tell you? Now I know why many are cold, but few are frozen. Me, I figure I've done my homework now, I deserve a little happy hour. I'm back at the hotel, Mountain Shadows, classy joint, I'm sitting at a table on the cement island that juts out into the pool, enjoying my first drink of the evening, waiting for Ed Cerabino to show. He's got a date with Jacques D'Arcy and the CBC producer and crew over at the Towne House bar at 8:30, but he wants to see me first. Sales pitch is coming, of course, but that's fine and dandy with me, gives me a chance to be alone with this character. He's twenty minutes late, but I don't give a shit, I'm sipping a very dry Beefeater martini on the rocks with a twist, picking up on the ambience. Huge red bulk of Camelback Mountain deepens to purple at dusk, seems close above the flat lanai rooms circling the pool. It's warm and pleasant here, I'm counting my blessings. When Ed finally shows, he looks strange in a suit and tie.

"Selling any hope chests?" I ask.

"Hope chests, yeah." He laughs, sits down. "Sorry, I got tied up down the shop."

"You open weeknights?"

"No, we had a shipment of falls come in today, I had to check them out. Also, I had my girl there type up some figures for you, I worked something out." He waves to the waiter, then glances at my drink. "How you doing there?"

"I'm fine."

"Come on, you're half empty. Martini, right?"

"Beefeater, rocks, twist."

He orders that and a scotch for himself, takes some papers from his inside coat pocket, puts on black horn-rimmed glasses. He wears a short-sleeved shirt under his suit coat and his thick wrists make his hands seem small.

"My wife's been wanting a fall," I tell him.

"Yeah?" He doesn't look up from the papers.

"Bet they're expensive, huh?"

"Yeah, they can run you money." He pushes at the nose-piece of his glasses, selects one of the papers, puts the others back in his pocket. "Okay, I been doing some work for you. Now, on the total package, you mentioned in the last letter you didn't have that insurance deal the New York people worked out, right?"

"That's right."

"Nobody would underwrite that?"

"My condition precludes that, Ed."

"Yeah, I remember you mentioned that in the first letter. Leukemia, right?"

"Chronic myelocytic leukemia."

"Yeah, that's right."

I nod, glance away. "Insurance companies are in the business of statistical reasoning, essentially, and life expectancy figures for this type of leukemia are quite consistent. Insurance was out of the question from the day the diagnosis was confirmed."

"Yeah, right. Anyhow, I just went ahead, I worked out some figures, assuming you wanted to finance it."

"That's right."

"Now, would that be from a bank in New York?"

"Yeah."

"Okay, so, just to give you an idea. If you financed it, say, just as an example, through a bank here in town, they'd do this. I require a down payment, usually one-third. Then they'd finance the balance for you over a period from twelve to thirty-six months. I figured you'd go for the thirty-six, right?"

"Not necessarily."

"I mean, it'd cut the payments way down."

I hesitate. "I'm afraid my condition rules out thirty-six months, Ed, I didn't mention that, it's my fault."

He adjusts his glasses. "I see. I didn't—"

"What would it be for twenty-four months?"

"Well, okay, I've got that here too." He takes out the papers again, selects another. "In other words, no matter which plan you take, my bank here charges only ten-point-five percent interest, deducted in advance. So, after you make the down payment, your actual loan on a two-year basis would be—let's see. Eighty-nine, two-ninety-four. That'd make your payments thirty-three-hundred forty-eight a month on that basis. I had the girl type up both plans for you." He hands me the paper.

Total cost (including Cryocapsule)	$127,500.00
(Minus) One-third down payment	42,457.50
Balance	$ 85,042.50

24 Months

Amount of loan	$ 89,294.63
(Minus) Interest @ 10.5%	8,929.46
Cash you receive	$ 80,365.17
Monthly installment	$ 3,348.55

"All banks around here have the same interest rate," he says. "Well, almost all. I don't know what kind of deal they have in New York. In other words, it might be more, it might be less, I don't know. Anyhow, this gives you an idea what kind of payments you'd be getting into."

"Do you always require a down payment?"

"Yeah."

"Why?"

"A number of reasons. Banks consider it sound financial dealing. It's a long haul over two or three years to pay off these things for the ordinary person. For example, if you had a straight loan of the full amount, same interest, same two-year deal, you'd be paying over fifty-eight hundred a month. Which is quite a strain for most people. Incidentally, I should tell you, many banks won't touch this thing yet. I've got a bank here that will, because they know my operation. You might get turned down by a bank in New York, I don't know."

"No, I'm all right there."

"You've inquired about that?"

"No, but my credit's good there."

"Good. And both you and your wife are working, right?"

"That's right. Plus, we have an IRA account."

"Enough for the down payment?"

"Just about."

"Well, no problem then."

I smile. "Except for the payments."

"Okay, well, can I speak frankly?"

"Absolutely."

"You think you can afford it?"

"Right now, yes."

"How long can you keep working?"

"Maybe a year or so, it's difficult to say."

"You got a lot of medical bills?"

"Not yet, just my regular therapy. With this variety of the disease, you can be maintained in almost normal health until the terminal stage. I'm losing weight consistently, but that's about it."

"It gets expensive later on?"

"In the terminal stage, it can become expensive, depending on what the physician wants to do."

The waiter comes with the two drinks on a tray. Ed pays the bill on the spot, lifts his glass quickly, takes a long swallow. We sit quietly for a while. I watch the reflection of the lighted water move on his face.

"What's the cost of the Ziegler and the wooden shipping container?" I ask finally.

"You wouldn't have to buy them. What I've done in all eighteen situations so far is use my own containers for shipping, transporting. I haven't charged anything outside of the freight charges."

"I read someplace they were about two hundred dollars."

He nods, shrugs. "Yeah, the wooden unit is eighty-four—that's with the fiberglass insulation—and the Ziegler's a hundred and twelve."

"I saw them at Erickson's."

"Well, you know, that's for show and all, he really doesn't need them. The only time people would buy those is when they're planning to store a person in dry ice for a relatively long period. I'm talking about people who can't afford to buy the whole package right away. Several are preserved temporarily that way; the families are trying to raise the necessary money for actual cryonic suspension here."

"Right, Bob told me about them."

He smiles, takes another drink. "That's one of the reasons people think I'm such a bastard, because I won't go the whole thing when they can't pay for it. In other words, they have an idea I'm some kind of a philanthropist here. I'll tell you the truth, if I did that, if I just said, all right, pay me when you can, I'd be out of business, I'd be bankrupt. That's a fact. In other words, I've sunk damn near half a million dollars into this thing and now I'm expected to give it away to people who can't even get credit from a bank to buy it on time, right? Either that, or they can't come up with the whole down payment, one or the other. I simply can't operate that way. I'd go bankrupt in no time flat."

"You're still the only firm offering the total service?"

"At the present time, yeah, but that's changing, you probably know that. Right now, we're the only firm in the world that's actually manufacturing permanent storage units as well as providing the complete range of cryonic suspension services. If we went out of business, it'd be the worst possible thing for the cryonics movement. I'll be honest with you, I welcome the competition that's supposed to be coming. Why? They'll make me look good in comparison. I mean it. I mean, if they think they can walk in and provide a total package, units and all, in a couple of years, they're absolutely nuts. It's taken us twenty-two years to get established here, plus twenty working capsules and a cash outlay of about half a million, as I said. I'll tell you the honest truth, I wish them luck. Know what I mean? They don't even begin to know what they're up against. It's not that easy." He looks at his watch. "Well, listen, I've got to get over to the Towne House and meet these guys from the CBC. Why don't you think it over, take your time, see what you want to do. How long you staying in town?"

"I leave tomorrow morning."

"Oh, God, that's right, you told me."

"Basically, I think we have a deal, Ed. I'd just like to ask a few more questions, small things that I'm curious about."

His face brightens. "Sure, absolutely, go ahead."

"How much of the money goes into the actual suspension process, how much into maintenance, how much into the trust fund? It was probably in the material you sent me, but I've got a lousy memory."

"No problem. Okay, normally, if it's a life insurance deal, as most of them are, about forty percent is used to pay for the suspension procedure, then sixty percent goes into a trust managed by anybody you choose—usually an attorney. Part of the trust is used for maintaining the deceased in the liquid nitrogen, that's a daily operation, and the cost averages about four thousand per year. All the rest is invested by your designated trustee to build up a nest egg for the future."

I nod, sip my drink. "Okay, I just wasn't clear on the exact percentages. Now, here's a stat I'm curious about. When I met with Bob, he said there were a total of twenty-one verified freezings in liquid nitrogen, including the two whole-body freezings in the single capsule at Trans Time in Oakland."

"Right."

"Is that the actual figure, twenty-one?"

He smiles, sits forward. "John, it depends on who you're talking to and it depends on that person's definition of freezing. In other words, some people count the three frozen brains up at Trans Time, some don't. Some people count those two bodies that were properly profused and are now being maintained in dry ice. The figures can vary widely."

"Bob was very specific. He said twenty-one *bodies* are suspended in liquid nitrogen right now. You have eighteen here. Trans Time has two. See what I mean?"

"Yeah." He frowns, glances at the pool. "All I can say, Bob might've been counting that woman in France. Not many people know about this. Some years ago, there was this physician in France who perfused his wife at the moment of clinical death, then placed her in a freezer at minus fifty degrees centigrade."

"No, Bob specified liquid nitrogen freezings. A few minutes ago, you mentioned that you'd manufactured twenty working capsules in twenty-two years. Counting the demo unit, you now have nineteen out there, right?"

"That's right, we've manufactured twenty. But that other capsule was never used in a freezing. It was one of the first few we made, not long after Professor Bradley was frozen in nineteen-sixty-seven. As you can imagine, that first freezing got a ton of publicity, not only in this country, but all over the world. We had reporters and photographers hanging off the rafters, thousands of telephone calls, big bags of mail. Unfortunately, not many of 'em wanted to buy anything, they just wanted information. Anyhow, we made—"

"Many are cold, but . . ."

"Yeah, right, tell me about it. Anyhow, we made only one other sale that year, that's the capsule I'm talking about. We corresponded with a physician in Trinidad. Trinidad, West Indies. He purchased the capsule outright. See, we didn't offer anything in the way of a total service back then, a total package, because it was all—we didn't have our act together, y'know? So he just bought the capsule itself. Back in those days—God, I haven't thought of this in years. Back then, know what we sold those early Cryocapsules for?"

"Peanuts."

He smiles, shakes his head. "Peanuts. Of course, a dollar was worth something back then. We sold those early models for exactly forty-eight hundred and sixty-five clams. Imagine that? I remember he paid us the full amount with a certified check from his bank, Barclays Bank, in Eastern Caribbean currency, they called their dollars 'beewees.' Exactly two beewees to the U.S. dollar back then, I remember that. The guy—his name was Leonard, Dr. Derek Leonard—he paid nine thousand seven hundred and thirty beewees for that Cryocapsule. Plus shipping charges, of course, I can't remember how much that was. Shipped it by air, I remember we crated it up and trucked it out to the air freight terminal. It was in the spring, April or May, nineteen-sixty-seven. That was the second capsule we ever sold. Shit, we thought—I mean, what'd we know?—we thought we'd sell *hundreds* of 'em! Right? We thought we'd be fuckin' *millionaires*!"

"Whatever became of the capsule?"

"Haven't got a clue, John."

"Never heard from the guy again?"

"Never heard from him again."

"You think it's possible that he used it? That a freezing took place?"

"No, I don't, and I'll tell you why. Whenever a freezing occurs, John, the media people are right on top of it. That's a fact. They have a field day with it. And that goes for anywhere in the world—well, with the possible exception of maybe Russia or China. I mean, they just eat it up. Newspapers, magazines, TV, radio, the whole shot, they all pick up on it fast. Believe me, I know, I been in this business since the very beginning. I mean, I'll give you a funny example, my so-called competition, Trans Time, up in Oakland, they froze a *dog* just a couple of years ago and it became a big media event—it even made *People* magazine." He reaches into his suit-coat pocket again, takes out his papers, selects a Xerox copy of a magazine article, hands it to me, then glances at his watch. "Read about my so-called competition up there. Really, you should get familiar with what their operation's all about."

"Will do, Ed, appreciate it."

"Look, I've got to split. Take your time, think it over, see what that bank in New York can do for you." He stands up. "Keep in touch, huh, let me know what's happening."

I stand, shake his hand. "Thanks for everything."

"Not at all. Take care now."

After he's gone, I sit quietly, sip my drink, then pick up the copy of the article from *People*. It's dated April 20, 1987, and it's a full page in the section called "Hero." Top half of the page is a photo of a healthy-looking beagle sitting in a big bucket, surrounded by four bags of Glacier Party Ice. Caption reads: "Celebrity hound Miles cools out 10 months after scientists froze him to death and then thawfully retrieved him."

A CLINICALLY DOGGONE BEAGLE, MEDICAL MIRACLE MILES IS A FORMER CHILLY DOG BACK FROM THE BEYOND

— Hero —

This time last year he was an unassuming little laboratory dog with no name. Today Miles, a frisky 3½-year-old beagle, is a living, breathing, barking breakthrough in medical science.

Last June at the University of California at Davis, Miles survived the following chilling laboratory procedure. First, physiologist Paul Segall and his team put the dog to sleep with sodium pentothal. Next, they gave him another anesthetic and immersed him into a vat of ice water, which quickly lowered his body temperature to 68°F. At that point, he was placed on a heart-lung machine. Then Miles's blood was drained from his jugular vein and replaced with a cooled blood substitute. (Had his blood not been removed, its cells might have grouped in tiny clumps, which could block arteries and blood vessels.)

His temperature began to drop rapidly, and at 38°F he lacked all signs of life—no heartbeat, no respiration and no brain activity. After 15 minutes of clinical death, Miles was thawed out, and his blood was put back into his body. After an hour, his body temperature was returned to normal.

Miles made a rapid recovery. "Within a few days, he was up and about," says Segall. "The wounds from the incisions had to heal, but apart from that he was fine." Named after Woody Allen's character in the movie *Sleeper,* Miles is the first dog to be revived from a deathlike, near-frozen state without apparent harm to life or paw. According to Segall, the beagle's 15-minute chill may one day lead to radical improvements in human surgical techniques and be helpful during deep space exploration.

Miles now leads a delightfully dull domestic existence in Berkeley, Calif. with Segall and his lab partner, Harold Waitz. Happily, there are no more medical milestones in store for the dog. "He has done his duty to science," says Segall. "Now Miles gets to be just a regular pet." And the only cold part of him these days is his nose.

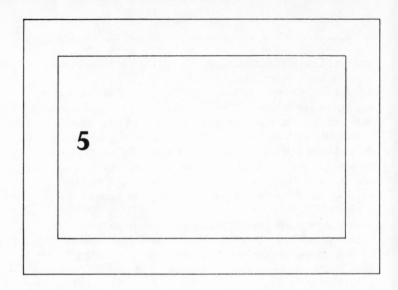

5

IT'S SNOWING IN MANHATTAN on Monday
morning, February 8, when I grab a cab at Penn Station and
head crosstown to the Police Academy, 235 East Twentieth,
that's where our Forensic Lab is located. Relatively modern
building, eight stories of light-tan brick weathered soot-gray,
dates back to 1964 when Abe Beame was mayor, remember
him? Security's very tight here because the Ballistics Lab occupies the top floor. I show my shield and sign in at the lobby
desk; when I get off the elevator I'm in a large steel cage. Show
my gold again, I'm buzzed in, I sign in again. Got a 9:45
appointment with an old buddy of mine, Lieutenant Louis
Diaz, commanding officer of Forensic. Louie and me, we go
back a long way—Brooklyn South, Robbery Squad, 1965.
Desk sergeant calls him, he comes out to greet me himself.
Still looks like a welterweight, which he used to be, excellent
amateur, champion of his army division, finalist in the Golden
Gloves, real fast hands. Grew up as the only Spanish kid in a
rough Sicilian neighborhood in the Red Hook section of

Brooklyn, graduated from Queens College. Haven't seen him in a couple of years now, but it's always a kick in the head. Instant marriage, know what I mean?

"Hey, John!"

"Louie!"

Shakes hands, smiles up at me (kid's only five-eight), dark hair, high forehead, dark complexion, thick lips, brooding Brando eyes. Terry Malloy from *On the Waterfront,* remember him? Only difference, Louie's got an IQ that goes off the charts. Never know it by listening to him, likes to keep a low-brow profile.

"So what's happening?" he asks.

"Got a case for you."

"No. Me? You and me?"

"Absolutely."

"Away from the desk, away from the phone, away from this fuckin' birdcage psycho ward?"

"Believe it."

Slaps me on the arm. "Little John, you just made my week. Week? Month! John, you're a fuckin' prince, y'know that?"

"You haven't heard the scenario yet."

"I don't care if it's a musical comedy."

Leads me back through the lab, he's got about twenty forensic technicians hard at work, reading the *News,* drinking coffee, breaking wind in their cubicles. Ushers me into his corner office, snowy southwest view, takes my topcoat and umbrella, gets me a fast cup of coffee, treats me like the prince that I am. Problem with Louie, he made the mistake of being an ambitious cop, he couldn't help himself, it was in his stone-washed genes. Always studying, taking exams, getting promotions. Irony is, he loved it as a street detective, he ate it up, he was a natural, particularly in undercover work because he's a born actor. Now he's a C.O., pushing papers, pulling down wholesome bread, but he's eating his heart out. I mean, it's painful to watch him, to see his eyes when you talk about street work.

I light up a panatela, glance out at the slanting snow. "So how're Iris and the kids?"

"Fine. Cindy and John?"

"Fine. Ever hear of cryonics?"

"John, you're talking to a forensic scientist here, okay? Cryogenics, that's the branch of physics that deals with the effects of very low temperatures."

"Didn't say cryogenics. Said cryonics."

"Cryonics?"

"Cryonics. Comes from the Greek word *kryos*—to freeze."

"Yeah? To freeze what?"

I reach in the pocket of my blue blazer, take out the neatly folded Xerox copy of the article about Miles in *People,* hand it across the desk. "This'll give you the general idea."

He smiles at the picture, reads the caption out loud. "Celebrity hound Miles cools out ten months after scientists froze him to death and then thawfully retrieved him." Now he reads the headline, chuckles softly, smiles as he reads the first paragraph. Smile disappears when he gets into the article. Whistles softly. Frowns. Blinks. Shakes his head. Finishes, gives me this look, says, "Ho-lee shit." Glances at the headline again. "John, is this the case you're—? Are we talking chilly dogs back from the beyond here?"

"Is this a great case or what?"

"Frozen beagles? I mean, who the fuck you working for, the ASPCA? Speak to me, John. Start from the beginning. Go slow. Take nothing for granted. Me, I'm just a forensic scientist, I don't know from frozen dogs."

I smile, sip my coffee, puff my cigar, start at the beginning: *Guinness Book of World Records*; meeting with Vadney and the investigators from BCI; undercover assignment; meeting with Professor Erickson in Oak Park; meeting with Ed Cerabino in Phoenix; tour of the Cryonics facilities in Tempe; discussion of financial arrangements; Dr. Leonard's Cryocapsule in Trinidad; all the way to Miles, the clinically doggone beagle.

"John, this is wild. I mean, I'll tell you the truth, this is the wildest fuckin' case I ever heard of."

"Beats work."

"So what's your next move?"

"Only got one lead, Lou. Slim one at that. Have to follow it, see what I come up with. Might come up empty, but I figure it's worth a shot, what the hell."

"Lead? What lead? You lost me."

"Dr. Leonard."

"The guy in Trinidad? How you figure that's a lead?"

I look out at the snow, blow smoke toward the window, watch it curl and rise slowly. "Hard to explain. I just feel it."

"Your famous intuition? Okay, but how you gonna explain that to Vadney?"

"Vadney knows I operate on intuition. He knows I play long shots. First off, I got spadework to do. Have to find out if this Dr. Leonard is still down there. Hell, this was twenty-one years ago, man might be dead now. If he's not, if he's alive and still down there, we play the lead."

Louie smiles, shakes his head. "Like my old man used to say, only three things an Irishman needs to get ahead in the world."

"Yeah? And *cajónes* are two of 'em, right?"

"Wrong. Nerve, crust, and *gall.*"

"Man should've added intuition."

"Gotta hand it to you, Little John, don't get me wrong, okay? You're looking to finagle a trip down there, right? Can't say I blame you, nice place to work a case, middle of winter. Tell me something, just between the two of us, how the fuck do *I* fit into all this? What, I tag along for protection? Chief'll never buy it. No way."

"Lou, know what's wrong with you?"

"John, y'got any idea how expensive it is in the Caribbean this time of year? This is high *season,* man. You're talking two, two-fifty a night, *minimum,* for a shithole room. *Air*fare? Forget it."

"Lou, what's the matter with you? Huh? Know what's wrong with you? You been sitting behind that tin desk too long. You been worrying about your budgets too long. We're talking about a twenty-four-million-dollar robbery here. Greatest robbery on record attributed to industrial espionage. It's in the *book,* for Christ's sake. A research trip to Trinidad is *peanuts.* You kidding? Top of that, you're a forensic *scientist,* this crap is right on target for you, couldn't be better. Besides, I need a drinking buddy."

Goes like so. First order of spadework, I call overseas, speak with the directory assistance operator in Port-of-Spain, Trinidad, ask if she has a listing for Dr. Derek Leonard. One moment, please. Yes, sir, Dr. Derek Leonard, Northern Coast Road, La Vache Bay, Trinidad, number is 827-3144. Bingo. Louie and I laugh like kids, which is what we are, even give each other high-five slaps.

Next thing, we have to nail down a game plan for Vadney, complete with facts and figures, leave no doubt in his mind that we did our homework. Louie gets on the horn, calls a buddy who's a travel agent, asks for up-to-date poop on travel to Trinidad: Airlines, round-trip fares, hotels, motels, guest houses, rental cars. Guy asks when we're planning to go. Louie says yesterday. Guy says he thinks we're out of luck, because the Trinidad Carnival runs February 13–16, all the flights and accommodations are usually booked solid months in advance, tourists pour in from all over, it's one of the most famous carnivals in the world. Louie's jaw drops, his eyes go sad, his voice chokes up. Tells him to check it out anyhow; if there's nothing in Port-of-Spain, is there anywhere to stay in La Vache Bay? Guy says he'll check it out carefully and get back to him.

Me, I'm optimistic about our chances. Tell you why: Black Monday, October 19, 1987, the big stock market crash. That was less than four months ago. Now, under normal circumstances, well-heeled Yuppies and snowbirds who routinely wing south for winter breaks just wouldn't think twice about taking in the Trinidad Carnival or Mardi Gras in New Orleans. Today? My opinion, most of them are playing it on the conservative side, cutting back on pricey jaunts like this for a while until the aftershocks are over and they can see exactly what's what. I mean, economic events like Black Monday wouldn't affect the very wealthy, the so-called old money class, but they'd probably opt for the Rio Carnival (which is supposed to be the best), if the spirit moved them. Yuppies and snowbirds, that's another story. I'm guessing, sure, but it's a guess based on the hard economic realities of February 1988.

In any event, while we're waiting to hear back from the travel agent, Louie and I get down to the serious business of discussing undercover strategies and ploys. Exactly how would we get through to this guy Leonard? What approach would seem the most natural, logical, convincing? With Erickson and Cerabino, it was relatively simple: I was in the market to buy a service they were selling. I'd set it up with careful correspondence, I'd studied most of the significant literature of the cryonics movement, I had the important questions and answers down cold, no pun intended. But what tactics could we use on Dr. Leonard that wouldn't arouse suspicion? For openers, we don't know anything about the man, we don't even know what he's a doctor *of*. Sure, we could call the police in Port-of-Spain, go through the standard callback routine (collect) to verify we're NYPD, then request the courtesy of a brief, basic employment check, based on the name and address; find out his occupation, principal place of business, and vital stats, if available. But we hesitate for one reason. On a relatively small island, it's entirely possible that the police could be acquainted with this man, particularly if he's an

M.D.; if that's the case, he may even have worked with them periodically over the years. If any of that is true, the knowledge of our call could very well get back to Dr. Leonard, which would blow whatever cover we decide to use. Two strangers from New York? Forget it. No, contacting the police is simply not worth the risk.

Now Louie comes up with another idea. He'll call directory assistance in Port-of-Spain, ask for the name and number of the largest hospital on the island (there can't be many), get through to that hospital's personnel department, and ask if Dr. Derek Leonard is on its staff. If not, can they tell him which hospital he's associated with—or if he's simply in private practice? Innocent enough, right? No need to give your name. Pure and simple shot in the dark, but what the hell?

Louie makes the call, he's really enjoying this international detective shit, you can see it in his eyes, hear it in his voice. Gets through to the directory assistance operator, asks the name and number of the largest hospital. Turns out to be Port-of-Spain General, number 854-9000; would he like to be connected? Yes, please. One moment, please. Gets through, asks for the personnel department. One moment, please. Gets through, asks if Dr. Derek Leonard is on staff. No more One moment, please: Dr. Leonard is chief of staff at the joint's Trauma Center. Thank you very much.

Firm ice for a change. Now we're on a roll, we talk it over, we bat ideas around. Through no fault of our own, the timing happens to be perfect. Black Monday or no, plenty of New Yorkers are sure to catch Carnival. Okay, suppose we mix fact with a pinch of fiction: I've just met with Ed Cerabino in Phoenix, he knows my condition, he knows I'm going to Port-of-Spain. Naturally, he suggests I touch base with Dr. Leonard so at least I'll have a medical contact down there. Tell him the specific type of leukemia I have, my medications, where I'm staying, how long I'll be there—just to play it safe, just in case I might need treatment of some kind. Right? I mean, that's done all the time, it's standard operating procedure for physicians whose patients are traveling, especially to a foreign country. Know the name and address of a doctor in that foreign city, make sure he knows your medical history. Finally, here's my trump card for a meet: I'll simply get a letter of introduction from that New York physician the guys from BCI selected for me. Fancy letterhead, all the quack buzzwords, I got it made.

"Just thought of something," Louie says. "Hold on a minute, John, I'm just playing devil's advocate, okay, but I think we got a potential flaw in our cover."

"What's that?"

"Two *guys* going to the Trinidad Carnival? *Alone*? I mean, John, I got an open mind, don't get me wrong, but it gives me—it makes me feel a little uncomfortable. Not from the gay angle, that's not all that important. But two men alone at Carnival down there, two men with obvious New York accents? Tell you what, if I was this guy Leonard, Dr. Leonard, and I had anything at all to hide, I'd be cautious in dealing with two men like us. Know what I mean? Especially with the letter and all, it just seems too pat."

I sip my coffee, think about it. "You got a point."

"We need a couple of broads, John."

"Couple of wives?"

"Okay, yeah, but young wives. Wedding rings, all that."

"Maybe you're right." I smile, glance out the window. Snow seems to be slanting down harder. "Wonder if Terri McBride's available?"

"Terri McBride, I heard of her."

"Detective from the Seventeenth, real looker. Worked a couple of cases with her. Excellent undercover cop, handles herself real good. Graduated from John Jay in—let's see—'eighty-one, I think. Kid's only twenty-nine now, she's got almost eight years of experience."

"Know any others?"

"Yeah, let's see. Only top one I can think of, Judy Cooper, detective from the Major Crimes Unit. Early thirties, very bright, attractive kid, worked with her once before. Trouble is, top undercover ladies like these, they're always booked, cases up the gazoo."

"Chief could get 'em unbooked."

Travel agent calls back, tells Louie it beats the shit out of him, but there are still some airline seats and hotel rooms available. Catch is, airline seats are first class only, plus the only hotel rooms left are expensive suites. Louie says, fine, what kind of bucks are we talking? He takes notes, relays the stats to me: Pan Am has one flight a day from JFK to Port-of-Spain, makes one stop in Caracas, Venezuela. Round-trip first-class fare, $1,280. However, there's a special deal if you book at least four days in advance and stay a minimum of three days: Round-trip first-class fare drops to only $886; saving of $394. Hotels? No cut-rate deals here. Suites are still available at the Trinidad Hilton, price range is $240 for a one-bedroom suite, goes all the way to $460. He asks the minimum for a two-bedroom suite. Guy tells him $330. Louie relays the stat, shrugs, gives me a look.

I shrug back; it's not my money. Now I look at the calendar. Four days from now is Friday. "Tell him to book four first-class seats and one of the two-bedroom suites. We'll hop the Friday flight."

Louie's all smiles, he can't believe this shit. Tells the guy, asks what that comes to. First-class fare, four persons, $3,544. One two-bedroom suite, minimum of three nights, $990.

"No, no," I tell him. "Let's make it—say, Friday through Thursday, one week, what the hell?"

Louie, he's trying not to laugh, he relays the dates, asks what that all comes to. One of the $330 suites, seven nights, that's a paltry $2,210. Bottom-line total, airfares and hotel? One moment, please. Damage comes to $5,754. Of course, that doesn't include food, booze, entertainment, or rental cars. Me,

I think it's a steal. Now all we got to do is sell Vadney. Is this a great case or what?

Cluttered *desks* make for cluttered *minds,* Vadney always says. Man says what he means. Means what he says. Delivers what he promises. So, naturally, you walk in his office, his desk is completely empty. By "desk," I mean his teakwood conference table that seats twelve. You should see this mother. Not a paper on it, not a pencil, not even a paper clip. Handsome high-gloss shine, of course, he insists that Doris Banks use non-aerosal York's Old English Real Beeswax Furniture Polish, made by Growner Products in Boroughbridge, North Yorkshire, England. Man accepts no substitutes. Special way to apply it, too. Once a week (usually Monday morning, first thing), he makes sure Doris holds the 500-milligram plastic container approximately six inches from the surface, then she sprays just a little over a ten-square-inch area, then she wipes it immediately with a clean dry duster to get that perfect long-lasting luster. Needless to say, when Louie and I take our seats at the far end near the Duke, flanking him, we hesitate to plunk our mitts on this mirror. Yeah, you can see your puss in it, clear as can be. Intimidating? You think that's intimidating to two old grunts like us? Me, I'd put my slushy *Guccis* up on that table, if I had a mind to. But, I mean, come on. Hate to see a grown man cry.

Another thing, you don't schedule a meet with the Chief unless you have a formal written presentation all prepared. I'm talking a neatly typed report or proposal or whatever, complete with a title page, an introduction, subheads for specific subjects, and a simple, declarative conclusion titled "Recommendations," step by step, that can be understood by a child. All pages double-spaced and numbered, wide margins for his little yellow stick-on "flags" with comments and questions. All copies three-hole punched, placed in NYPD-blue Duo-Tang 51240 presentation folders, as distinguished from the Duo-Tang 5-3558 folders with the NYPD logo on the cover, which Press Relations Director Jerry Grady uses for all press packages. See, the practical advantage of the 51240 style, it has a clear plastic cover, so you can see the title, case number, writer(s), and date at a glance, plus the big red rubber stamp reading CLASSIFIED, if it happens to be classified intelligence, which almost everything relating to this case happens to be.

I hand Vadney the original manuscript of the proposal. He hands me the original manuscript of my classified trip report, which I submitted last Friday.

"Good solid report," he tells me. "Clear, concise, excellent insights into those people and what they're up to. I've flagged about half a dozen pages there, Little John, I need clarification on some of the technical stuff. Also, I approved your expense report. Approved it, signed it, sent it on to Mat Murphy. It's in the works now."

"Thank you, sir."

"Okay, now, what's this thing? 'Proposal for Undercover Operation in Trinidad, W.I.,' what's all this about?"

"Uh, you want to review it first or—?"

Glances at his watch. "Yeah, I'd like to, I know how much work you put into these things, Little John, but I only got half an hour here. Got an appointment with Commissioner Reilly at four-thirty. Summarize it, give me a brief synopsis, I'll study it later."

"All right, okay, fair enough. Well, sir, I met with Lieutenant Diaz this morning, I briefed him on the case to date. Naturally, as a forensic scientist, commanding officer of the lab, he has a thorough *technical* knowledge of cryonics. I need his expertise on this trip. He's an excellent undercover—"

"Trip? What trip?"

"To Trinidad, sir."

"Trinidad. Why Trinidad?"

"That's where Dr. Leonard lives."

"Oh, yeah, Dr. Leonard. I remember that name from your trip report. Refresh my memory on him, huh?"

"He purchased a Cryocapsule from Ed Cerabino back in nineteen-sixty-seven. They shipped it down to him."

"In Trinidad?"

"Right."

"Okay, I'm with ya, go ahead."

"Chief, to make a long story short, Dr. Leonard is my only lead in the case so far. There's something about that whole episode that—well, to my ear, it just doesn't seem to ring true."

"What, specifically?"

"First off, Professor Erickson told me there're exactly twenty-one verified whole-body freezings in liquid nitrogen. Even the people from BCI believed the figure to be twenty. Second, Ed Cerabino claims there are twenty—he has eighteen of 'em—and he went on at considerable length to explain how that Cryocapsule was shipped down to Trinidad empty. I mean, he was in a hurry, he had another appointment, but he went out of his way to explain the whole thing to me. Why would he do that?"

Chief nods. "But y'got nothing solid to go on, huh?"

"John," Louie says, "why would Erickson say twenty-one in the first place?"

"I don't know. It seemed to me—like he let the number slip. We'd had a couple of drinks, we hadn't had dinner yet."

"Okay, let me get this straight," Chief says. "You think there's some kind of connection between the guy we're looking for, Dr. Mailer, and this Dr. Leonard, that right?"

"Yes, sir."

"But y'got no hard evidence to back it up."

"Just his infamous intuition," Louie says.

Chief grins, shakes his head. "Yeah, well, it's paid off plenty of times before. Right, Little John, your intuition?"

"It's been helpful."

"So, bottom line, you want to follow it, you want to get down to Trinidad, and you want Diaz to go with you."

"Yes, sir."

"So what's your cover?"

Louie sits forward, taps a finger on his copy of the proposal. "We've been doing spadework, Chief. We found out that Dr. Leonard is chief of staff of the Port-of-Spain General Hospital Trauma Center."

"Yeah? So?"

"They got their annual Carnival going on," I tell him. "This weekend—four days. We'll just be there for Carnival, like everybody else. Ed Cerabino told me to check in with Dr. Leonard."

"He did, huh?"

"Uh, no, sir, I'm just—"

"No, huh?"

"—making that part up. For the cover, okay? Next, I'll get a letter of introduction, a medical courtesy letter, from that doctor—y'know, the one recommended by BCI?"

"Dr. Veritas," Chief says.

"That's the guy, I can never remember his name. He'll tell Leonard everything he needs to know about my leukemia, my medications, all like that. We'll take the letter right to the hospital, meet the man, it's a beginning. I'll tell him Ed Cerabino sends his regards, I'll give him an update on the cryonics facilities, ease into that, come in through the back door. From that point on, we'll have to wing it, play our roles."

Chief sits back, hands behind his head, narrows his eyes at the ceiling. "I see what you're getting at. I see the role-playing part. Obviously, you don't want to talk about it, I understand, but let me be candid with you guys. Personally, I wouldn't buy it. If I was Leonard, a doctor and all, I wouldn't buy it. I'd smell a cop. Two cops."

"Yeah?"

"Yeah, Little John. Know why? I'll tell you exactly why, I'll be candid with you." Sits forward now, glances at us. "I mean, just look at you guys. You don't look the part. Know what I mean? No way, José. You don't *look* like gays, you don't *act* like gays, you don't *talk* like gays. I mean, even if you had the right clothes and jewelry and all, I still wouldn't buy that cover, Times Square, New Year's *Eve.*"

I exchange a glance with Louie, I know he's going to break up any second if I don't jump in fast. "Chief, that's not—"

"Know what you guys *really* need, Little John? I'll tell ya. I'll tell ya exactly what you guys need, what I could buy all the way if I was Leonard. Huh? Know what you need for the perfect cover down there at the carnival?"

"What?"

"What?"

"A couple of *broads,* that's what!"

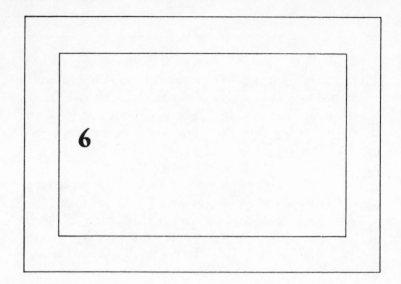

6

GETTING TO PORT-OF-SPAIN from Piarco Airport, you roar down Golden Grove Road and it's lined with forests of coconut palms black and heavy against a red-streaked twilight and your jalopy Chevy taxi bombs along the left side of the road and when you hit the straightaway you see the big mountains of the Northern Range in gray haze as the headlights come at you. They come at you almost head-on, single file, shimmering in heat waves, blurred, melting upward, and your Trinidadian driver with the bashed felt hat and sunglasses and nonstop commentary dims his brights and they dim theirs and tear past on your right so close you feel something grab in your gut. Then you hook a left and squeal onto the new blacktop of Churchill-Roosevelt Highway and it's wide and straight and packed with cars and you pass through Arouca and St. Augustine and there are farms and factories and billboards and houses with yellow lights and boys carrying home fish they caught in Caroni River and off to the left beyond the river is Caroni Swamp and with the windows open you don't need anybody to tell you it's there. Then you're on Beetham Highway where Shantytown sprawls stinking with miles of shacks and huts and outhouses and finally you come into the city, into Port-of-Spain, into the deafening mob scene at sundown, traffic backed up, horns blaring, streets teeming with men, women, children, horses, dogs, donkey carts, bicycles, street vendors, steel bands, motorcycles, trucks, scooters, buses, cars, and tourists, into the Big Night, the night all hell breaks loose, the buildup night, the countdown night, the night the lid blows and life explodes in a wild, drunken, freewheeling frenzy of excitement, of bacchanal, of street dancing, of doing anything you want, wearing anything you want, being anything you want, the night starting madness so intense you can't believe it's happening—the night before Carnival.

Our taxi climbs Belmont Hill and stops at the jammed entrance arcade on the top level of the Hilton. Driver says it's called the "upside-down" hotel because you enter the lobby on the top floor, then take the elevator down to the seven floors of rooms built into the sides of the hill. Judy Cooper, Terri McBride, Louie, and me, we're all half bombed from the unlimited booze in Pan Am's first class, we follow the bellboy with our luggage along the wooden walkway, and off to our right on a lower level we can see the lighted pool in the shape of Trinidad, surrounded by candle-lit tables. On the lawn beyond the pool, a small steel band is beating soft calypso, and silhouettes shuffle on the dance floor.

Louie and I register at the desk, we both put "Mr. & Mrs.," of course, but we give our legit names and addresses, no reason to fake it down here, plus we'll be using our legit credit cards for a lot of stuff. Lobby's packed, noise level high, lots of people wearing weird getups. Now we have to wait for another bellboy to escort us to our luxurious suite, I glance around, take in the architectural ambience. Quite a joint. There's this dining area on a level down to our left, below a white circular stairway, big colorful room designed to look like a tropical summerhouse-type deal, enclosed by floor-to-ceiling glass on three sides, overlooking that romantic lighted pool. Must be hundreds of lush tropical plants scattered around, well-kept jungle atmosphere, supposed to give the illusion of open-air dining, just misses, nice try. Judy and Terri, they're pointing at the chandeliers, these things are exact imitations of steel-band drums. Yeah. Even to the carefully contoured note sections, drums of all sizes and shapes, all painted bright primary colors. I mean, this is no chintzy decor here, Hilton's talking authentic chichi elegance all the way.

Bellboy finally grabs our loaded luggage trolley, runs interference for us to the elevator banks. We manage to squeeze in one, go down just three floors, we're exchanging raised eyebrows, our suite must have a fabulous view. Should have, $330 a pop. Does. Me, I let Louie handle the tip, he's the ranking officer, I head straight for the terrace, Judy and Terri right on my heels. Slide open the glass door, step out into Disneydad: *Oooohhh! Aaaahhh! Hot daaamn, Vietnaaam!* Picture postcard this: Downtown Port-of-Spain is a distant, dizzy halo of gold beyond the darkening mountains and the red-streaked sky. Gulf is changing color. Three large cruise ships are anchored near the dock area, portholes blazing, throwing yellow across the water. Temperature? I'd guess high seventies. Balmy. Fragrant breeze. Men and women from the frozen north could go crazy in this atmosphere. Crazy. Shed their inhibitions, as it were. Particularly during a carnival where, it's been said, revelers often shed clothes as well as inhibitions.

Speaking of which, when the girls change in *their* bedroom (we're working cops, we don't fool around) and bounce out to join Louie and me in the living room, their fashion signatures could be described as kicky but cautious Caribbean cop. Terri, you'd have to see this kid to believe she's been a detective for almost eight years now, still looks like she just stepped out of a Pepsi ad: Silky light brunette hair, brown eyes, five-six, maybe

115. Tonight she sports an obviously brand-new (expense account) red-and-white horizontal striped sweater, sleeveless, white cotton capri-length pants, white Keds without laces. Plus big red-plastic circle earrings and a matching bracelet. Judy, she's a couple of years older, early thirties, around five-four, 118, sexy frizz to her short blond hair. Dark brown eyes, thick lashes all her own, high cheekbones, teeth so white that even Tammy Bakker would kill for 'em. Now, get this. Ever hear of *ice*-washed denim? New to me, but that's what she's wearing. Ice-washed denim jumpsuit. I mean, how tony can a cop get? Swear to Christ, this kid looks like she's poured into cracked blue ice. Snaps up the front, three-quarter rolled sleeves, slash pockets, almost-matching blue thongs.

Louie's conservative all the way. Flowered trousers, orange pullover with a big bronze medallion, white Reeboks. Me, I don't look all that tight-assed myself, new short-sleeved sport shirt with blue-and-white horizontal stripes, new white denim jeans, old Top-Siders. Piece of gear we all miss, of course, our service revolvers. When you live with one every day, you tend to feel very, very uncomfortable without it. Republic of Trinidad and Tobago has a strict prohibition against all firearms. Police here don't even carry 'em. Last time I had to leave mine home was back in December 1985 when I went to Egypt on a case. Wound up staring down the business end of a helium-neon gas laser drill held by the thief, who was also a killer. Time before that, April 1982, went to England on a case, wound up staring down the barrel of a .38 held by the thief, who was also a killer, happened to be a young lady. Crazy young lady, at that. Felt naked without my piece both times, feel the same way now.

Well, the way we figure it, tonight might be the only night we won't be working, so we want to make the most of it, move around town, catch some of the action, get in the Carnival spirit. Lots of literature in the room about the various events scheduled, plus a good street map, and a map of the island itself. We decide to study this stuff over a drink in the Carnival Bar, top floor, we received four chits for complimentary drinks when we checked in. Then we'll head downtown and see what's going on.

It's about 6:15 when we get up there, 5:15 New York time, perfect timing for Happy Hour. Louie's paired off with Judy because she's the shorter of the two; me, I'm the giant of the gang at five-ten, I got a good four inches over Terri in her tennies. Carnival Bar turns out to be a pleasantly cool, relatively quiet, softly lighted place with thick green carpeting, intimate little tables, and a long, low, blond mahogany bar. Area where the bartenders stand is sunken—only their heads and shoulders are visible—so that you have an unobstructed view through the tall windows. With the oncoming darkness, houselights are yellow dots all over the mountainsides. We opt for the bar, sit in comfortable leather armchairs, hand in our cards for the complimentary drink, called Coco-n-Oak.

"What's in it?" Judy asks the bartender.

He smiles, speaks in a kind of musical patois. "All kinds of good things. Rum, gin, coconut milk, a little carypton."

"Beefeater gin?" I ask.

"Yes, sir, if you want it."

"My man," Louie says. "Could you recommend some good nightspots downtown?"

Bartender laughs as he mixes the drinks. "Well, it all depends on what you mean by 'good,' sir. Are you in the mood for—"

"Nothing posh," Terri tells him. "We're in the mood for some real earthy entertainment."

"Right," Judy says. "Emphasis on *earthy.*"

"Well, in that case, ladies, you'll want to stop in the Mariner Club down on South Quay." He glances at me. "But make sure you ask for a table in the balcony, sir. It gets a bit—well, earthy down on the floor."

"Floor shows?" I ask.

"All night long, sir."

"Far from here?" Louie asks.

"No, sir, it's just down on the waterfront." He pours our drinks in green coconuts with floating lilies and tiny plastic monkeys holding the straws.

Judy holds up her coconut. *"J'ouvert!"*

"Watch your language," Louie tells her.

Sips her drink, looks at the ceiling, shakes her lovely frizzy hair. *"J'ouvert!* It's French, it's a popular Carnival shout. It means, I'm free, I'm liberated, I'm open, I'm ready to let it all hang out."

"Both of 'em?" Louie asks.

Terri turns to me, unbuttons my shirt to the chest. "Know what's wrong with you guys? You're—basically, on a very basic level, you're a couple of tight-ass senior citizens here. Good looks, great sense of humor, top physical shape, but your *asses* are too tight."

"It's called 'hardening of the sphincter muscles," Judy says.

"The dreaded hard-ass syndrome," Terri says. "Classic symptom of the dreaded male moon of pause. Judy and me, we're swimming in *The Blue Lagoon* here and you guys are *On Golden Pond.*"

Me, I consider myself halfway between, but I play basketball every day, what can I tell you? In any event, it goes like so at the bar, we're not ready for dinner, we had a huge late lunch in first class, and we're not tired either, we all managed to grab a few hours of sleep after the movie, *Ironweed,* with Jack Nicholson and Meryl Streep, they've both been nominated for Oscars. Okay, we study our maps and brochures, finish our drinks, go out, grab a cab, head for the Mariner Club.

Traffic is heavy all the way down, streets alive with crowds, and as we get closer to downtown we can hear the sounds of many of the big steel bands marching around. With the windows open, we can smell the warm evening air, a damp, strange smell, like fruit or vegetables rotting. Stars are bright, seem very close, millions of them visible, extending all the way down to the bold outlines of the mountain ranges. Taxi driver, he's a happy young guy, he tells us the big groups are following their favorite steel bands, or "orchestras," as they're often called, and each band is playing its own original "road march." Says many steel bands number over a hundred players, almost all young, few over thirty, all dressed in colorful uniforms. He goes slow so we can get a good look at some. They all march inside long, low, rectangular scaffolds made of metal pipes and with wheels of every description. Scaffolds are sometimes ten drums wide and fifteen drums long, each drum painted with the colors and insignia of their sponsor, firms like Texaco, B.W.I.A., Hilton, Shell, Kodak, Pan Am, Coca-Cola, and Esso. Driver says the first rows hold high-toned kettle-drums, next rows hold progressively larger drums, then finally the last rows with the loud bass booms and the clang of the "steel-cutters"—auto brakes—dominating. Mounted policemen in white cork helmets are all over, helpless in the mob, and street vendors are doing a good business in the heat and dust, selling rum, mauby, oranges, coconuts, all kinds of fruit drinks, and flavored ice-licks.

Driver says there isn't any order to it tonight, they just march wherever they want. Says there are bands here from every corner of the island, each the best in its area. Forty-eight of them competed in the preliminary eliminations held last Sunday at the Savannah (that's a racecourse with a big grandstand up near the Hilton, where most of the major events of Carnival take place), and the number was narrowed to ten finalists for the Panorama Steel Band Championship held just this afternoon. Shell won this year, driver says they deserved it, they were the best.

Good sharp kid, this driver, says that to tourists one band probably sounds like all the others, but most Trinidadians can distinguish one steel band from another blocks away. Says there's very little guesswork. Says most people spend long evenings judging for themselves in the neighborhood "pan yards" months before Carnival. Neighborhoods where there are no streetlights, where the only light comes from open windows and bare bulbs strung on wires over the yards, where the bands practice seven nights a week for as long as six months before the eliminations. Says people go to as many as a dozen yards a night, whole families, to stand back in the warm dark, silent, serious, respectful, hearing how the new "kaisos" are being arranged. Says it's an honor for a small boy to be allowed to stand inside; inside where the sign on the tree says *Panmen Only;* inside where he's allowed to stand next to his favorite player, right by his side in the unreal light, allowed to watch, to listen, to learn, to see the rubber-headed batons go like hell over the kettle or boom, all from memory because in steel band there's no written music. Never knew that. None of us ever knew any of this stuff.

Louie gives the driver a big-league tip, he's told us more about steel bands in half an hour than any of our fancy brochures with their posed four-color spreads and no information about the real world down here. Kid thanks us kindly, jumps out, opens the door, helps the ladies out. Last time a New York cabbie did that, Teddy Roosevelt was commissioner of NYPD and the carriages were drawn by nags.

Mariner Club is jammed with tourists from the cruise ships *Maracaibo* and *Orion* (yuppies wear name tags in case they get lost), plus hundreds of sailors from the Canadian ship H.M.C.S. *Bonaventure* who look like a motley crew despite the clean white uniforms. This joint is simply a waterfront imitation of New York's once-famous old Latin Quarter, remember that? Remember Billy Martin getting Mickey Mantle in a fistfight in there, back when they were still players? Wooden dance-floor/stage in the center, surrounded by ringside tables pushed in close, more circles of tables back from ringside, a raised area with tables along the windowed wall, and a high balcony over the long, crowded bar. Louie slips the maître d' something, we're shown to the VIP balcony where all the Christians sit. Before the waiter gets to us, we have a nice view of several fistfights and the wide-open soliciting of wonderfully foul-mouthed hookers, lesbians, pimps, transvestites, gays, you name it. Waiter finally takes our order, says there's a "nonstop all-night floor show" all right, but it stops every fifteen minutes.

Tell you what, after you get a few drinks in you, the shows aren't all that bad, if you go for offbeat entertainment. For example, Judy and Terri, they get their rocks off by the Bottle Dance. The Bottle Dance of the followers of the sacred Shango Cult. Master of ceremonies, who, as Louie pointed out, really does bear a striking resemblance to Richard Nixon in a fright wig, but has a gravel-throated Brooklyn accent, he introduces 'em like so: "Under fast-changin' disco strobes, these here nearly nude male and female dancers, overpowered by supernatural spirits, will gyrate to the eerie rhythm of African jungle drums, jumpin', whirlin', prancin', and rollin' on broken bottles that you folks in the audience will be allowed to supply and break yourselves. Nothin' phoney about this, folks, come on, come down and start breakin' bottles!"

Louie jumps up, joins in the yelps, grabs two of his empty beer bottles, maneuvers his way downstairs, laughing like a madman. They got a sheet spread on the dance floor, people are smashing bottles by the dozen (some of 'em full), sounds like a greenhouse in an earthquake. Louie slings his two in, comes running back, the girls are standing now, yelling, screaming. Me, I'm sipping my Beefeater martini on the rocks with a twist, puffing calmly on my Dutch Masters panatela, wondering how any dancers can possibly pull this shit off.

Houselights dim, colored strobe lights start pulsating, eerie rhythm of African jungle drums gets louder and louder. Spotlight hits the dressing room door, out they come, a line of about a dozen young guys and gals wearing jocks and smiles. You can hear the tinkle and crunch as they jump and gyrate around barefoot, arms flailing, eyes wild, obviously getting in the mood. Terri and Judy are wincing, cringing, laughing, this is real earthy shit. Louie's delighted, he's moving his shoulders and arms to the rhythm, swigging his beer, not bad duty for a Spanish kid from Red Hook.

I nudge him. "What's your instant diagnosis?"

"They don't *bleed*! The fuckers got no *blood*!"

"How do they *do* it?" Terri shouts.

Louie does his madman laugh. "Didn't ya hear Nixon? They're *overpowered*! Overpowered by super-fuckin'-natural *spirits,* that's how they do it!"

Back in the audience, about a half-dozen kids who apparently belong to the sacred Shango Cult too, they're overcome by the spirits now, they start letting go with high-pitched screams, they leap up on their tables, they even roll on the floor. Okay, that's all the encouragement the dancers on stage need, they live up to their billing now, they're whirling, prancing, and *rolling* around in the glass. No, this is straight, I mean I saw it with my own eyes. No skin-colored body stockings, nothing like that, they're sweating like crazy, they're wearing jockstraps, period. Okay, they might be covered in oil, that's possible, that'd prevent a lot of friction, but that glass down there is real. I know, I hear you, there's a scientific explanation for all this, the body secretes certain protective fluids under certain life-threatening situations, that's how the firewalkers get away with it, right? Still, you see this kind of weird crap, it gives you pause.

After the Bottle Dance, master of ceremonies introduces two rugged-looking women wrestlers, "both of 'em lesbians," he announces proudly, who will preform with no holds barred, "wearing just jocks," while a beautiful Polynesian stripper, who hasn't appeared yet, "herself on the AC-DC current, if ya get my thought," will dance around them with a specially designed foot-long dildo to hold her clothes and do other things, "if ya get my thought," he concludes. Spotlight swings to the dressing room door and follows the stripper out as the steel band plays something exotic and the room goes wild again.

"Let's go to the Penguin Club," Judy says out of the blue.

We don't pay any attention to her; she's reading brochures.

"Let's go to the Penguin Club!"

I look at her. "The Penguin Club?"

"Says here it's the most sophisticated club in town."

"In these clothes?" Terri asks.

Judy shrugs. "Doesn't matter. It's almost Carnival."

"They'd never let us in," I tell her.

"You ever been there?" she asks me.

I sip my martini. "We'd need coats and ties, you'd need cocktail dresses, all that. What's wrong with this place?"

"This place's—*tawdry.*"

We ignore her. Wrestlers are hilarious, big beefy things, and the stripper's timing is excellent. Crowd's breaking up. Judy sulks, sipping her rum, staring at her glass. Show ends with a loud ovation as the stripper squirms away from a tangle of arms and legs on the floor and runs nude to the dressing room door, dildo rammed in her ass, fatso wrestlers in hot pursuit. Crowd goes nuts, spotlight picks up Nixon, arms up, giving the victory sign with his middle fingers, eyes rolling. Steel band segues into soft dance music, houselights come up, we're into another fifteen-minute break. All of us agree with Judy that it's tawdry as hell, finish our drinks, head for the sophisticated Penguin Club.

Streets are even more crowded than before, many people carrying torchlights now, big steel bands marching around, traffic's slowed to a crawl. We maneuver along South Quay toward Frederick Street, following our map, pausing to take in the costumes and bands. Whole scene is beautiful by torchlight, totally unreal. If this is what they do the night before Carnival, makes you wonder what's coming up.

Penguin Club's on the top floor of an office building on

Frederick. Take the elevator to the fifth floor, get off, follow the signs, walk up two more flights. Heavy glass door, then we walk into pleasant air conditioning, soft lighting, thick carpeting. Maître d' comes over in a tux, Louie makes with a paper handshake, guy doesn't give our duds a second glance. Shows us to a window table in the corner of the bar area. Girls are all smiles now, wide windows give an excellent view of the downtown streets, plus the clusters of house lights spilling down the mountainsides. It's very crowded, but even from here we can see part of the floor show in the other room. A classy calypso singer's walking around the empty dance floor with a mike, making up lyrics about the people at the tables. Kid's a real comedian and the crowd loves it. He points to some couple, spotlight picks them up, then he sings a quick little story about who they are, where they're from, what they're up to, or hope to be up to—all in rhyme—and the crowd howls. As my eyes adjust, I glance around the bar itself. Casually dressed tourist types, quite a few Americans, plus a sprinkle of classy-looking hookers, very young girls, some in their teens, light-skinned, smartly dressed, obviously working for the club.

"See anybody in a coat and tie?" Judy asks us.

"Nope."

"Nope."

"Nope."

"See anybody in a cocktail dress?"

"Yeah."

"Yeah!"

"*Yeah*!"

"Not *them,* ya wimps! The *real* people."

We order a round of drinks from our tuxedoed waiter, then the girls go off to the ladies' room. When they come back, the calypso singer's finished his gig, the band's into a relatively slow number, and people are getting up to dance. Terri grabs my hand, flicks a thumb toward the dance floor. Off I go, but under mild protest.

"Keep a secret?" I ask.

"Yeah."

"I can't dance calypso."

"No, huh?"

"Never danced calypso in my life."

"So improvise."

"Can't. Got two left feet."

"Yeah? Whaddaya do on Golden Pond?"

"Waltz. Fox-trot."

Gets a laugh out of her. *"Tight."*

"I know."

"Ass."

"I know."

We get on the dance floor, she tells me to watch her, then copycat. Do my best. Must say, kid's got natural rhythm, does calypso like a native, in an almost stationary shuffle, knees bent slightly, arms in close and pumping softly, like trying to walk with her feet glued to the floor. Makes it look easy, smiling, really feeling the beat, peaches-and-cream Pepsi ad. Me, I'm doing okay now, I'm finally getting into it. I mean, I can almost feel the old sphincter muscles begin to loosen up.

Then it happens. I see this man at a table in back, just a glimpse at first, his right profile in candlelight, talking to a girl at his table, can't be his wife, she's too young. Take another quick look. I know this guy. *Who, what, when, where?* He's laughing, holding hands with the girl, looks to be in her late twenties. Man's about my age, mid-fifties. Full head of hair, gray-white at the temples, at least it seems that way in candlelight. High forehead, thin black steel-framed glasses, aviator style. Handsome profile, straight nose, strong chin. *Who, what, when, where?* Know him, know him, know him. Know his face by heart. Must've seen him dozens of times, close range. Who is he?

One thing I know for certain, he's not a cop. Can't explain exactly how I know that, I just know. Call it instinct, gut feel, whatever. Instinct also tells me this guy may very possibly be somebody I put away. When? Don't know. Must've been quite a few years back, because I'm usually good at matching names and faces. *Who, what, when, where?* Face draws a blank, at least temporarily, but it gives me an unpleasant feeling. Don't know why. My radar just picks up bad readings about this particular guy. You stay in this line of work thirty-two years, primarily robbery squad, you put a lot of crooks away. How many? Knew you'd ask. Okay, you work robbery, say you arrest and help to convict an average of fifteen to twenty people a year, conservative average. That works out to between 480 and 640 people you helped send to prison in thirty-two years. Lot of people. Sure, some of 'em are repeaters, career criminals, but you still wind up with a hefty total. Ninety-nine-point-nine percent don't give you any grief when they get out, they don't take it personally, particularly the pros. But there are always a few who do, almost always the real wackos. They brood in the can for, say, seven to ten years, they think about you, they blame you personally, they build up a festering hatred, they fantasize about how they're going to get revenge. They get out, they come after you. Happens. Ask any cop who's been around awhile. If I'm honest about it, that's one of the major reasons I feel so vulnerable without a weapon. Because you never know who's out there. And you think about it, at least on a subconscious level, frequently. And you think about what one of these sick animals might do to your family.

Question: Does this guy see *me*? I mean, the floor's crowded, sure, but it's a relatively small floor, and here I am, dancing up a storm, bright striped shirt, white jeans, full view of practically everybody. Calypso number finishes, Terri and I leave the room, I don't look over there again. But now, back at our table in the bar, I'm thinking about him, I can't help it, I'm trying to match a name to that profile. I don't tell the others, of course, I don't want to spoil their fun.

Next twenty minutes or so, they got another floor show going on in there, dancers doing the limbo, typical tourist stuff. When it's dance time again, I ask Judy, Louie asks Terri, we all go in together. Fairly fast calypso this time, I'm watching Judy, doing my copycat thing, I try not to look over there for the first few minutes. Then, when Judy's between me and a straight-line view of this guy's table, I take a fast glance. Young couple sitting there. At first, I think I'm looking at the wrong table, I wait, then I scan the other tables back there. Man's gone. In a way, I'm relieved. But I can't stop thinking about him and the strange feeling that face gave me. Did he see *me*? Is that why he left? Since I remember his face so vividly, it's odds-on that he'd remember mine. Christ, what's the matter with me? Why should I let something like this get to me?

Time flies on your night off. We stay at the Penguin until almost midnight and dance a lot and drink a lot and I begin to feel happy and relaxed again. The four of us come out of there *singing*. Yeah. Crowds in the street are still carrying on, Carnival's official at midnight, everybody's bombed. No taxis in sight, we walk up Prince Street, where traffic's moving, and hang around until we get what's called a "drop taxi" heading up Charlotte Street. Driver's going all the way to Maraval, but says he'll drop us at the foot of Belmont Hill, where it's a short walk up to the Hilton.

Taxi already has four passengers, we squeeze in, the girls on our laps. Driver makes frequent stops along Charlotte. People getting in and out all speak fast "Trinidadianese" that's difficult for outsiders to understand. It's a language of their own, like Brooklyn street vernacular, hurried, abbreviated, full of four-letter words, rich in repartee, sounds like it's got an African-French-Spanish-English base, but with English dominating, if you listen carefully. They speak with their hands and faces and bodies and there's nearly always emotion and music in their voices. Tonight, they're especially happy and excited, of course, and it's enjoyable to hear them.

Hop out at Belmont Hill, Louie pays the driver, we walk up

the hill in moonlight, singing. Three, four cars pass us, squealing around the curves, going very fast. Terri holds my hand tightly. Louie swears at the cars after they pass, calls 'em fuckin' assholes, shakes his fist at 'em. Kid's a pisser, you'd have to see him in his flowered trousers. Judy's blond hair looks beautiful in the moonlight.

It's around one o'clock or so when we get up to the hotel. Judy and Terri call it quits, they've had it, but I feel wide awake for some reason. Louie and I go out to the pool for a nightcap.

Still a few people at the circular grass-thatched bar, but the hotel's steel band is gone. Umbrellaed tables and deck chairs have been pulled back from the cement to the grass, cement hosed down, grass watered too, smells good in the cool air. I order a Jack Daniels, rocks, Lou has a Drambuie. Sign the tab, take our glasses away from the bar, and sit in deck chairs on the grass, back from the glow of the lighted pool, under one of the palm trees. Lights in the trees are off, big fronds are dark against the stars.

"Question," I say. "Ever hurt anybody in the job? I mean, when you were on the street?"

"Not real bad, no. Busted a few beaks, kicked ass, the usual. Why?"

"Never used your gun?"

"Never had to, John, thank God. Drew it a few times working Brooklyn South, never had to use it. But I just wasn't on the street that long, know what I mean?"

"Yeah. That's true."

"You?"

I sip my bourbon. "Yeah. Yeah, I had to use it a few times."

"And?"

"Got involved in a couple of scrapes, Harlem, late 'sixties. Never hit anybody, far as I know."

"Talk to me, John. I mean, I know that tone of voice too well. What's happening?"

Underwater pool lights brighten and dim in very slow pulsation, two sets of four lights each at both the deep and shallow ends. First red, painting the water gradually from pale to intense, then joined by blue, same deal, pale to intense, then green, then yellow. Now the cycle is completed, water fades to black, stars reflected on the surface.

"Talk to me, John. Something happened tonight, I know it, you know it, okay? This is me, remember? Happened at the Penguin, happened just after you danced with Terri that first time. It was in your eyes, man, you can't hide shit like that from me."

"It's probably nothing. I saw a guy in there tonight. Table in the other room. I know the man, Lou. Don't know his name, but I know his face, I'd know it anywhere."

"Black guy?"

"White."

"Then you can rule out the Harlem shit."

"Yeah."

"Somebody you sent up?"

"Got to be."

"Can't remember his name?"

"Can't remember it."

"Must be a face from long back."

"Must be."

"How old a guy?"

"About my age. Fifty-three, fifty-four."

"Okay, come on, what actually happened? He say something to you? He threaten you in some—"

"No. Nothing like that."

"What, he give you a look or—?"

"No. I'm not even sure if he—well, no, he must've seen me."

"What makes you think so?"

"He left fast. At least, I think he did. Maybe he just moved on, I don't know. He was with a young girl, late twenties."

Louie nods, sips his drink; his face reflects red from the

pool. "I hear you, John, I know where you're coming from. It's something every street cop has to live with. You put a guy away, sooner or later, he'll be out. The longer you're in harness, the more of 'em out there. I'm sure you've faced—what, hundreds of 'em, right?"

"Lots. Truth is, it never really bothered me all that much. Never lost any sleep over any of 'em. Know why? Swear to God, as far as I know, I never hurt anybody real bad in this job. I always made a conscious effort never to hurt anybody unnecessarily."

"So what's the hang-up about this guy?"

"His face. For some reason, his face draws a blank."

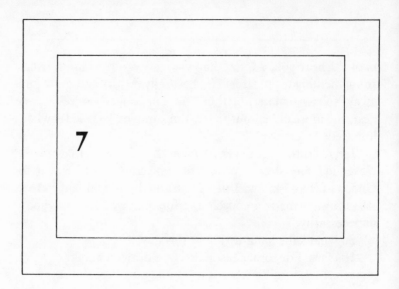

7

GENERAL HOSPITAL is on the main drag, Charlotte Street, big old seven-story building, and the Trauma Center is a modern two-story wing with a separate entrance. We figure, Dr. Leonard being chief of staff and all, he'd be on duty over Carnival weekend, probably day shift, so we arrive about 9:15, four casually dressed tourists. I go up to the main desk in the lobby, take out the envelope with my letter from Dr. Veritas to Dr. Leonard. Introduce myself to the young lady there, show her the letter, tell her I'd like to deliver it personally, if that's possible. She jots down my name, picks up a phone, punches some buttons, waits. Healthy-looking kid, dark hair, dark eyes, teeth as white as her uniform. Identifies herself as Coogan, Reception, explains the situation, asks Leonard if he can see me. Answer is yes, but he's busy right now, could I wait about half an hour? Sure thing. Lobby's modern, spotless, surprises me that only a handful of people are waiting around, after all the wild celebrating we saw last night. Hate to think what it'll be like in here tonight, first official night of Carnival.

My uneducated guess, total bedlam. Blood? Like the Red Sea was a dirty bathtub. Price you pay for mass hysteria.

We sit and wait, read the morning paper, *The Guardian.* Banner headline: J'OUVERT! Judy's gloating about that, says Terri and her got all the Carnival buzzwords down cold, wants to know when the Odd Couple gets up-to-speed here. Most of the paper's devoted to Carnival, of course, and there are some interesting stats: Radio Trinidad predicts that up to three million people will take part in the festivities today through midnight Tuesday. Kickoff is noon today up at the Queen's Park Savannah (the big racecourse), where they'll stage the huge, traditional costume parades, including forty-eight steel orchestras, then the major event of the night will be the calypso king and queen contests. Happen to have box seats for all this merriment, courtesy of the girls, who simply tacked the tickets on the expense account. I got my excuse all re-hearsed in my head: Chief, Dr. *Leonard* attended all these events, he had box *seats* for the whole four days, we were doing *surveillance* on him, catching crooks ain't *cheap*!

Exactly 9:55, Dr. Leonard walks briskly into the lobby, in-troduces himself, shakes hands all around, his lean body tow-ering over us. I'd judge him to be about seventy-five years old, six-three, 170. Trim white hair, bald pate, tortoiseshell-framed glasses, speaks with a crisp British accent.

"Now, I understand you have a letter for me?"

I hand him the envelope. "Yes, sir, from my physician."

LUXET VERITAS, M.D., P.A.

1065 Park Avenue

New York, NY 10028

(212) 860-4900

February 10, 1988

Dr. Derek Leonard

Chief of Staff

Trauma Center

Port-of-Spain General Hospital

700 Charlotte Street

Port-of-Spain, Trinidad, W.I.

Dear Dr. Leonard:

My patient, Mr. John Rawlings, has been undergoing
treatment for chronic myelocytic leukemia for approximately
two years. During that period, X-ray therapy has proven
reasonably successful, and he has reacted well to busulfan,
regulated on the basis of biweekly blood counts.

Mr. Rawlings and his wife, together with Mr. and Mrs. Louis
Diaz, will be attending the Trinidad Carnival, and plan to be
in Port-of-Spain, February 12-18, staying at the Trinidad
Hilton.

Although it is unlikely that Mr. Rawlings would require
medical attention during this one-week visit, I thought it
would be judicious for him to have the name and hospital
affiliation of a physician in Port-of-Spain, as a
precautionary measure. Naturally, I would be pleased to

extend the same professional courtesy to any of your patients
who may be traveling to New York.

    Mr. Rawlings obtained your name and address from Mr. Edward
Cerabino of Phoenix, Arizona, who recommended you.

    If you should need any further information about Mr.
Rawlings's medical history and/or present therapy, please do
not hesitate to telephone me collect.

Sincerely,

Luxet Veritas, M.D.

LV/alb

    Dr. Leonard smiles. "Edward Cerabino. I haven't heard
from him in—many, many years. May I ask how you became
acquainted?"

    "Met him just a couple of weeks ago," I say. "Dr. Veritas
and I had corresponded with him for some time."

    "I see. And you met him in Phoenix?"

    "Yes, sir. When I told him I was going to the Trinidad
Carnival, he recommended you as a medical contact. Dr. Veritas didn't know any physicians in Trinidad."

    "Yes, I see. Well, rest assured that I'll be available for any
assistance you might require."

    "Appreciate it, Dr. Leonard."

    "How are you feeling now?"

    "Just a little tired. It was a long flight yesterday, then we did
a little celebrating last night."

    "Ah, yes. Well, the next four nights always tend to be a bit
hectic, so I'd suggest you get as much rest during the days as
possible. Conserve your energy."

    "I'll do that."

    He glances at the others, smiles. "That's sound advice for

all of you. Try to conserve your energy."

"Right."

"Yes."

"Right."

Now he takes out his wallet, removes a calling card, hands it to me. "Please don't hesitate to call at any time. The top number is my office at the hospital, the other is my home number. I have an answering service during the evenings. If it's an emergency, they'll call me and I'll call you back immediately."

I shake his hand. "That's very kind of you. Thanks very much for taking the time to see me. I appreciate it."

"Not at all."

"Ed Cerabino wanted me to give you his best regards."

"How very nice of him. How is he getting on these days?"

"He's doing quite well. I was very impressed with his facilities there."

"In Phoenix, yes. Still in the cryonics business, is he?"

"Yes, sir. That's what I was seeing him about. I've been making the necessary arrangements for cryonic suspension."

He nods, frowns, adjusts his glasses. "Ah, I see. I see. That's very interesting indeed. Fascinating science. Some years ago, I was actually conducting research in the general field of cryonics. Did he mention that?"

"No, sir. But he said he did business with you years ago."

"Yes. Quite a long time ago, actually. It must have been—let me think. I believe it was sometime in the nineteen-sixties, if memory serves."

"Have you kept fairly current on the subject?"

"I'm afraid not, other than the odd newspaper or magazine articles over the years." Glances at his watch. "I'm terribly sorry, but I really do have to get back. It was a pleasure to meet all of you—Mrs. Rawlings, Mr. and Mrs. Diaz. Perhaps we can—you'll be here a week—perhaps we can arrange to get together for a drink or something before you leave."

"We'd really enjoy that," Terri says.

He gives her a bright smile. "All right? Frankly, I'd like to pick your husband's brain about what's going on in cryonics these days. I'm afraid I've got a lot of catching up to do."

"Any time at all," I tell him. "It'd be a pleasure."

"You're just up at the Hilton," he says. "I'll see how the work load goes, perhaps I'll be able to call and stop by for a chat on my way home one evening. Probably not during Carnival, it gets pretty busy around here, as you can imagine, but surely before the week is out."

Queen's Park Savannah is chaos at noon. Huge "bands" of costumed people march through the narrow streets leading to Park West by the tens of thousands and crowds stand five and six deep from the curbs, lean out windows, and perch on roofs and walls, straining to see. The big steel "orchestras" that are supposed to accompany each of the bands on stage arrive in stake trucks, wagon trucks, tongue trucks, dump trucks, lorries, open and closed buses, or march on foot inside the rolling scaffolds. They all converge on the Savannah within the same hour and the noise is terrific. Traffic is snarled as far as you can see in all directions and horns blare from hundreds of vehicles simultaneously, so that inside, as the bands boogie across this enormous wooden stage that's about the length of a football field, it's difficult to hear the orchestras. To make matters worse, the sky is overcast and the humidity is very high.

Terri and Judy aren't with us. They take one look from the terrace of our suite about eleven o'clock and that was it. No way. They rent a car and take off for Maracas, which is the only decent beach on the island. We don't blame them. In fact, Louie and I rent a car at the same time and tell them we'll be out there in the early afternoon. But first we want to catch a little of this action here.

Grandstand, temporary stands, and bleachers are filled to capacity, and thousands more are sitting in the aisles. We have four box seats in the grandstand, and we're beginning to feel guilty, when a young couple comes down and takes the two empty seats; we welcome them. They're Trinidadians in their late teens, good-looking kids, wearing colorful straw hats. Program says there are forty-eight bands registered for today, together with their own steel orchestras, and we don't see how it's going to be possible to finish this thing before sundown. A band is announced and the roar starts and the music plays and they parade or dance across the long elevated stage over the track, waves of them, sometimes looks like over a thousand members, in some of the most imaginative "theme" costumes we've ever seen. There are floats and props and elaborate headdresses and almost all the bands stage a brief skit of some kind for the judges. In the Ancient History category we'd arrived too late to see "She and the Tibetians," "Golden Age of the Assyrian Empire," and "Golden Age of Athens," but we saw "Mesopotamia B.C.," which was excellent. Then, under Modern History, we saw "This Was France," "Roya-line du Dahomey 1442–1890," "Les Fetes Galante des Versailles," and "Splendour of Ancient Java." Distinction between ancient and modern is debatable, but what the hell.

They come on and on and each seems bigger and more splendid than the last, particularly "Fan Fare" in the Original category. Members of this one hold enormous rainbow-colored fans on poles and have costumes to match, so that when they dance, filling the entire stage area and waving the fans in rhythm with the music, it's really spectacular. Sun breaks through for short periods and when it does Louie takes some snapshots with his little automatic Nikon. Takes shots of the bands, then the crowd, and gets me in the foreground of a few.

We decide to leave about one o'clock. I tell the young couple next to us that we'll be gone for the rest of the afternoon and give them our ticket stubs, plus the tickets intended for Terri and Judy, to give to their friends. Outside, there aren't any taxis around. There's a big crowd at the west end of the grandstand; the bands are leaving from a gate there and marching back through the side streets. Another crowd is at the far east end of the bleacher section, where the bands are forming to go in, backed up all the way to Queen's Park East and down Charlotte Street. We walk toward that crowd, maneuver through, then turn left, walk along Queen's Park East, and finally up the hill to the hotel.

Now we go into the Carnival Bar, have a beer and a sandwich, and watch the festivities at the Savannah through the tall windows in air-conditioned comfort. We're wearing our swim trunks under our jeans, so we go directly to the Hertz counter in the lobby, pick up the keys, go out and jump into our gray 1988 Chevy Beretta. It's a little more expensive than some of the others, but Louie's rented Berettas before, he likes them, and he wants to drive. Fine with me. I mean, I figure, a man in my condition shouldn't be driving anyhow. I'm the navigator with the map, I'm in charge of the radio, air conditioning, all the sophisticated shit, like telling him to drive on the *left* side of the road.

We follow Circular Road around the north edge of the Savannah, then take Saddle Road northeast toward the town of Maraval. Pleasant drive, gives us a chance to talk. Very little traffic in either direction. Louie's happy with the car; gooses it on the straight stretches, then slows to a moderate speed when we hit North Coast Road and start to climb. It's a first-class road, winding northeast through the green mountains of the Northern Range, two lanes of asphalt with adequate shoulders, but there are no guardrails even at the sharpest turns; I make a mental note to leave Maracas long before sundown. As we climb higher, the views are really something. Water of La Vache Bay sparkles a deep, transparent, sapphire-blue far below us in the early afternoon. From that elevation, we can actually see the mountains of Venezuela across the Paria peninsula. There are heavy clouds over there, the mountains are quite dark, and the water near the coastline is gray. Looks like it's raining in the mountains. Sun is still making a fight of it on our side, clouds are white and seem to move quickly in the breeze from the bay, but we know it can't last much longer.

Louie turns down the radio. "Question. If you were really dying of something, leukemia, heart disease, whatever, would you want to be frozen?"

"Couldn't afford it."

"Say you could."

"I've thought about it, Lou. First reaction, no. No way. But, according to all the research stuff I've been reading, more than forty thousand people, worldwide, are dues-paying members of one cryonics outfit or another."

"That a fact?"

"That's what it says."

"Forty thousand people can't all be wrong, right?"

"Keep in mind that a lot of 'em live in California. They tend to pick up on weird shit like this easier than we do."

He adjusts his sunglasses. "What I been thinking, I suppose it depends on the situation, know what I mean? Like, take a guy, he's about thirty-five, he knows his family's got a long history of heart disease, okay? Grandfather died young, father died young, all like that. Maybe he figures, what the hell, who knows, maybe in twenty, thirty years, artificial hearts might be commonplace. Huh? Maybe he figures, what's he got to lose? I mean, he's got the money, he can't take it with him, there's a high probability he'll be dead before he's forty. What's he got to lose? What're his alternatives? Rotting in a grave or being cremated, that's what his alternatives are. At least with cryonics, he's got some small degree of hope."

"Unless he's flattened by a steamroller," I say.

"Yeah." He smiles briefly, but he's serious. "Whatever condition the body is in at death, it remains unchanged indefinitely in liquid nitrogen. There's no cellular deterioration whatsoever."

"Okay, you're a scientific guy, answer me this question: How come only twenty-one people have been frozen in all these years?"

"That surprise you?"

"Yeah. Well, no, I suppose not."

"Doesn't surprise me."

"Lou, Erickson's book was published in nineteen-sixty-four, the first edition, the American hardback. The book that really started the whole movement, okay? Okay, now, twenty-four years have gone by. Movement's had its ups and downs, but there're still quite a few active cryonics societies all over the world. And at least one private corporation, Cryonics, in Phoenix, offers facilities for very professional cryonic suspension. With others on the way. Yet only twenty-one people have been frozen—I'm talking verified whole-body freezings. Know why? My opinion, it's because the movement can't get backing by the real eggheads, the scientific community."

"Yeah, fine, let me tell you something about the so-called scientific community. I mean, I happen to know something about it, because I'm in it. Let's put public acceptance aside for just a minute. John, the lag between scientific discoveries and acceptance by scientists has always been the ball-breaking part. Give you a couple of examples. Okay, take anesthetics. The first anesthetics were tested and proven in the early eighteen-hundreds, but *forty years* passed before they were used in surgical operations. Forty years, and it took even longer before they were offered to women in childbirth. I mean, I could cite you dozens—"

"Penicillin," I tell him.

"Yeah, right, there's another. Fleming discovered penicillin in nineteen-twenty-eight. Tested the hell out of it, realized its value, busted his ass to convince other scientists, but it wasn't in general use until nineteen-forty-four, and it took World War Two to do it, at that. What I'm saying, it's the rule, not the exception. It's not just the usual scientific caution and conservatism, it's because—it's what we call 'hardening of the categories.' Guys like Erickson know what they're up against. Changing scientific perspectives takes a long, long time. Particularly on a subject like this. When you're challenging ideas on the very nature of death."

"But there's been a lot of publicity. In the States, at least. Millions of people know the general idea."

"How many of 'em understand it, John?"

"Yeah, okay."

"How many of 'em have actually studied it, taken it very seriously?"

"I think a lot of 'em take it seriously now."

He gives me a look.

"I think they do," I tell him. "Most of 'em."

"I think you're optimistic there."

"If they know anything about it, I mean."

"Yeah, John, but what do most of 'em *know*? I'm talking the literate public, okay?, masses of people. In America, for example, what do they really know? If they read *People* magazine, they know that some outfit in California froze a beagle and brought him back to life. Okay? Or maybe they saw him on the Phil Donahue show, he was on that one, plus some others, I don't know. Okay, fine, they read about Miles, the Wonder Dog, they see him on TV, and maybe they think about it for a couple of minutes. Or laugh at the idiocy of the idea. Or bring it up for a laugh at the office or the next cocktail party. John, *that's* what they know. And, believe me, that's all they *want* to know."

"Why?"

He takes a deep breath. "Okay, how many people you know who want to talk about death? Or even think about it for any length of time? How many of your friends know the distinction between clinical death, biological death, and cellular death?"

"I don't know the technical definitions myself."

"Oh, sure you do."

"No, just in general—in layman's terms."

"Well, it's academic to most laymen, but death is a relative term, John. It doesn't occur all at once, in most cases. Fact is, it occurs very gradually over a period of hours. When your heart stops beating and your breathing stops, you're clinically dead. That's not necessarily final; in fact, it's often reversible. Countless numbers of people have been revived by CPR methods after clinical death. Today, death is thought to be final only when the decision is made that the body has deteriorated to an irreversible degree—for example, when the brain is deprived of oxygen for a number of minutes. But here's the thing. Here's the important thing to keep in mind. The decision is arbitrary today, because the criterion for irreversibility is constantly changing. I mean, a great many pathologic conditions that were considered irreversible only ten or twenty years ago are easily reversible today."

"And you think that's academic to most laymen?"

"Yeah, I think the general public considers it that way. But I didn't answer your question and it's important. Why doesn't the public *want* to know about cryonic suspension?"

"Because death isn't imminent to most of them."

"I don't think that's the real reason."

"It's got to be part of it," I tell him. "If it wasn't for this case, I honestly don't think I'd've studied the subject. Okay, I'm interested now that I've started, but I don't think I would've started on my own. I mean, I'd heard about freezing over the years, I knew it was happening, just like most people, but I wasn't interested enough to go out and buy a book about it. I didn't want to."

"Weren't you curious?"

"I suppose so, vaguely."

"You were curious, but you didn't want to find out about it?"

"I was too busy, Lou, I was occupied by other—"

"You just said you didn't *want* to read about it."

"I didn't. I didn't want to."

"Why?"

"Christ, I don't know."

"You think it's possible you were afraid of it?"

"*Afraid* of it? Why the fuck should I be afraid of an idea to extend life?"

He frowns, concentrates on the road. "Because the idea of extending life indefinitely is frightening. Think about that. I mean, you and me, like most people, we grew up, we went to school, we went to church when we were kids, we were educated to a specific set of absolutes: People are born, they live maybe as long as seventy-two, seventy-four years or so, if they're lucky, and they die. It's not long, but it's about as long as most of us can reasonably expect. So we grow up, we become adults, we adjust ourselves to the reality of it. And when you accept the fact, it's not too awful a piece of knowledge to live with. We even get comfortable with it. I mean, it's a dependable cycle and there's a strange kind of security about it. Then something happens. Some professor comes along, he says: Wait a minute, I don't agree; most of you have a logical chance of physical life after death, a scientific probability of revival and reanimation. It's not a joke, he says. It's not a hoax. It's a genuine possibility. Alter your perspectives, he says. You have a chance *right now* to avoid permanent death if you'll only listen, if you'll only act. It's a prospect that represents the greatest promise in the history of mankind, he says. A revolution of the species, the possibility of the indefinite extension of human life. If it turns out to be an impossible dream, what have you lost? If it succeeds . . ." He glances at me, pauses, then looks back at the road. "But maybe people don't want it to succeed."

"Yeah."

"And notice. We're talking about fear of living."

I start to answer No, but check myself.

We arrive about three o'clock and Maracas looks just like the color pictures in the brochures, only better: An extremely wide, clean white beach, curving for about a mile, bordered by tall rows of coconut palms, and surrounded by mountains. Fewer than a dozen cars are parked in the lot by the Casa de Maracas and sunbathers are only specks along the glare of sand. Surf rushes in long, flat, far up, then slides back slowly, leaves a quick mirror image of palm trunks, like dock pilings.

We spot the girls' rented red Mini Minor easily and park next to it. Louie, he's like a kid now, he can't wait, he jumps out, pulls off his shirt and jeans in a flash, he's laughing, he's going, "Holy shit, there's *nobody* here, look at that fuckin' *beach,* I can't *believe* it!" Off he goes, breaks into a sprint, straight down the beach, past the girls, into the water without breaking stride, then eight or ten high splashing steps, and into a running dive. Saturday afternoon at Coney Island, what can I tell you?

Me, I'm a civilized adult about all this, I mean when you've been to as many exotic tropical island beaches in the blue Caribbean as I have, it gets to a point where it's almost boring, know what I mean? I remove my T-shirt, jeans, and Top-Siders in a quasi-dignified fashion, place them in the car, pick up the keys Louie left carelessly on the seat, put on my stylish Porsche-Design Carrera sunglasses, lock the car, and walk leisurely toward the girls, who, I note, follow every ripple of my hard, lean, basketball-disciplined body. As well they should.

Terri holds up her drink. "Just in time for the rain!"

"Timed it perfectly," I say. "You two *drinking*?"

"Hair o' the dog!" Judy says.

"What the hell're you drinking?"

"Rum punches!" Terri says. "Liquid sunshine!"

Can't help laughing. They're wearing wide-brimmed straw hats and oversized sunglasses and they're covered with suntan lotion. Their bikinis are about as brief as they come, but they have the figures for 'em, and they're wearing their wedding rings, of course, to show the beach boys the bacon's taken.

Louie's wading now, lifting with the waves before they break. Water's a light blue-green in the sun, changes to a deep blue when the clouds pass over. Looking west, we can see the heavier clouds coming. It's very humid even near the water and the sand is hot. I sit on one of the two extra towels the girls brought along for us, borrow their big plastic container of genuine Ambre Solaire Advanced Tanning Filter with Moisturising Tanning Milk and the all-important "6 Protection Factor" that allows me to stay in the sun without burning six times longer than when unprotected. I slobber it all over me. Louie, he's out there completely unprotected, but I don't give a shit about him. I figure, he's a dark-skinned Spanish kid from Red Hook, he wouldn't know genuine Ambre Solaire from axle grease.

Sun breaks through frequently over the next hour or so and there are periods when we have good direct sunlight for as long as five minutes or more. We all go in the water occasionally to cool off, but spend most of the time on the beach. It's quiet and relaxing. Terri and I go for a walk all the way around the bay to the promontory. She looks great in the bikini and I can see she's getting the sun, particularly on her face and shoulders, despite the straw hat. Must be the strong reflection from the water. It's quite a long walk, but we enjoy it, picking up shells as we go.

Sun's almost gone when we get back and the clouds in the west seem much closer. They're black except for the edges. Land colors are intense in that light. There are whitecaps in the bay and the water is steel-gray. You can smell the rain on the wind, a warm rotting smell from the mountains. Nobody's left on the beach. Only our two cars are left in front of the Casa de Maracas. It's a low wooden building with a red clapboard roof and a big open porch. There's a long white sign on the roof with the name of the place in red letters and a Coca-Cola

symbol at each end. Small cottages are off to the right and in
back. Inside, it's dark and a bit cooler and there's a stale smell
of beer.

Judy and Louie are leaning over the lighted jukebox, drinking rum, reading the titles out loud, laughing at them. Louie
sees us first, raises his glass.

"Hey! The return of the lovers!"

Judy glances up. "Ain't love grand!"

"Nice of you to join us," he says.

"Nice of you to wait," Terri tells him.

"Well, you do owe us a round, y'know."

"Kiss my what?" I ask.

"We've got to get moving," Terri says.

I glance at my watch. "I know."

"Before it gets really dark," Terri says.

"Right," I tell them. "It's an hour's drive."

"In daylight, yeah." Terri turns to me, lowers her voice.
"John, they can't drive like that. They've had too much to
drink."

"He'll be all right."

"No," she says. "Not on these roads."

"Okay, let me handle it."

We walk to the jukebox. Louie's just dropped in a coin and
Judy's starting to press the buttons, their faces lighted by the
machine. Buttons stay down a few seconds, then click back up.
First record is a calypso number.

"Lou, let's shove off," I say.

He looks up. "What's the hurry?"

"It's getting dark out there."

He squints at the windows, turns his watch to the light. "It's
only—it's not even five-thirty."

"These roads will be hell in the dark, Lou."

"Fact is," he says, smiling at Judy. "Fact is, we better have
something to eat first. Judy and me, we're beginning to feel
these suckers."

"They don't have anything to eat here," Terri tells him.

"Certainly do," he says. "Certainly do, chicken-in-the-basket. Their specialty."

I make a face. "Chicken-in-the-basket?"

He laughs. "Well, what the hell'd you expect—filet mignon?"

"No."

"Yeah, I bet you did."

"No. Maine lobster would be perfectly okay."

Judy goes off and dances by herself, snapping her fingers. We watch her silhouette against the lighted bar.

"Listen, Lou," I say. "We'll be up all night, we need a good dinner, really. It's only an hour's drive."

"Don't sweat the driving," Terri tells him. "We'll drive."

"Okay, okay," he says. "Maybe you're right."

Bartender begins turning on lights around the room. They finish their drinks and Louie pays the bill and we all go out on the porch. It's already very dark now and the rain's just started, a steady drizzle, drumming on the roof, making a soft spattering sound on the blacktop. We lean on the railing and watch, listening to the jukebox. Heavy clouds cover the tops of the mountains. We can hardly see the bay beyond the rows of palms. Light from the windows behind us throws pale yellow rectangles on the blacktop and our four shadows are long and clear. Air is cool and feels good, but the rotting smell is strong.

"Well, we're dressed for it," Judy says.

Terri takes the keys from my hand. "I'll drive Louie, you guys follow. Drive carefully, huh?"

Judy gives me the keys to the Mini Minor and we all run off the porch. Rain feels cold and pleasant, it's still only a drizzle. Soon as we get the car doors open, Terri gives Judy her clothes and shoes, Louie gives me mine. None of us change, we're too wet now.

Five minutes later, Terri's driving the Beretta at a moderate speed along North Coast Road, climbing southwest into the mountains. I stay about fifteen, twenty yards behind. There's no traffic in either direction, which doesn't surprise me. As she approaches the first sharp curves, she sounds her horn and touches her brakes cautiously several times, her taillights flashing to warn me, and I slow also. She'd disappear briefly around the curves and then come back into view. Road has a solid white line down the center and I have to keep reminding myself to stay well over in the *left* lane; haven't driven on the left since the trip to England in 1982. Terri's brights outline the steep wall of rock to the left, but it's impossible to see very far ahead because of the curves. In the absence of guardrails, I'm glad to be in the inside lane.

After only ten or fifteen minutes, we're well up in the mountains and the road starts to level some. Rain seems to fall harder at this elevation. Sprays in sheets through my headlight beams and we can hear it drum on the roof above the fast clicking of the wipers. Off to the right, I can see the long red horizon line of the sea.

We start going downhill just after La Vache Bay and it happens so fast I can't even react for a few seconds: Terri's taillights flash in quick spurts, like she's pumping the brakes, but her speed is increasing. Judy sits forward. I step on the gas, straining to see, but she's far down the road already, a good fifty yards ahead of us, nearing the next curve. She sounds the horn and we hear her tires screech as she turns, but her taillights have stopped flashing. She disappears around the curve.

"What the hell's she *doing!*" Judy yells.

"She didn't even *slow* for it!"

"John, she's lost her *brakes!*"

I blow the horn, hit the brakes, take the curve quickly, tires squealing. She's up ahead, hazard lights flashing like crazy now. She takes the long inside curve next, then seems to accelerate at a tremendous rate, rock wall flashing past in her brights. I pick up speed and start blowing my horn. I don't know what else to do. My hands start shaking, I'm out of breath.

"Watch your speed, John!"

"I gotta catch up!"

"For God's sake, slow down!"

"I'm all right, I can handle it!"

After the inside curve, we're on a fairly straight stretch going down, but the incline's not as steep as before. I'm speeding now, but I'm not gaining on her at all. I don't dare hit my brights, but I pound my hand on the horn and keep it there. I'm still shaking, I'm dizzy, I'm out of breath. Judy's shouting at me, but I can't hear what she's saying because of the horn. It's becoming difficult to see the Beretta in the rain. Judy's hands are braced against the dash.

"John, for Christ's sake, *slow down*!"

I punch the horn with my fist and hold it down.

She grabs my shoulder. "God damn it, man, *slow down*!"

"Get your hand away!"

At the curve, Terri tries to slow her speed by turning into the rock wall, sideswiping it. First she bumps it lightly, like she's testing, and sparks spew crazily in all directions. Now she starts hitting it harder, slamming into it in a kind of rhythm, sparks shooting like small explosions. Toward the end of the curve, the car begins to fishtail wildly, then spin around like it's on ice, headlights whirling in a fast circle, completely out of control, tires burning and squealing across the solid white line. Headlight beams suddenly jerk straight up as she hits the shoulder on the other side and catapults out over the edge. Beams seem to hang for a moment, straight up, long white shafts in the dark, rain flashing through them at an angle, before they drop and vanish.

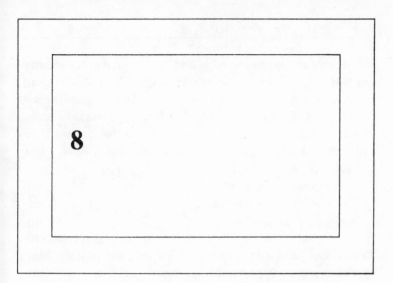

8

WE'RE SCREAMING. I slam on my brakes and we swerve crazily on the wet asphalt, tires squealing, and before we stop dead in the middle of the road we hear the first heavy crash from below. We fling open the doors and run out in the rain and our horn is stuck and blowing. There's a second, more distant crash of metal and glass, then a quick red flash outlines the curved edge of the road an instant before the explosion that sounds like a bomb. It's so loud that my legs buckle as I run and I fall to my knees in the road. It's echoing in the mountains. Judy's running down the road in the light of our headlights. I try to run again, but my legs won't work and I fall ahead sprawling. Judy's screaming and the car horn keeps blowing. I scramble up and run after her, shouting. She's crouched at the edge, looking back at me, white in the headlights. Far behind her, black smoke starts billowing into the shafts of light.

"Watch *out*!" I yell.

"Go for *help*! We gotta get *help*!"

I crouch and go to the edge and look over. I can't see anything at all. It's pitch black down there. Glare of the headlights makes it worse. There's a strong smell of gasoline and the smoke drifts up now and flashes into our headlight beams far out beyond the edge. I get down on my hands and knees and look again. I'm shaking and my arms won't hold. I hear waves hitting the rocks, but I can't see anything.

"Go for *help!*" she yells.

"We've gotta get *down* there!"

"Get back, John, it's slippery!"

I inch forward on my elbows and look down again. It's very dark. Gasoline smell is so strong my eyes begin to sting. Horn keeps blaring. Judy grabs the waist of my trunks.

"Get back, John, I mean it!"

I push back from the edge, but she keeps hold of my trunks. I look at her in the glare. Rain pours down on her. I hear the rain hitting her skin. Then, what happens next, this always seems like a bunch of fragments from a dream, maybe because I'm in a state of shock, I don't know, but here's what happens, here's how I remember it: *Above the horn, above the rain, way off to the right, I think I hear a voice, a man's voice, making loud, rhythmic sounds. I stand up slowly, I look in that direction, I can't see anything because of the headlights. I walk in that direction, out of the shafts of light. Voice stops. Can't see anything in the dark. But now I hear the voice again, from somewhere ahead in the road, rhythmic sounds, like a hurt animal.*

"Lou!" I yell.

Horn. Rain. No voice.

"Louie! Where are you?"

I hear Judy's feet slapping behind me, I turn, see her silhouette in the headlight shafts, running toward the car.

I walk ahead, squinting in the dark. "Lou! Lou!"

Fifteen seconds later, the horn stops. Seems suddenly very quiet except for the rain spattering on the road. Judy slams the hood shut, gets in the car, starts the engine, backs up, turns, faces the headlights in the direction I'm yelling. Lighted part of the road is empty. Now she clicks on the brights. Way off to the right, I catch a glimpse of him, flat on his back, arms and legs spread. I run over there, see that he's bleeding badly; he was thrown at least fifty feet across the asphalt. Judy runs over with beach towels; we place them carefully under his head and neck. Seems to be breathing okay, he's making soft sounds in his throat now, but he's unconscious. We have no way of knowing how badly he's hurt, but we've got to move him, get him into the car. I tell Judy to drive it over as close as possible. While she's doing that, I take a closer look at his head, arms, and legs. He's only wearing swim trunks, so he's scraped up pretty bad, but he's not bleeding from the head, and there are no obvious breaks in his arms and legs. That's all I can tell. I figure, we can get him to the hospital in about half an hour. He's in shock now, of course, and if he has trouble breathing on the way, Judy and I can help, we're both trained in CPR, but that's all we can do.

She drives the car over slowly, maneuvers it so the passenger-side door is as close to him as possible. Gets out, opens that door, pushes the passenger seat forward, transfers our clothes from the back seat to the driver's seat. I sit Louie up carefully, get behind his back, rest his head against my chest, get a firm grip under his shoulders and around his chest. Judy faces us in a crouch, grips his legs under the knees. On a count of three, we lift slowly, stand. I walk backward, I'm straining, I'm out of breath, but I manage to get him into the back seat without undue pressure on his neck or head. Judy hands me one of the beach towels, I prop it under his head. He's on his back, knees bent, and his breathing still seems okay to us, but he's starting to shiver. We cover him with the other beach towel, tuck it in all around, then place our jeans and shirts on top of that. There's no room for either of us to sit back there, so we get in front now, close the doors.

I'm driving, but before we leave, I turn the car around in a
slow circle, brights up, and we both scan every foot of the road
that's visible. Nothing. Silence now, except for the windshield
wipers and the drum of rain on the roof. Just to be absolutely
certain, I drive ahead about ten yards, then do another circle,
very, very slowly this time. Nothing. Finally, we realize we'll
have to leave a marker of some kind to indicate exactly where
the car went over the edge. I get out, open the trunk, grab the
tire iron, walk to the edge, and leave it. Gasoline smell is still
strong. And, standing there in the rain, I'm very much aware
of the reality that I've been trying so hard to deny, to push
back in my mind for as long as possible: Terri's dead. There's
no way she could've survived. Terri McBride. Twenty-nine
years old. Dead. I'm too numb to deal with the question why. I
get down on my knees now, crying finally, shaking with it.
Saying the only prayer I ever say anymore, saying it from the
deepest part of me: *God, please have mercy.* When I look up,
Judy's there kneeling beside me.

It's not raining in Port-of-Spain when we arrive at 6:55. As we
speed south on Queen's Park East, past the Savannah, traffic's
relatively light, and the big costume parades are still going on
in the twilight, steel orchestras blaring. Turn left off Charlotte
Street into the emergency entrance of the Trauma Center, stop
slowly in front of the large sliding glass doors. Judy jumps out,
runs inside, comes back fast with four people in green scrubsuits, wheeling a modern gurney. When they get the beach
towel off Louie, he's still unconscious, bleeding all over, shiv-
ering badly, and his breathing is labored. They're extremely
careful in lifting him out and onto the gurney, working as a
team, a young male intern giving orders. Louie's covered with
a blanket, strapped in, then they wheel him inside quickly.
Judy and I run in with them.

Inside, there's a long semicircular counter flanked by six or
eight individual trauma rooms, half of which are occupied and

alive with activity. Louie's wheeled into the nearest empty one, Room 4, and the same team of four stays with him. Judy and I, we're ushered to the center of the counter and asked to check him in. Judy takes over, talks to a woman sitting at a computer terminal. I go to Room 4, stand just inside. Louie's been transferred to a table surrounded by all kinds of emergency equipment, most of it computerized. They've got a respirator over his mouth and nose, wires taped to his forehead and chest, and a blood-pressure cuff around his upper right arm. Young intern in charge sees me, steps over quickly; he's wearing a surgical mask now.

"You'll have to wait in the lounge, sir."

"Okay. What's his condition?"

"We're checking his vital signs. His blood pressure is low, so we've taken a sample, it's being typed and cross-matched now. That's all we—"

"For a transfusion?"

"Yes, sir. Now, if you'll be kind enough to wait out in the lounge, I'll come out and give you a report as soon as possible. My name is Dr. Kitchener."

"I'm John Rawlings. Thank you, Dr. Kitchener."

Outside, Judy's still answering questions at the counter. She turns as I come over. "John, we gotta move our car."

"Right."

"They want it in the parking lot."

"Okay."

"They've notified the police."

"Good."

"Police are on the way here now."

"Fine. I'll move the car, meet you in the lounge out front."

"Okay. Bring in our clothes, huh?"

"Will do."

Soon as I get outside, I hear the steel orchestras and the crowd in the distance. Twilight is fading fast and the air seems much cooler. I drive the car around to the front, park in the lot. Remove my wet swim trunks, put on my jeans, shirt, shoes, make sure my wallet's still in my back pocket. Pick up Judy's jeans, check her wallet. Now, for the first time, I realize we'll have to tell the police who we are. I mean, we can take them aside, we can explain the situation and request the courtesy of confidentiality, but we'll have to identify ourselves. A girl is dead. In my judgment, there's a very high probability that she was murdered. I mean, a brand-new 1988 Chevy Beretta just doesn't suddenly lose most of its brake fluid. My guess, it was drained in the parking lot of the Casa de Maracas. By somebody who thought Louie and I would be driving it back. Who? Who knew we rented that particular car this morning? Who knew exactly where we were going? If we were followed out there, it's a good bet Louie would've picked up on it, he's a pro. Still, maybe not, because North Coast Road is the only road from Port-of-Spain to Maracas Bay, and that beach is supposed to be the only decent one on the whole island, so it's the most popular. If somebody was tailing us, he'd be able to do it from a considerable distance, too, because Maracas is the first village of any size on the whole road. Until I get cold, hard, solid evidence to the contrary, I have to assume that somebody's trying to kill us. That guy in the Penguin Club last night? Face continues to draw a blank in my mind. *Who, what, when, where? Mid-fifties, full head of hair, gray-white at the temples. High forehead, thin black steel-framed glasses, aviator style. Handsome profile, straight nose, strong chin. Who, what, when, where? Know him, know him, know him. Know his face by heart. Must've seen him dozens of times, close range. Who is he?* Don't know. Grab Judy's clothes and shoes, get out, lock the door.

What Dr. Kitchener called the lounge turns out to be the lobby just inside the front entrance where we were this morning. Seven people waiting in here now, all West Indians, most young. Judy's standing at the reception desk talking on the phone. She finishes, comes over, I hand her the clothes.

"Just notified Hertz," she says. "We'll have to see them, bring along the police report, and fill out the accident forms as soon as we can."

Glance at my watch. "It'll have to be later tonight."

"Also, I asked the receptionist if Dr. Leonard was still on duty. Negative. He left at about five-thirty, she said he planned to catch the end of the costume parades with his wife, have dinner in town, then head home. But he carries a beeper, so they can contact him at any time. What do you think?"

"I'd like him to see Louie, yeah."

"Me, too. Just tell the receptionist. I'm gonna change in the bathroom down the hall. Be right back."

I get Dr. Leonard's card out of my wallet, go up to the desk, tell the receptionist my name, show her the card, explain that Dr. Leonard gave me permission to call him any time of the day or night. I ask her to beep him. She agrees without hesitation.

Less than two minutes later, Dr. Leonard calls. Receptionist asks him to hold, waves me over, pushes the flashing extension button.

"Dr. Leonard, it's John Rawlings."

"Yes, Mr. Rawlings."

"Sorry to bother you, but it's an emergency."

"What's the trouble?"

"My wife was killed in an automobile accident."

"Oh, my God, I'm terribly sorry."

"And Mr. Diaz was seriously injured. He's here now, he's—"

"Who's the physician in charge?"

"Dr. Kitchener."

"Has he given you a preliminary report?"

"No, sir, not yet."

"All right, listen. We're at the Hotel Normandie, that's about a five-minute drive from the hospital. I'll be there just as quickly as I can."

"I appreciate it, Dr. Leonard."

"And please accept my condolences about your wife."

"Thank you."

When Judy comes back, we discuss our game plan about identities. Status quo with Dr. Leonard, we'll stay undercover as long as possible. When the police get here, we'll explain the situation in private, ask for their cooperation in not revealing our NYPD affiliation to any outside parties, including the hospital administration and staff, for the duration of our undercover activities. Naturally, we're not at liberty to divulge any details about the exact nature of our operation here, unless and until we require official police assistance. However, we intend to cooperate to the fullest extent possible in their investigation of the accident and death. And we'll suggest they call or telex Chief Vadney in New York to verify our credentials and undercover status.

True to his word, Dr. Leonard arrives about five or six minutes later—it's now 7:16—tall, lean, white-haired, looking scholarly despite his sport shirt and khaki trousers. Comes straight over to us.

"Mr. Rawlings, I'm terribly, terribly sorry about your wife. You said it was an automobile accident?"

"Yes, sir."

"And Mr. Diaz was in the same car?"

"That's correct."

"Has Dr. Kitchener spoken with you yet?"

"Not yet," Judy says. "We're still waiting."

"I'll see to your husband immediately. Do you recall what time he was admitted?"

"About six-fifty-five," she says.

He looks at his watch. "Twenty minutes ago. We should have a workup on him now. I'll come back and give you a preliminary report just as soon as I can."

Off he goes, past the desk, down the hall, walking briskly. Thought occurs to me that he didn't ask any questions about the accident itself. Obvious questions that people seem to ask almost automatically: Where did it happen? When? How? Not even the professional questions: Where is the deceased now? Was she examined by a physician? Was she pronounced dead on arrival? All right, I hear you, as chief of staff at the Trauma Center, maybe he delegates questions like these to his staff. Maybe fatal auto accidents are commonplace on an island of this size. Also, let's face it, we're virtual strangers to this guy. He's elderly, he's British, he's certainly reserved, from what I've seen. Still, I can't fight it, my intuition waves a red flag here. Maybe it's because I've been a cop for so long, I don't know. Didn't tell the others this, but this morning, during that first brief meeting, I experienced a vague suspicion that the man was being evasive about my cryonics-related questions. Choosing his words carefully. Can't recall anything specific, all I can tell you, I just experienced a quick blip on my radar. Same thing now. This time, it's not what he says, it's what he neglects to say.

Okay, now, I'm sitting back, I'm glancing around at the other people in the lobby, here's this guy walks in the front door, I know he's a cop instantly. Instantly. West Indian kid, mid-thirties, five-eleven, I'd guess 210–215, should be 175–180, takes a fast swipe at his dark unruly hair; light complexion, high cheekbones, wears a sweat-stained short-sleeved flowered sport shirt that hangs out loosely over his dark trousers. Ambles up to the reception desk, dusty black cordovans, walks like his feet hurt. Then I see the little bulge in the small of his back, right side. I know it's not a gun, they don't carry 'em down here, so it's got to be a walkie-talkie. But I didn't see it when he walked in the door, okay? Didn't have to. Knew. Instantly. Takes a small notebook from the breast pocket of his shirt, flips it open, glances at it, talks with the receptionist. She points us out, he walks over, glances at the notebook again, then speaks quietly.

"Mr. Rawlings?"

"Yes, sir."

"Mrs. Diaz?"

"Yes."

"Detective Gordon Kinch, Port-of-Spain Police Department." Reaches in his back pocket, shows us his badge and ID card.

We stand, shake his hand. I take a good look at the color photo on the card to make sure it's him. I always do that, no matter what my instincts tell me. Learned it the hard way. Got burned once, but only once. It's Kinch, all right, but taken about ten years ago; kid in the photo is smiling just enough to show the gap between his front teeth.

"Mind if we talk outside?" I ask.

"No, not at all."

We follow him to the front door, he holds it open for both of us. Like his style. It's darker now, but we can still hear a steel orchestra from the Savannah. Judy and I stand near the outside light, take out our wallets, show him our ID cards with photos.

"Detective Judith Cooper, New York Police Department."

"Detective John Rawlings."

Kinch narrows his eyes at the photos, takes a swipe at his hair. "What's going on?"

"Working undercover with two other detectives," I tell him. "One of them was killed in the auto accident, the other's injured, inside, no report on his condition yet."

He pulls a pen from his breast pocket, flips open the notebook, copies our full names and badge numbers from the cards. Then: "Where did the accident occur?"

"In the mountains above La Vache Bay," Judy says. "The car went off the road, fell into the canyon, and exploded on second impact."

He's writing. "Approximate time?"

"Six-fifteen this evening," I tell him.

"Name of the officer killed?"

"Detective Terri McBride," Judy says. She spells it out for him slowly.

"Badge number?"

"Eleven-forty-seven," she says.

"Age?"

"Twenty-nine."

"Nature of the accident?"

"Brake failure," I tell him. "Brake failure on a brand-new rental car." I wait for him to get it down. "Nineteen-eighty-eight Chevy Beretta. License Zelda-Barbara-Anthony five-seven-eight-three." I wait again. "In our judgment, suspicious circumstances. Possibility of the brake fluid being drained. Parking lot of the Casa de Maracas. Maracas Bay."

He finishes writing, glances up. "Was Detective McBride inside the vehicle when it went over?"

"As far as we know," Judy says. "She was driving. It was raining at the time, visibility poor."

"We were in the car behind them," I explain.

Judy waits for him to finish writing. "We searched the area and found Detective Diaz, who either jumped or was thrown from the car."

"Detective Diaz?"

"The officer undergoing treatment," she says. "Louis Diaz, D-i-a-z. John, you know his badge number?"

"Nine-eighty-nine."

Kinch jots it down. "Will you people be available tomorrow morning to help recover the body?"

"Certainly," I say.

"Where're you staying?"

"Hilton."

"Eight o'clock all right with you?"

"Fine," I tell him. "We've marked the approximate place where the car left the road. How do you get down into the canyon?"

"From that elevation, up there overlooking La Vache,

we've never used a crane, it's just not practical. So we can't recover the vehicle itself. Last time we recovered a body from that area—this was some years ago—we used a simple tow truck with a cable and winch. Two officers from Emergency Service climbed down the cable with a body bag, then the winch hoisted them back up. I'll check it out with my C.O., but that's what we'll probably do."

Goes like so. Kinch also says he'll check with his commanding officer about respecting the confidentiality of our NYPD affiliation, but he doesn't see any particular problem with that. He wants one of us to accompany him down to headquarters to fill out the necessary papers on the accident and death, then he'll file the official report. Says it won't take longer than an hour. Judy volunteers to go with him, says she'll meet me back here.

It's 7:25 when Dr. Leonard comes back into the lobby. Now he's wearing a green scrubsuit and cap. Motions for me to stay seated, takes the chair next to me, removes his glasses, rubs the bridge of his nose. "Well, I have relatively good news."

"Oh, thank God."

Replaces his glasses. "Mr. Diaz is conscious, his vital signs are beginning to stabilize, his condition is listed as fair at this time. Specifically, he suffered a slight concussion, but there is no apparent disturbance to the cerebral function. He suffered multiple abrasions and cuts, of course, especially on his arms, legs, and back, resulting in significant loss of blood. Five small but deep wounds on his knees and elbows require stitches; that surgery is being done right now. Our preliminary series of X-rays show no fractures, but we'll want a more comprehensive series in the morning. His condition will require observation for twenty-four to forty-eight hours, possibly longer, so I'm having him admitted to the hospital immediately after the minor surgery is completed."

"Is he in much pain?"

"Not at the moment, no. Dr. Kitchener administered an initial injection of Demerol. He'll be given more tonight as needed."

"When can I see him?"

"Just as soon as we get him settled in next door. Do you want a private room or semiprivate?"

"Private, please."

"All right then, I'll see to it. Mr. Rawlings, may I ask, have you made arrangements for your wife's body? Do you need any help?"

"No, thank you, the police are taking care of that."

"I see." He stands. "Well, if you should need any assistance, please don't hesitate to ask. And, again, please accept my deepest condolences."

I stand, shake his hand. "I appreciate all you've done for us, Dr. Leonard."

"Not at all. Where is Mrs. Diaz now?"

"She went to police headquarters to fill out the necessary forms. She's supposed to be back in about an hour."

"I see. In that case, I think you'll have sufficient time to go back to the hotel, freshen up, meet her back here, then you can both go over to the hospital. You should be able to see Mr. Diaz"—he looks at his watch—"at about eight-thirty. Just ask for his room number at the front desk."

Louie's sitting up in bed when we arrive about 8:35. Face looks like Brando's in *Waterfront,* after the boys worked him over, near the end, remember that? Big bandage on his left forehead, left eye half closed, socket black and swollen, both elbows heavily taped, plus the knuckles of his right hand. Gives us a grin as we come in.

"How y'doin', champ?" I ask.

"That bum never laid a glove on me."

"Hey, Louie," Judy says.

"Hey, Coop. Where's Terri?"

I sit on the side of his bed; Judy walks to the window. He frowns at me, then glances over at her. His eyes fill quickly.

"Oh, no, John."

I take a deep breath, look away.

"Oh, my God, no."

In the silence, Judy's lighter makes two fast, sharp clicks. We hear her snap the cigarette from her lips, then inhale deeply.

"Talk to me, John."

"She didn't get out."

"She went over?"

I nod slowly. I can't look at him.

"Got anything on you?"

I reach in my back pocket, pull out a pint of Beefeater, hand it to him. He winces as he unscrews the cap, takes a good belt.

"It exploded in a matter of seconds, Lou."

He hands the bottle back. "I heard it. That's the last thing I remember clearly."

Judy turns around. "We think somebody drained the brake fluid in the parking lot."

"No question," he says, "and they didn't stop there, they also disconnected the hand brake. Soon as we started downhill, she realized we had no fluid. She pumped it, she tried everything. I grabbed the hand brake—nothing, disconnected. That's when we decided to start ramming the rock wall, we had no other choice, we couldn't even gear down. Just before we went into the spin, I yelled, 'Jump, jump, jump!' I was out of my seat belt, I was trying to get the door open. Next thing, it felt like the road came up and hit me from the side and I couldn't stop rolling."

We wait for him to continue, but he shakes his head, reaches for the bottle, takes another belt. Now he blinks at the ceiling.

"Easy," I tell him. "Take it easy."

He nods. "John, who the fuck's trying to kill us?"

Who, what, when, where? Mid-fifties, full head of hair, gray-white at the temples. High forehead—

And then I remember. Suddenly. Clearly. Face, name, circumstances, everything. No doubt in my mind.

And I know why he's trying to kill us.

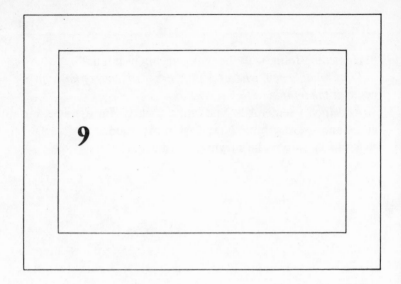

9

NOW IT GETS BIZARRE. Next morning, I explain the basics to Judy at breakfast (room service in the suite so we can have complete privacy) and halfway through she stops eating and just stares off into space. Judy, she's a good listener, she's bright as they come, she's worked plenty of weird cases in her career, but she's obviously flabbergasted. Glances at me, narrows her eyes, keeps asking if I'm absolutely sure. Yeah, I'm sure. I'm positive. She's never heard anything this wild in her life. Neither have I. But it's a fact. Now all we have to do is find the man and prove it. Our game plan for this morning, she'll meet Detective Gordon Kinch in the lobby at eight sharp, as planned, go with him and the tow-truck guys to try and recover Terri's body. That could be an all-day job, but one of us has to be there. Me, I'll be in Louie's hospital room when visiting hours begin at 8:30, see how he's doing, then call Chief Vadney at home about 9:30 (we're an hour ahead of New York) and give him a comprehensive report, which may or may not include the bizarre part, depending on how long he's been up and the severity of his Sunday-morning hangover.

Turns out Louie's had a rough night, woke up at 4:30 in considerable pain, had to have his third shot of Demerol. Dozed for the next couple of hours, woke up in pain again, asked for another shot, nurse gave him an argument. Dr. Leonard made his rounds with Dr. Kitchener about an hour ago, authorized another shot, told him the pain wasn't unusual after what he'd been through. Now he's had breakfast, he's been watching TV news, he's scheduled for a new series of X-rays at 9:25. I tell him where Judy's gone, that she'll be in to see him as soon as she gets back, and that I'll be calling Vadney in about an hour, but I decide not to discuss the case with him now, he's too groggy to even read the newspaper.

Try to cheer him up, read him the section of the paper on American news. Presidential primaries are in full swing, biggie in New Hampshire is coming up Tuesday. No less than twelve candidates still hanging tough. Democratic front-runners are Dukakis and Gephardt, followed by Simon, Jackson, Gore, Babbitt, and Hart. Yeah, Gary Hart's still in it. Republicans, it's neck-and-neck between Bush and Dole, then Kemp, Du-Pont, and Robertson; Al Haig called it quits on Friday. Quite a field. Here's a knockout sidebar: *Times* of London polled 500 New Hampshire residents, found out one in five would swap their favorite contenders for—this is no shit—Margaret Thatcher. Yeah! That's what it says. Which means Maggie Thatcher would actually be *the* front-runner today if she were running. Tell you what, these New Hampshire folks don't take kindly to snow jobs.

Soon as Louie's whisked away for his X-rays at 9:25, I grab the phone, get out my AT&T card, dial Operator, give her my international number, then Vadney's home number in Manhattan.

His voice sounds sleepy. "Hello."

"Chief, it's John Rawlings."

"Rawlings? What's happening?"

"Sorry to call you at home, but it's an emergency."

"What's happening?"

"Detective Terri McBride was killed in an automobile accident last night."

"Oh, my God. The kid, the girl?"

"Yes, sir. Detective Lieutenant Diaz was in the same vehicle, he was injured, but not seriously. He's in the hospital now, I'm with him. He's in stable condition."

"How'd it happen?"

"Brake fluid in their car was drained. They were driving in the mountains just outside town. Couldn't stop the car, it went over the edge into a canyon and exploded. Diaz jumped from the vehicle, but McBride was driving, she couldn't get out in time."

"So you think it was murder?"

"That's our opinion, sir."

"You got a suspect, John?"

"Yes, sir, but we haven't—"

"You gotta work through the local police there now, you can't take matters into your own hands, you don't have the authority."

"We know that. We're already working with the police."

"Terri McBride. Jesus, she was just a kid."

"Twenty-nine, Chief. Less than eight years on the job."

"Christ. Have you recovered the body?"

"Police are attempting to do that this morning. Detective Cooper is with them, Judy Cooper."

"Judy Cooper. You two all right?"

"Yes, sir, we're fine."

"And Diaz, he's not badly injured?"

"Slight concussion, cuts, bruises, but he's stable."

"Who's your suspect, John?"

I hesitate, then: "Dr. James Mailer."

"Dr. James—*who*?"

"Mailer."

"The guy we're *lookin'* for?"

"Yes, sir."

"The guy who actually pulled the *robbery*?"

"Yes, sir."

"Holy Jesus *Christ,* Rawlings! So you've actually *seen* him, *talked* with him?"

"Seen him. Not talked. He's here. Positive ID."

"Wait a minute, hold on now, buddy-boy, let me get this thing straight. Nobody's seen this guy since he disappeared with all the documents and vials in nineteen-sixty-six. That I know, I know that for a fact. He was fifty-four years old in nineteen-sixty-six. That would make him—let's see. That was twenty-two years ago. So that'd make him—seventy-six years old now, right?"

"Right."

"Okay, now, listen up, Little John, I know you've been under tremendous stress and all, but listen up. All those pictures of Mailer you studied in the file, the very *latest* you saw is that good black-and-white blowup of him and Dr. Stegmueller, taken in the lab in—I believe it was nineteen-sixty-five. That's the very latest. So that's twenty-*three* years ago. So, I mean, what I'm trying to get across here, how the fuck could you possibly recognize the man *now*? At the age of seventy-six? I mean, shit, he's an old man now."

"It's Mailer, Chief. Positive ID."

Pause. Then: "You sure you're not in shock—or like that?"

"I'm sure."

Long pause. Then: "I'm comin' down there, Little John. Now. Today. It's—eight-thirty here. What time's that flight leave?"

"Ten-thirty. Pan Am. Only flight of the day. Makes one stop in Caracas, arrives Port-of-Spain five-thirty, Trinidad time."

"And you're staying where—Hilton?"

"Trinidad Hilton. We got a two-bedroom suite."

"Okay, buddy-boy, I'm gone, I won't even have time to pack. Meet me in the lobby about—how long's the drive from the airport?"

"Half hour."

"Meet me in the lobby at six. You got a fugitive warrant?"

"Never leave home without one."

"Good man. Okay, last thing, listen up. Both ears. Direct order: Don't make a move on this guy till I get there. He's *mine*. I waited twenty-two years to nail this fucker. Now the statute of limitations doesn't even come into play. He's murdered one of my officers. For that, I'm gonna take pleasure in nailing his ass *personally.*"

Bang. Hangs up. Never fails. As usual, I keep talking into the receiver: "Have a pleasant trip, asshole. Sorry you have to go first class, nothing's left, what's a motherfuck to do? Oh, and don't forget to tell your dog-breath wife to buy a new scrapbook, huh?"

Twenty minutes later, Louie's back from his X-ray series, still groggy from the Demerol. When they get him back in bed and we're alone, I tell him I called Vadney, explained the situation, and that he'll arrive tonight about six. I don't tell him anything about Dr. Mailer, I figure I'll wait until he's sharper. Anyhow, he says he's real tired, he wants to catch some sleep now. Says the new series of X-rays are being sent to Dr. Leonard. Says we should have the results sometime this morning.

Gives me an idea. I tell Louie I'll be back this afternoon, then head straight for the Trauma Center. Go up to the young lady at the desk, Miss Coogan, she recognizes me from yesterday morning. Tell her my name again, ask if she'd be kind enough to call Dr. Leonard, ask if I could see him privately. I'm in luck, he happens to be in his office, in conference with Dr. Kitchener, but tells her to send me up in about fifteen minutes. Perfect; gives me time to plan my strategy.

Lobby's crowded this morning, just as I thought it'd be, at least twenty people, every seat taken. No ashtrays in sight, I decide to wait outside. Nice sunny morning, I light up a cigar, lean against the wall in the shade. Question is, should I continue to play cat-and-mouse with Leonard for a while longer, or drop my cover and see what I can get? Instinct tells me to play it safe, to wait for Vadney, to let him stumble around like always. Emotion tells me I've had enough of this shit. Terri McBride is dead. Whoever killed her was after Louie and me, that's for sure, so why not face facts: Mailer knows who we are. How? Haven't a clue. This guy Leonard, I've been giving him a lot of thought. I changed my mind about him, I don't think he was involved in the murder or had any knowledge of it. And I don't think he knows who we are. It's just a strong gut feel about the man.

About ten minutes later, I go inside, Miss Coogan motions to me. Dr. Leonard called a couple of minutes ago, he can see me now. Second floor, office 227. Take the elevator up, walk down a long antiseptic hallway, knock on his door. Voice tells me to come in.

Large modern office, single window is flanked by two bookcases; another bookcase to the left near his desk, graceful Queen Anne style, looks like rosewood. Leonard's standing behind it, his back to me, studying X-ray films on a large wall-mounted light box.

"Please sit down, Mr. Rawlings, I'll be right with you."

I sit on the three-seater couch facing his desk.

"Mr. Diaz is a fortunate man," he says, switching off the light box and turning. "No fractures whatsoever, even to the elbows and knees."

"That's a relief."

In his white jacket and trousers, he seems somehow taller. He removes his tortoiseshell-framed glasses, rubs the bridge of his nose as he sits down slowly. "Apparently, he suffered quite a bit of discomfort during the night. To be on the safe side, I recommend that he remain hospitalized for at least one more night."

"I agree. I just came from his room. He was very tired."

He nods, replaces his glasses, rubs a hand over his bald pate and short white hair. "You've been under quite an emotional strain yourself, Mr. Rawlings. How are you feeling today?"

"Depressed, naturally, but I'm okay."

"Would you like me to prescribe a mild antidepressant?"

"No, thank you, Dr. Leonard. Reason I asked to see you, I'd like your opinion on a medical subject, if that's all right."

"Surely."

I sit forward. "As I mentioned yesterday morning, I'm in the process of making arrangements to be cryonically suspended."

"Yes."

"You said you'd conducted research on the subject. I'd just like to know your opinion on the—what's the word I want?—feasibility. On the scientific feasibility of cryonic suspension."

He glances out the window, nods slowly. "Yes. I know what you're asking. I've been away from it for years now, as I told you, but I think an idea that should be stressed more is that cryonics has never made any wild claims or guarantees, as far as I know, and it doesn't take anything away from the dignity of man. If anything, it enhances his dignity, it's one more struggle in a long series of struggles for survival. The problems are immense, but so are the possibilities. The foremost obstacle in the way right now is the same as it was some twenty years ago, the job of changing public attitudes. When that happens, research funds and facilities will be readily available. In my judgment, it's bound to happen, but it's going to take time, and it will be an uphill battle all the way. When I was doing research in New York some years ago, I was in touch with an intern at a hospital, a man in his late twenties. He had been a member of the Cryonics Society of New York for a year or so and was finally in the process of getting his legal documents drawn up. Then, quite suddenly, he died of a heart attack. He had no previous record of heart trouble, he just had an attack and died. I was called about two hours after his death by two of his friends, both interns. They asked my advice. They said they'd had a hell of a time locating me. Nothing had been done, they hadn't even attempted to cool the body to reduce the rate of deterioration. They both knew his wishes, they'd talked about it at length, they knew the basic steps to be taken. But they just hadn't done anything. I told them what they already knew, that the situation was extremely unfavorable because of the delay. I told them what had to be done immediately and offered the full assistance of the Cryonics Society of New York—immediately. They asked the man's wife and brother. I held the line. Six or seven minutes, as I recall. The answer? Negative. His wife and brother considered his wishes briefly and then shoveled dirt in his face. They felt terrible about it, of course. But they had to be practical, of course. They embalmed him and buried him."

"Was that a typical reaction back then?"

"He was one of seven near misses during the year I spent in New York."

"And the relatives were to blame in each case?"

"Five of the seven, I believe."

"I suppose you felt a bitterness toward them."

"Toward the relatives? No. Bitterness wasn't justified, Mr. Rawlings, not at that point in the game. We were on the defensive. The people still left in the movement are still on the defensive. Few prominent scientists will say publicly, today, that cryonic suspension is worth the effort even under the most ideal conditions. What was demanded of the wife and brother in the case I just related was not just concurrence but *initiative.* They would have had to help convince physicians and hospital authorities to cooperate, to take unconventional and perhaps awkward steps under conditions of intense emotional strain. Who failed? His family failed. In understanding, in courage. Who failed? I failed. I wanted to make damn sure the difficulties were appreciated so I couldn't later be accused of misleading anyone, so they wouldn't hesitate midway and back out, giving the program a bad name. Who failed? The scientific community, too conservative to offer leadership—waiting, waiting, waiting around for public demand to force massive research funding and facilities. Too cagey to place their own reputations on the line, even when they admit privately they're in sympathy with the program. Who failed over the past twenty years? The physicians, the morticians, the cemetery operators, the insurance men, the attorneys, the hospital administrators. Oh, many of them keep expressing interest, many of them accept articles for their journals now, some even promise to cooperate. But why must they be *led,* why must they be *spoon-fed,* why must they be pampered and wheedled and *coaxed*? Where's their initiative, their enterprise, or even their instinct for self-preservation?"

In the pause, I study his eyes, then speak quietly. "Maybe they're waiting for a miracle."

"A miracle?"

"A scientific breakthrough."

He nods, narrows his eyes. "Of what kind?"

"A scientific breakthrough of such magnitude that it would stagger the scientific community—as well as the public."

"Please be specific, Mr. Rawlings."

"Maybe they need scientific documentation about what happened to Dr. Mailer."

"Dr.—who?"

"Dr. James Mailer. The first human being to be cryonically suspended, thawed, and successfully reanimated. The first human being to survive death."

He frowns, blinks. "How much do you know, Mr. Rawlings?"

"I know that Dr. Mailer died of a coronary here, probably in nineteen-sixty-six. I know that you perfused him at the moment of clinical death, under ideal conditions, and suspended him in liquid nitrogen in the Cryocapsule you purchased from Ed Cerabino. I know that recently, probably within the past several years, you thawed his body successfully, using artificially constructed virus particles to repair cells damaged by freezing. Artificially constructed virus particles that Dr. Mailer stole from the International Cryogenics Corporation in nineteen-sixty-six. Artificially constructed virus particles that required twelve years of research and development, and cost ICC twenty-four million dollars. I know that a team of cardiological surgeons, led by you, using the most advanced techniques in heart surgery, either replaced or repaired his heart. Successfully. I know he recovered. I know he's alive and active. I've seen him with my own eyes."

He adjusts his glasses. "Exactly who are you?"

"Detective John Rawlings, New York Police Department." I take out my ID cardholder with the gold shield, flip it open, let him take a good look at my photo.

"Exactly what do you want, Detective Rawlings?"

"We want the police here to question Dr. Mailer."

He leans back. "I see. All right, let's consider a purely hypothetical situation. Let us assume that most of what you just told me about such a man actually did happen. Let us assume that a man named Dr. James Mailer committed the crime you related, moved to this island, died of a heart attack, was cryonically suspended in nineteen-sixty-six, and then, just a few years ago, he was thawed by some magical process, reanimated, underwent successful heart surgery, and recovered. Let us assume such a man is living in Trinidad today. Now, correct me if I'm mistaken, but in New York State, the statute of limitations on a robbery of this kind, industrial espionage, a Class C felony, is only five years. Is that correct?"

"We're well aware of that."

"I'm sure you are. So, to continue our hypothetical situation, the five-year statute of limitations on such a crime, committed in nineteen-sixty-six, would have expired in—let me think. Would have expired in nineteen-seventy-one. Seventeen years ago. So I fail to see why you would want the police here to question such a man."

"On suspected first-degree murder."

"*Murder*? Of *whom*?"

"Detective Terri McBride, the woman who was killed in the automobile accident."

"So she wasn't your wife?"

"The four of us were working undercover."

"I see. Tell me this, Detective Rawlings, how do you know she was murdered?"

"We have sound reasons. I'm not at liberty to divulge them."

He looks out the window, shakes his head, speaks so softly I can hardly hear: "Oh, no. Oh, my God, no."

"We'd appreciate your cooperation, Dr. Leonard. If necessary, we can ask the police here to serve you with a summons."

"That won't be necessary. If, as you say, you have sound reasons for suspecting the man of first-degree murder, then I will certainly cooperate with you to the fullest extent possible. There's something you should know about Dr. Mailer—as he is today."

"The man's obviously quite dangerous."

Leonard nods, takes a deep breath. "Yes. First, let me give you a very brief history of what actually happened here. Your assumptions about the cryonic suspension of Dr. Mailer were largely correct, except for the dates. To start at the beginning, Mailer and I had been friends since college. He elected to go into the field of scientific research; I chose to be a physician. Most of my younger years were spent as a practicing private cardiologist. But we remained friends over the years; in fact, we often visited each other. In nineteen-sixty-five, he developed symptoms that seemed to him nothing more than a common cold, a stubborn virus. Then, gradually, his symptoms seemed to go haywire. Fluid filled his lungs, breathing became difficult, and there were chest pains. Before the end of that year, a prominent Boston cardiologist reached a dire diagnosis: Cardiomyopathy, a progressive, almost always fatal weakening of the heart. When he came to visit me in late August of nineteen-sixty-six, I had absolutely no knowledge that he was a fugitive, that he had traveled here on a forged passport. He didn't tell me anything about the robbery until much later. His visit was planned months in advance, of course, because he wanted my personal diagnosis. Unfortunately, my tests confirmed the disease to be cardiomyopathy."

"And I assume heart transplants weren't possible back then."

He smiles briefly, shakes his head. "Compared to the revolutionary techniques in cardiology today, Detective Rawlings, we were just emerging from the Dark Ages back then. We simply didn't have the technological expertise to attempt anything as dramatic as a heart transplant. Of course, experimental heart surgery was taking place in various countries. But the first moderately successful heart transplant—performed by Dr. Christian Barnard—didn't occur until December of nineteen-sixty-seven. In any event, Dr. Mailer was dying and wanted to be cryonically suspended at the onset of clinical death, under the best conditions possible. That's when I began corresponding with Ed Cerabino. The Cryocapsule was sent to me by air freight in mid-April, nineteen-sixty-seven. Jim Mailer died on September tenth of that year. He had lived here for well over a year by then. And, of course, he had told me everything. Long before he died, I was thoroughly familiar with virtually all aspects of cryonics. Including the classified intelligence that no one else had—how to administer the artificially constructed virus particles during the thawing process."

"Where was the capsule stored?"

"In my home, in a specially constructed basement room, air

conditioned to a constant cool temperature, windowless. The vacuum pump was in constant use, of course, and I monitored the pressure levels and liquid nitrogen supply on a daily basis. I did that for exactly nineteen years, one month, and fifteen days."

"So he has thawed in—the autumn of 'eighty-six?"

"That's correct. The thawing process began October twenty-five, nineteen-eighty-six."

I'm taking notes now. "Why did you select that time?"

"Why? A variety of reasons, based on nineteen years of significant progress in cardiology. Among the primary reasons was the escalating survival rate of human-heart transplant patients. I've always been a cardiologist of the old school, conservative, dedicated to the discipline of the conventional 'scientific method,' involving exhaustive research and experimentation. However, at the time of the operation, I was seventy-three years old. I realized that I couldn't put it off very much longer. The time and circumstances just seemed to be favorable."

"And I assume the transplant was a human heart."

"Human, yes. By that year, it was becoming increasingly obvious that artificial hearts were not the answer. While the device seemed to work quite well, the biology didn't work. The human body just couldn't seem to tolerate it. As you probably know, Barney Clark was the first recipient of an artificial heart in December of nineteen-eighty-two. He died the following March. To date, four other patients have received permanent artificial hearts. William Schroeder was the longest survivor, living nearly two years. In the United States, the National Institutes of Health will stop funding artificial-heart research several months from now."

"When did the operation take place?"

"November third, 'eighty-six."

"At this hospital?"

"Here at the Trauma Center, yes. Now, when I said earlier

that the time and circumstances seemed to be favorable, let me be specific. A major factor—I should say *the* major factor—that influenced my decision to actually begin the thawing process on October twenty-fifth was largely a fortuitous factor. To wit, the growing probability that a suitable donor would be available. As you know, that's always the most critical problem in all transplant surgery. And, of course, to be absolutely candid about it, as chief of staff here, I'm in a prime position to identify potential donors and to speak with their families. So, naturally, for several years, I had been alert to the possibility of finding a suitable donor for Mailer. Now, in mid-October of that year, a youngster, a nineteen-year-old boy with the same A-positive blood type as Mailer's, had drowned at Blanchisseuse Bay, that's quite a distance northeast of the city, but he was revived by CPR within seven to eight minutes. He was rushed here, severely traumatized but breathing, with an unstable EKG reading and a flat EEG. We placed him on a respirator. Within twenty-four hours, all of his vital signs had stabilized, but his EEG was still flat. Obviously, his brain had been deprived of oxygen for too long a period. He was brain dead. I talked with his parents at length, explained the situation, told them the truth, that we could keep him on the respirator indefinitely, but that the probability of his ever regaining consciousness was nil. I asked them to consider taking him off the respirator soon, before the expense became impossible for them, and I asked them to consider donating his organs to people who were in dire need of them."

"Dr. Leonard, let me interrupt you for just a minute. I'm curious. Were there any other coronary patients on the island who were—I don't know how to put it—on the 'waiting list' for a heart transplant?"

"Yes, quite frankly, there were three on the island, but none of them had the A-positive blood type that was required. It was that simple."

"I understand. Please go ahead."

He adjusts his glasses, looks out the window. "So, to continue, I'll make this as brief as I can. Eventually, they agreed, the boy's parents agreed. The following day, I started the thawing process. Forty-eight hours later, Dr. Mailer was here, on a respirator, breathing, unconscious, vital signs quite unstable, but his EEG was not flat. The artificially constructed virus particles injected during the thawing process had prevented significant damage to the brain cells. Within a thirty-two-hour period on the respirator, the man's vital signs had improved to the point that he was strong enough, in my judgment, to withstand heart-transplant surgery. Meanwhile, the brain-dead boy remained on the respirator, comatose, heart beating normally. At seven o'clock in the morning, November third, our heart-transplant surgical team began the operation, concentrating first on the boy. After several hours, we removed his heart while it was still beating, which is of critical importance. Other surgeons had already cut Mailer's breastbone to gain access. The transplant itself required more than five hours, which is about the average time, and it went remarkably well. At about two-thirty that afternoon, Mailer was finally sent to intensive care. We had done everything we could do. He was breathing with the help of a respirator, his young heart was beating weakly, and his EEG reading was close to stable. Now it was just a matter of time."

"Were you optimistic?"

He thinks about it. "As a matter of fact, yes, cautiously optimistic. But, Mr. Rawlings, it's important to keep in mind that no one had ever attempted to do anything like this before. Ever. In the history of medical science. I mean, on the face of it, in retrospect, it was frightening. For me, at least, it was frightening. None of the other surgeons knew the man, knew anything about him, except that he was a friend of mine who was dying of cardiomyopathy. The first time any of them saw Dr. Mailer, he was on the respirator, vital signs unstable, but strong enough for the operation."

"So you're actually the only one who knew?"

"Correct. In any event, he didn't regain consciousness until the next morning. I remember it vividly, of course. When I walked into the intensive care unit, his eyes were open. Of course, he was still on the respirator with the oxygen mask, surrounded by the most sophisticated life-sustaining equipment we have here—but he was awake. I looked down at him and his eyes moved to mine. He blinked several times. There was definite recognition in his eyes. I'll never forget those few seconds as long as I live. I thought: My God, my God, we've actually done it. We've made one of the most important discoveries in the long history of medical science. This man has been legally dead for nineteen years and we've actually brought him back to life."

"Question, Dr. Leonard: If you—and now Dr. Mailer—are the only ones who know what you accomplished, how can you prove it? I mean, to the satisfaction of the scientific community?"

"Excellent question, Mr. Rawlings. A question we addressed at considerable length before Jim Mailer died. Answer: I filmed the entire event. In fact, I even rehearsed the clinical death, the profusion process, and various stages of the liquid nitrogen suspension, using Jim as the model, to make certain I had the best camera angles and lighting. Back then, I used sixteen-millimeter film with a sound track and professional lighting. Photography has always been a hobby of mine. I locked the camera in place for every scene, turned it on, walked into the frame, and narrated exactly what I was doing, using scientific language as well as layman's terms. And I didn't cut or edit one foot of the developed print. I have a total of four and a half hours of it. Enough to convince even the most skeptical."

"And you filmed the thawing process?"

"Videotaped it, yes. By then, I'd long since had videotape equipment. And I narrated every scene, giving the elapsed time."

"Including the injection of the virus particles?"

"Oh, certainly. Especially that part of it, every detail, sometimes quoting brief excerpts from Dr. Mailer's original documents."

"And you videotaped the heart transplant?"

"That's correct. Actually, I had it done professionally by a cameraman and sound technician from one of our local television stations. And, again, I narrated the entire operation, from the moment the boy's heart was about to be removed, still beating, throughout the transplant. Five hours and sixteen minutes of videotape. Let me add that no one on the surgical team found this to be unusual in the least. We routinely videotape other, mostly shorter, operations to be studied by students in the School of Medicine at the University of the West Indies. But to conclude, twelve days after the operation, when Dr. Mailer was still recovering in a private room in the hospital, I had the same cameraman and sound technician videotape a half-hour conversation between Jim and me. He was quite stable and alert by then, even eloquent at times. And during that conversation, he revealed precisely why he had stolen the documents and vials. Fascinating half hour. So, all in all, start to finish, I have a grand total of eleven hours and forty-three minutes of film documentation."

"Quite a movie."

"Quite an event, Mr. Rawlings."

"Question: Where's Mailer now?"

He shrugs. "At home, I should think. Doing what he's been doing eight hours a day, six days a week, for the past—over a full year now. He's writing a book, a first-person account of what happened."

"A book based on the film by—?"

Gets a smile out of him. "Yes, you might say so."

"Should be a best-seller."

"Best-seller? Mr. Rawlings, at the risk of overstating the case, it should be a blockbuster, an international sensation."

"What's the title?"

"His working title is: *The Man Who Survived Death*. He says he's about three-quarters of the way through the first draft, about four hundred manuscript pages, something like that."

"Book like that could be worth millions."

He nods, glances down and away. "Yes, and quite frankly, it's that aspect that troubles me. I only see him occasionally these days, in the evenings, and I've expressed my concerns. He's a changed man, Mr. Rawlings, quite changed. He's become something of a recluse. He's so paranoid about the book that he refuses to let *me* read it. I haven't seen a single page. All he's told me is that he has a—God, I know how wild this must sound—that he has a marketing strategy all planned, that he wants a major agency to represent him. The agency will read the manuscript and view highlights of the film. At that point, they will more or less follow his marketing strategy. Copies of the finished manuscript will be submitted to all major commercial publishing houses in the United States, England, France, West Germany, and Japan. They will be asked to submit sealed bids against what he calls a 'floor price' of—it embarrasses me to say this—against a floor price of five million dollars. Simultaneously, the agency is to hold private screenings of the film highlights, in New York only, for executives of all the major television networks of the five countries I've just named. The executives will then be asked to submit sealed bids against a floor price of fifteen million dollars. Last, all major motion picture studios in those five countries will be given the same opportunity as the television networks—private screenings, sealed bids, floor price of fifteen million. I'm seriously worried about him. I've told him that a scientific breakthrough of this magnitude should, by its very nature, transcend this kind of rank commercialism. He simply won't listen to reason. He seems—to me, at least—to have developed the symptoms of what could be a serious mental disorder. There are even times when he seems disoriented, completely irrational. I'm not a psychiatrist, but I'll simply say this: Please be careful with him."

I wait, then: "Where's he living?"

"La Vache Bay, the house closest to mine on the grassy cliff overlooking the sea. There are no numbers, but the houses have names on them. Mine is named 'Silver Sands.' His is named 'Landsdown.' It's not difficult to find."

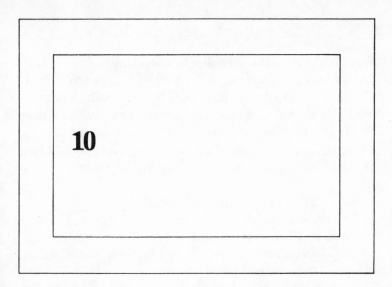

10

CHIEF VADNEY sashays into the Hilton lobby at 6:05 that evening, fat and sassy, blue blazer, striped shirt, red tie, gray trousers, attaché case, and I can tell in a twinkle that he's enjoyed the unlimited booze in Pan Am's luxurious first class. Doesn't spot Judy and me in the milling crowd, strides up to the check-in desk, grabs a pen, begins to register. We go over there just in time to catch his conversation with the ritzy room clerk. We decide to stand back and not interrupt. Wouldn't be polite, know what I mean?

"Reservation, sir?"

"No. Didn't have time."

"I'm sorry, sir, we're completely booked."

"*Booked?*"

"We're in the middle of Carnival, sir."

"*Carnival?*"

"Yes, sir."

Chief whips out his ID holder, slaps it on the desk, flashes his gold. "See if you can find that one you always got tucked away, huh? I'm on official police business here."

Clerk shrugs. "Sorry, sir, we're booked to capacity."

"You're—? Don't pull *that* routine on me, huh? I mean, I *know* you guys always stash one empty room in case of last-minute politicians and dignitaries and them. *Find* it."

I step over now, diplomatic as Ed Koch, place my hand on his shoulder. "Chief, you're all set, you're staying in our suite."

"Rawlings! Nice to see ya, buddy-boy!"

"You remember Detective Cooper, Judy Cooper."

"Yeah, sure." Shakes hands, looks her up and down.

Judy's in no mood for it. "Chief, I think we should all go straight to the suite and talk."

"Yeah, right. I got no luggage, just this case, let's go up."

We maneuver through the crowd to the elevators, Chief's checking out all the young talent in revealing Carnival costumes. Elevator doors open, spew out more revelers in even less attire, Chief's eyes are dancing quick calypso. We squeeze in, cheek-to-jowl, I hit the third-floor button, doors close, down we go. Fast.

Happy-hour crowd goes: "*Whooooooo!*"

Chief goes: "We're goin' *down!*"

I go: "It's the upside-down hotel!"

Chief goes: "*Huh?*" Eyes go: "**+.*" Mouth goes: "O." Reactions to that effect.

Doors open at the third floor first, Judy and I squiggle him away from the bulging bazooms and bare midriffs. Out we get, doors close, down they go. "*Whoooooo!*"

"The upside-*down* hotel?" Chief asks.

"It's built into the sides of a hill," Judy tells him. "The lobby's on the top."

"Weird," he says. "Totally fuckin' weird."

Once we get in the suite and settle down in the living room, things get even weirder. Judy tells him what I already know, that the police finally recovered the dismembered remains of

Terri McBride during a five-hour underwater search. Frame of the car was discovered fifteen feet deep in the bay, parts scattered over a wide area, and they used scuba-diving equipment, working in shifts, to recover her remains. Coroner's office arranged for a casket through a local funeral home; it will be hermetically sealed before shipment back to New York. Funeral home is awaiting our instructions. Next-of-kin should be notified by Chief Vadney's office as soon as possible.

Chief gets on the phone, calls Doris Banks at home, briefs her, asks her to make the necessary arrangements. Tells her the casket will be on the first Pan Am air-freight flight in the morning. Details when he knows them. Naturally, Detective McBride will have a full-dress departmental funeral, the works.

Next, I brief him on the bizarre developments here, chronological order, from the time I spotted Dr. Mailer in the Penguin Club on Friday, to the fatal accident Saturday, to my confrontation with Dr. Leonard this morning. Now, when I get to the technical stuff about Mailer—freezing, thawing, reanimation, heart transplant—I go slowly, refer to my notes, repeat the key facts, figures, dates, times, all like that. Keep telling him I know this shit's difficult to believe, but it's all true, it happened, Leonard's got eleven hours of narrated film to document it. When I'm finished, the Duke just sits there, stares off into space, eyes narrowed to slits.

Finally, he looks at me, frowns. "So, what we're talkin' here, bottom line, we're talkin' a fuckin' *nut* case, a paranoid psycho murderer. Brain-damaged. Brain-damaged geek of medical science. Huh? Real-life Frankenstein monster who's writin' a *book* about himself. He cheats death, robs his own grave, so to speak, engineers the greatest grave robbery of all time, with him as the main character, now he's lookin' to cash in on it. Still mid-fifties, he figures he's got a lot of living to catch up on. Huh? Talk about *celebrity*? *Fame*? Talk about worldwide *mass-media* attention? He could be the most famous man on earth. He could have a face-name recognition factor greater than that of—Muhammad Ali, Gorbachev, and Brooke Shields *combined*. Brand-new heart, heart of a nine-teen-year-old kid, figures it should last him another fifty years easy. Hell, if we can't prove he killed McBride, this guy might still be on the lecture circuit forty years into the next *century*."

I nod, glance at Judy. "If his kidneys hold up."

Chief gets up, goes to the sliding glass door of the terrace, takes in the view. "Thought just occurred to me. God *damn*. Jesus H. Christ *wept*. Never thought of this before. *Nobody* ever thought of *this* before." Turns, faces us, hands on hips. "Listen up, you guys, here's a legal question that'd freeze the bowels of Chief Justice Warren *Burger*. How we gonna collar a geek who's been legally *dead* for nineteen years?"

A sudden silence.

"Now, there's a good question," I admit.

"One thing's for sure," Judy says. "You won't find any legal precedent for this one in any law book ever written."

"Tell me about it," Chief says. "Sucker's been deader than a doornail for nineteen years, now he's brought back to life, madder than a hatter, proud as a peacock, with an ego as big as all outdoors, lookin' to make hay while the sun shines."

"Not only that," I say. "This guy's young at heart."

"Guess we'll have to play it by ear," Judy says.

Chief looks at his watch. "Still plenty of daylight left, it's only five-thirty, how about—"

"Six-thirty," I tell him.

"Six-thirty?"

"We're an hour ahead of New York."

"Oh, yeah." Adjusts his big Omega Astronaut Moon Watch carefully. "Six-thirty-*what,* exactly?"

"Six-thirty-one," Judy says.

Click. "Check. Listen, you guys, I don't want to waste any more time than necessary. Judy, how about you get that detective of yours on the horn—what's his name again?"

"Gordon Kinch."

"Gordon Kinch. How about you get him on the horn and the four of us drive out and pay this guy Mailer a surprise visit? See if Kinch can meet us out front at about, say, seven o'clock? How long's it take to get out there?"

She goes to the phone. "Half hour tops."

Turns out Kinch knows the La Vache Bay area quite well, he used to swim there as a kid, still takes his family there for occasional picnics on the beach. He knows Dr. Leonard, of course, he's worked with him many times over the years, and he met Dr. Mailer once, about a year ago. Says Dr. Leonard's house is right near the edge of a small cliff overlooking the beach; closest house to that is about fifty yards back from the edge. Says it's been for sale, furnished, for at least five or six years now and he thinks Dr. Mailer just rents it. We get there about 7:25, light traffic going out of town because of tonight's Carnival events. Absolutely beautiful area, wide grassy cliff overlooking the sea, long whitecaps coming in from the reef. Trees here are flat-topped and permanently bent northeast by the trade winds. Grass is trim because, Kinch says, farmers use it for grazing goats and sheep.

Mailer's house is white coral, two stories in the center, white pillars at the entrance, and one-story wings sweeping back to enclose a patio. Looks megabucks. Faces east, so that now the front facade is in deep shadow, but the windows blaze with sunlight coming through from the back. Strong light, gold, continuing into the semicircular driveway and reaching the car parked to the right of the entrance, an old Jaguar XKE sports coupe, black, classic lines, top down, looks like it's kept in mint condition.

Kinch parks behind it, we get out, walk slowly to the steps. Climbing them, I wonder if he's watching us from a window. Beauty of a door, polished redwood, big brass knocker in the center that Judy recognizes instantly as something called

Fatima's Hand, the slender left hand of a woman wearing an emerald ring and holding a ball. I ask Judy what it's supposed to symbolize. She says Fatima was the fabled daughter of the prophet Mohammed, wife of Ali, seventh century. Says her symbol is often displayed in Shiite processions.

Kinch uses the knocker, three taps that sound sharp and metallic in the silence. We hear footsteps almost immediately. Door opens wide, strong sunlight comes through, so that his face and figure are in shadow.

Low, friendly voice: "Hello, Mr. Kinch, nice to see you."

"Sorry to bother you, Dr. Mailer, but these people are detectives from New York, and they'd like to ask you a few routine questions about an automobile accident in this area last evening."

"Yes," Mailer says pleasantly, "Derek Leonard called this morning and told me you might stop by. Which one of you is Detective John Rawlings?"

"I am, Dr. Mailer." I stick out my hand. "Nice to meet you."

Firm handshake. "Pleasure."

I turn sideways. "This is Chief of Detectives Walter Vadney and Detective Judith Cooper."

He shakes their hands, exchanges greetings. "Please come in."

We follow him down a hallway floored by coral slabs and out to a little bar on a porch overlooking the patio. He motions for us to sit on the stools, says he knows we can't drink on duty, asks if we'd like soft drinks. All very polite and friendly. I get a good look at him as he takes our orders. Dark hair, gray-white at the temples, high forehead, thin black steel-framed glasses, aviator style, non-smoker teeth, strong chin. Tanned complexion has the normal mileage of mid-fifties, particularly around the eyes and mouth, but no scars, no sores, no blemishes; his tan might mask some additional wear and tear, but not all that much. Of course, he's had more than a year to recuperate, fifteen months, to be exact, and he's got a healthy ticker now, which makes a big difference. Body looks lean in a long-sleeved blue shirt and dark trousers. Up close, looking at me to take my order, his eyes seem to dominate. Light blue, almost transparent in this light. Anything unusual in those peepers? Any subtle hint of instability—mental, emotional, physical? Nope. Not a trace. Absolutely natural.

It's cool and somewhat shady at the bar, the porch is enclosed by thick coral arches with overhanging bougainvillea. All the windows and doors opening on the porch are black wrought-iron grillwork without glass. Patio itself is a large circular area of coral slabs, white table and chairs in the middle, little coral benches at the edges, surrounded by trim, well-watered grass, and two old but fruit-bearing lime trees with full crowns. Dozens of ripe limes are on the grass.

Kinch leads off: "So you know about the accident, sir?"

"Yes, Derek Leonard told me about it this morning. Horrible. They went off North Coast Road in heavy rain?"

"That's right," Kinch says. "One detective was killed, a young lady. The other detective, a man, managed to jump out before the vehicle went over. It exploded on second impact and finally landed in the bay."

Mailer nods. "I was terribly sorry to hear about it."

"It happened late Friday afternoon," Kinch goes on. "Where the road starts sharply downhill, not far from here."

Mailer sits on his stool behind the bar, sips his vodka martini. "Yes. Detective Kinch, could we please get to the point? May I ask what the accident has to do with me?"

Chief clears his throat. "Yeah, you may. I sent the four officers down here to determine your whereabouts."

"For what reason?"

"Restitution," Chief snaps. "Let's stop playing games here, huh? You stole twenty-four million dollars' worth of research and development from ICC. They want it back. They want the stolen documents and vials. You're protected by the statute of limitations now, but they have every legal right to recover their property. Dr. Stegmueller is prepared to initiate a civil suit against you, effective immediately."

"That won't be necessary," Mailer says calmly. "At this point, I'll be only too happy to cooperate. Derek Leonard has all of the original documents in a safe at the hospital, and twenty-four of the thirty-six remaining vials are under refrigeration there. He's at Carnival with his wife tonight, but I'll call him first thing in the morning. Now, to get back to the accident. Derek told me that Detective Rawlings considers me a suspect in *causing* the accident. Is that correct?"

"That's right," I tell him.

He glares at me. "That's absolute nonsense. How could I have possibly *caused* an accident of that nature?"

"Easily," I say. "Most of the brake fluid was drained while the car was in the parking lot out at Maracas Bay. Also, the hand brake was disconnected. Question: Can you account for your whereabouts on Friday afternoon between the hours of three and five-thirty?"

"Certainly. I was here at home, working on a book I'm writing. I work from eight-thirty in the morning until roughly five, five-thirty in the afternoon. Every day of the week except Sunday. I've been on that schedule for well over a year now."

"Can you prove you were here?" I ask.

"Of course not. I work alone. I live alone. I have a housekeeper and a gardener who both come in once a week, on different days, but neither of them on Fridays. Question: Can you prove I *wasn't* here? Because the burden of proof is on *you,* under the law, as I'm sure you understand only too well."

Kinch to the rescue: "Dr. Mailer, these gentlemen are merely asking questions, they're not accusing you of anything. You agreed to answer questions about the accident."

"Then let's get down to *facts,*" Mailer says. "Facts, rather than illogical speculations with nothing to back them up. For example, let's examine the question of *motive.* All right? Motive. Now, even if I had known you were looking for me—and, clearly, I had no way of knowing that—but even if I had known, what possible *motive* would I have for wanting to *kill* you? None. None whatsoever. I'm certainly not a fugitive from justice now. You can't arrest me for a theft committed some twenty-two years ago. You're seventeen years too late for that. You can't touch me. So look at this thing logically. The last thing in the world I'd want to do at this point is to commit a crime of *any* kind, much less murder. What would I have to *gain*? What would be the *purpose*? I'm not attempting to hide anything. Quite the contrary. In my book, which is nearly completed now, I freely admit to the theft. As a matter of fact, I go into it at some length. And I give my rationale in considerable detail. No, gentlemen, you're being illogical. You have absolutely no motive, no evidence, nothing. Not even prima facie evidence. Now, I've agreed to make restitution, I understand the legal requirement of doing that. In fact, I knew I'd *have* to make restitution before the book was published, and I had every intention of doing so long before the actual publication. As I said, I'll call Derek Leonard in the morning and make arrangements for him to give you all of the original documents and the remaining vials. My only requirement prior to that transaction is to have you—and the authorities here—sign a statement, a receipt, as it were, of exactly what I'm giving you to return to ICC. I'll ask Derek to contact his attorney and have an appropriate document drawn up as quickly as possible. We'll need witnesses to the transaction, we'll need to have the document notarized, simply for our mutual protection. I'm sure you'll agree to that. Chief Vadney?"

"Agreed. Set it up."

Mailer looks at his watch. "And now, if you'll excuse me, I've got a date with a young lady and I don't want to keep her waiting. We've got tickets to the Calypso King and Queen Finals at the Savannah. I recommend this particular event to

all of you, it's one of the most entertaining shows of the Carnival. You still have time, it begins at eight-thirty. I'll see you to
the door."

As we follow him down the hall, some of Dr. Leonard's
statements come to mind: *He's a changed man, Mr. Rawlings,
quite changed. He's become something of a recluse. . . . He
seems—to me, at least—to have developed the symptoms of
what could be a serious mental disorder. There are even times
when he seems disoriented, completely irrational.* Recluse?
What about the girl, what about the Penguin Club, what about
tonight? Serious mental disorder? Disoriented? Irrational?
Can't buy it. Not after what I've just seen and heard. Doesn't
add up.

We get back into town about 8:20, we want Kinch to drop us
off at the hospital so we can visit Louie, but as soon as we pass
the Hilton and get on Queen's Park East, traffic is so bad it's a
disaster area. Cars, trucks, vans, RVs, motorcycles, taxis are
pulling off the road, tearing along the grass, dust billowing in
the headlights, horns blaring, people singing, yelling, laughing
hysterically. Wish you could see Vadney's face, he can't believe this shit. "Real animals," he calls 'em, "dogs in heat,
drunken savages." Me, I'm up front with Kinch, window
open, smoking a stogie, soaking up the ambience, what do I
know? By the time we get close to the Savannah, the Calypso
King Finals are going full swing, taxis and cars are surrounded by mobs of scalpers, kids, food and drink sellers, all
pushing in on them, screaming, shouting offers, hands waving,
grabbing, Vadney's going totally nuts. Loudspeakers in the
stadium blast the calypso singer, crowd inside roars with
laughter, falls silent listening to the next chorus, boos loudly,
then cheers again, breaks into applause. Song goes like so:

> *Put a tiger in meh tank,*
> *That is what the woman say,*

Put a tiger in meh tank,
An ah want it right away;
So she get meh in a rage,
Ah open the tiger cage,
Man, ah didn't fail,
Ah gee she the whole ah the tiger tail.

Well, is now she fly in a rage,
Ah pull out the pump an ah watch the gauge;
Five gallons a gas an you still want more,
Woman, what the dickens you take meh for?
Ah prefer to go down Petit Valley
Ah buy meh gas from Lord Melody,
Don't mind he hair gray an he down in age,
He does pack in the pump an does watch the
gauge.

Well, we start to argue as male,
She not satisfied with meh tiger tail:
Just a little bit more, you shouldn't get on so,
'Cause you know the distance ah have to go;
When I go in the gas station by Birdie,
Ah does get meh service free;
Ah boun to like Sparrow till ah dead,
He does gee meh the tiger from the head.

So ah finish serving the lady,
Ah stretch out meh hand to collect the money;
In pulling out the pump, the drain fall,
So ah tear piece a cloth an ah wipe up all;
All an a sudden, friends, ah feel whap,
Is meh girl friend giving meh a slap:
You dreaming brute, kick meh on the floor:
Tell meh why you tear piece a meh nightie for?

Finally get down to the hospital about 8:55, Kinch drops us
off, says to call him in the morning; we'll hoof it back to the
hotel, it's twice as fast, if we don't get run over, mugged, or
both. Take the elevator up, floor is booked solid, TVs in every

room tuned to the Calypso King Finals, even most of the nurses are watching.

Louie's propped up in bed, watching the same thing, gives us a big smile when we walk in. Fresh bandage on his left forehead, left eye is open more now, socket black but not as swollen, elbows and knuckles still taped heavily.

"Diaz!" Chief says. "How y'doin', buddy?"

"Better, much better, Chief, thanks for coming."

"You sure *look* better," Judy tells him.

I give him a soft high-five. "Hey, champ."

Chief sits on the side of the bed. "You're a lucky man, Lou. John and Judy briefed me on everything."

"No fractures," Louie says, "not even a hairline. I'm due to get out of here tomorrow morning. So what's new, what's happening?"

"We just went to see Dr. Mailer," Judy says.

Louie snaps off the TV. *"Mailer*? Holy shit, you actually— you *found* him? Where? How?"

I sit on the other side of his bed. "Dr. Leonard told me everything this morning. Mailer died of heart disease here in 'sixty-seven. Dr. Leonard, he's an old friend, he began the perfusion process at the moment of clinical death, then placed him in liquid nitrogen suspension, using the capsule he bought from Ed Cerabino. Mailer was frozen for just over nineteen years. Then, about fifteen months ago, Dr. Leonard found a suitable heart donor, a brain-dead nineteen-year-old boy. At that point, Leonard began the thawing process, introducing the stolen virus particles. Meantime, the kid was kept alive on a life-support system at the Trauma Center. When Mailer was thawed and revived, Leonard rushed him to the Trauma Center and placed him on the life-support system. Thirty-two hours later, Leonard and a team of surgeons performed a successful heart-transplant operation. Hard to believe, Lou, but it's all true. Dr. Leonard filmed the whole thing, every step, from the clinical death all the way through to the heart transplant and recovery."

"Mailer's writing a book about it now," Judy adds.

"A book based on the film," Chief says. "He's lookin' to make a fortune out of this thing. He will, too, if we can't nail him on McBride's death."

"We recovered her body this afternoon," Judy tells him.

Louie glances away, shakes his head. "What'd Mailer have to say about that? Has he got an alibi or what?"

"The fucker's got no alibi," Chief says, "but we've got no proof and he knows it. No motive, no evidence, no witness, nothing. We questioned him at length, we came up empty. Well, not completely empty, we nailed him on the restitution angle. We're getting full restitution, all the original classified documents, plus twenty-four of the thirty-six stolen vials. At least we got that. That should make Stegmueller happy after all these years."

"John," Louie says. "You got any ideas? Like, does your intuition pick up on anything about this guy?"

I hesitate. "Yeah. Yeah, picked up on a few things, I'm planning to play a couple of hunches."

"Good man, Little John," Chief says. "Play every hunch that crosses your mind. Wanna talk about 'em now or—?"

"Not ready yet, Chief. You know me, gotta have time to— y'know, cogitate."

Chief nods quickly, then frowns. "Time to what?"

"Think things through."

"You do that, buddy-boy, it's paid off in the past, right?"

Glance at my watch. "Matter of fact, I want to check something out right now. Gotta go see Dr. Kitchener at the Trauma Center. He's on duty, he works this shift."

Off to see the wizard. Lobby of the Trauma Center isn't that crowded at 9:15, revelers haven't chugged enough rum yet, the night's still young. Receptionist Coogan doesn't work this shift, there's an older lady at the desk, looks mean, looks like she'd rather be at the Savannah, looks like she'd be a shoo-in winner in the Calypso Pit Bull Finals. Me, I smile, turn on the charm, I've always had a way with the canine crowd. Tell her my name, tell her I'm a friend of Dr. Kitchener, ask to see him for just a minute. Don't show ID because, as far as I know, Kitchener's not aware I'm a cop; want to keep it that way. Receptionist bares her teeth in a lovely smile, rings the trauma desk in back, asks for Dr. Kitchener, waits, speaks to him in playful barks. He'll be out to see me shortly. If I had a box of Milk-Bone biscuits, I'd give her the whole thing. Stuff cleans teeth, freshens breath naturally, says so on the label. Down, Fido, down!

Shortly means shortly to this guy, Kitchener comes out at 9:20 in his wrinkled green scrubsuit and cap, mask pulled down, he's peeling off his surgical gloves as he walks toward me. Good-looking West Indian kid, but his face seems tired, especially his eyes.

I shake his hand. "Just wanted to thank you personally for taking such excellent care of my friend Louie Diaz. He sends his best, he says he'll never be able to thank you adequately."

Kitchener nods, sits down tiredly. "You're both quite welcome, Mr. Rawlings, I appreciate the thought. As it turned out, he was very fortunate, no broken bones, nothing of a serious nature. We have him scheduled for discharge tomorrow morning."

"What time should I be here?"

"Right after Dr. Leonard makes his rounds. I'd say between eight-thirty and nine."

"I'll be here at eight-thirty sharp. I want to thank Dr. Leonard too. Bet you're in for a busy night tonight, huh?"

"Yes, but we have extra staff on duty every night until Wednesday, so we can all take short breaks once in a while."

I glance around. "You should be very, very proud of this new Trauma Center. It's one of the most modern, first-class facilities I've seen anywhere. When was it built?"

"Just three years ago. We needed one badly, believe me."

"Dr. Leonard was telling me about the successful heart-transplant operation you people performed here about a year ago. That must've been fantastic. Was that the first one done here?"

"No, actually, it was the second. We did the first one just about a year prior to that. Both recipients survived, they're both still living, so we're quite proud of that."

"Were you involved in the operations?"

He smiles. "No, no, Mr. Rawlings, I'm still an intern here. I don't participate in major surgical events of that nature. No, Dr. Leonard put together a team of specialists for both operations. I was just an observer."

"I see."

"And I also studied the films."

"Did you meet the patients?"

"Well, no, but I was on duty the night that Dr. Leonard brought in the second recipient. So I participated in the sense that I assisted in the trauma room, I helped him get the man on a life-support system."

"That must've been memorable for you."

"Yes, it was."

"Is it true that the man was near death when he got here?"

"Near death? No. No, his vital signs were quite stable."

"Was he conscious?"

"Oh, yes. Wide awake. We were talking with him."

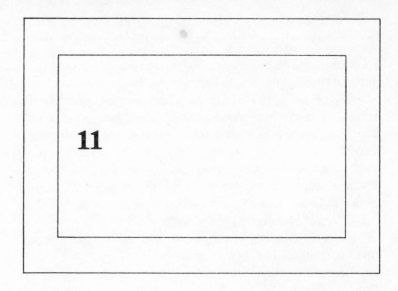

11

BRIGHT AND EARLY next morning, Monday, February 15, we're all in Louie's room when Dr. Leonard gives him a final check before discharge. Mailer already called Leonard, asked him to contact his attorney and have a simple document drawn up to be signed by the relevant parties prior to the actual restitution exchange. Leonard tells us the transaction can take place in his office at five o'clock this afternoon. His attorney will be present, two of his staff as witnesses, a notary public, Kinch, Mailer, and us. About 8:45, when Leonard's gone and Louie's getting dressed, Chief makes a credit card call to Dr. Stegmueller at his home in New York. Talk about a one-way conversation? More Vadney explains what happened here, more the actual reality of the whole wild situation begins to hit him. Adrenaline starts pumping like crazy, he's out of breath, his face turns red, his voice jumps an octave. Begins to dawn on him that he's now in a position to release the whole incredibly big and bizarre story to the sensation-hungry mass-media folks worldwide.

Beads of sweat glint on his forehead as he continues non-stop: "I mean, Steg, you realize what we're *talkin'* here? I'll tell ya what we're talkin' here. We're talkin' the first human being in the history of the fuckin' world to be brought back from the fuckin' *dead*! Huh? I mean, okay, other than what Jesus Christ did, know what I mean? But that doesn't count, him being God and all, right? This thing, we can prove it beyond the shadow of a fuckin' Doubtin' Thomas. I mean, we got it all on *film*, narrated film, facts, figures, dates, times—and we got it *live*, too, we got a walkin', talkin', fartin' Frankenstein monster here, happens to be a media freak, he'll knock 'em dead, he'll tell 'em stories that'll send icicles straight up their assholes! This thing, we're talkin' lead-story network TV around the globe! This thing, they'll interrupt *soaps* for this type shit. We're talkin' front-page banner heads from the *New York Times* to fuckin' *Tass*! Cover stories in every magazine from *Time* to *Playgirl*! Huh? Tell ya what, buddy, after I talk to you, I'm gettin' Jerry Grady on the horn—what time's it there?—seven-forty-eight, that's right. I'm gettin' Grady at home, he's our director of media relations, I'm tellin' him to call every top media man in Manhattan and get their butts aboard that Pan Am ten-thirty flight this morning. I'll tell 'im to tell 'em I hit the fuckin' mother lode of media gold down here—guaranteed!—my ass on the line! By six o'clock tonight, this place will be crawlin' with cameras! *Crawlin'* with 'em! A carnival of crawlin' cameras smack in the middle of a carnival of costumed crazies. Huh? Talk about an exotic backdrop? Steel-band calypso driftin' on the balmy breezes of the blue Caribbean? Huh? Then—crack!—*The Iceman Cometh*! Talk about the right—"

"Chief," I say softly.

"—man in the right place at the right time! Yeah, sure, Steg, you can come down, too. Absolutely, positively. You got a stake in this action, too, you got a role to play here. Hop that ten-thirty—"

"Chief," I say louder.

"—flight with all the others. Rawlings, I'm talking long distance here, what's the matter with you?"

"Don't do it," I tell him.

"Don't do—*what*?"

"Don't call the media yet."

"Don't call the—? Why *not*?"

"Wait till seven o'clock tonight."

"Wait till—?"

"Tell Dr. Stegmueller to get Mailer's personnel file, including his fingerprints from the security clearance material, and send it down by courier on the ten-thirty flight this morning. Tell him that everything you just said is strictly confidential until further notice."

"Rawlings, what's the fuckin' *point*? We got a positive *ID*. We've *seen* the man, we've *talked* with him, he's *admitted* everything, we *know* it's him. Leonard's got eleven hours of *film* to prove it."

"Chief, don't put your ass on the line yet. Give me until seven o'clock tonight."

He glances at the receiver, then at me. Shakes his head. "Steg, I gotta get back to ya, buddy. Right. Ten minutes max. Right." Hangs up, gives me a look, shakes his head again.

Louie's out of the bathroom now, fully dressed. Judy's sitting by the window with a quizzical expression, she's never seen the Duke in action like this before. She keeps her mouth shut. Wisely.

Chief sits on the bed now, tugs at his open collar. Forehead flattens just a split second before his ears jut back and he's into his patented left-sided molar-shower. "It's funny, y'know, when ya look at shit like this in perspective. Y'gotta keep a sense of humor about all this. Lou, Judy, listen up, I want you to learn something here. Now, Little John, don't get me wrong. I know what you're tryin' to do here. I appreciate the fact that you're tryin' to cover my ass on this. But, bottom line, buddy-boy, it's *my* ass that's on the line, not yours. I've stuck it out before, moons up, it's nothin' new for me. Comes with the territory. Like the man says, y'gotta know when to hold 'em, know when to fold 'em. I'm holdin' 'em this time around, 'cause I'm experienced enough to know what I got. Full house, aces high. Now, okay, I know you're playin' hunches here, Little John, I know you're listenin' to your famous intuition, as usual, and I don't blame ya. I mean, I don't blame ya one little bit, it's paid off a lot of times in the past. It's like a gift ya got, it's what makes ya such a damn fine detective, head and shoulders above the pack. But this time, I think—rather, I know—you're being too conservative. Look at the facts, buddy. Forget the hunches and intuition and radar and stick to the flat-out facts. We can't nail Mailer for murder, we got nothin'. You know it, I know it, he knows it. We got squat. We can't touch him. But, wait a minute here, hold on, we're not comin' away from this thing empty-handed, right? What we *do* have is somethin' very, very special. We *do* have restitution, recovery of most of the stolen property. Which is worth *what*? Which, after twenty-two years, countin' inflation and all, is worth maybe a hundred million dollars, that's what. Huh? Probably more. Think about it. Probably a lot more. Know why? I'll tell you why. Listen up now, this is the whole key to my thinkin'. Because Mailer is living, breathing *proof* that it *works*! Huh? That what he stole back then actually *works*. That whatever combination of chemicals is in those twenty-four remaining vials, along with the intelligence on how to administer it, is capable of bringing frozen people back to *life*. Huh? Now, that's news, Little John, that's major, major news. That's a scientific breakthrough the likes of which will send ICC's *stock* soaring through the stratosphere. Follow my thinkin'? The secrets we're recovering and returning to their lawful owners could eventually be worth billions. That's right. *Billions*! Know why I want the press to find out? I'll tell you why. Number one, to prevent insider trading. To prevent unscrupulous Wall Street stockbrokers from finding out before the rest of the public, then sinking millions into ICC stock at rock-bottom prices. I mean, they'd realize windfall profits that'd make guys like Ivan Boesky look like penny-ante *ragpickers*. So that's number one, protecting the little guy out there in the market. Number two—I admit it, I'll be up front about this—it makes *us* look *real* good. I'm talkin' NYPD now, I'm talkin' our national and international *reputation*. I mean, try to look at the big picture, look at what we've accomplished here. We've solved one of the greatest robberies of all *time*. Huh? A robbery so great that it's earned a listing in the *Guinness Book of World Records*. Little John, you saw it with your own *eyes*. Right?"

"I saw it."

"Think of what that'll do for our public image, our reputation. Think of what this'll do for the pride and morale of the whole department, twenty-five thousand of New York's finest, from Commissioner Reilly all the way down to the rookie cop on the beat in the sticks of Staten Island."

"It'd be nice," I admit.

"Twenty-two years on this case and we never closed the file, never gave up, never caved in to pressure. Kept our heads high and our ears to the ground. Methodical, tenacious, ploddin' old grunts like me. So what happens? Hot-fuckin'-diddly—*damn,* if we don't up and hit the world media jackpot, that's what, the shot heard 'round the world. Huh?"

"Right."

"Then why the fuck don't y'wanna tell the *media*?"

I shrug. "Because I'm not totally convinced that this guy is the same man that was frozen. Only one way to find out for sure."

"Fingerprints?"

"Fingerprints."

"And just how you gonna get Mailer's fingerprints *here*?"

"Simple. Five o'clock this afternoon he'll be in Leonard's

office to sign the papers of restitution and give back what he stole. He'll be handling the new papers, plus the original re- search documents, plus—if we get lucky—maybe even some of the vials. We'll have his latent prints on a lot of material, Chief. Louie, Judy, and me, we stand back, keep our hands off the stuff. Papers of restitution will be handled by too many people—Mailer, Leonard, his attorney, Kinch, witnesses, the notary public, and you. But the only latents on the research documents and vials might turn out to be Mailer's, Leonard's, and finally yours, if you have no choice but to handle them. After the meeting, we go straight to police headquarters with Kinch, have his lab technician dust the research material and vials, come up with the clearest latents he can find. Next, we fingerprint you, compare your prints with the latents, elimi- nate yours. My opinion, there's a strong possibility that might leave us with only two sets of prints, Leonard's and Mailer's. Pan Am flight arrives at five-thirty with the courier, he goes straight to headquarters, gives us Mailer's prints from his per- sonnel file. We get out the scope, see if they match up with the two sets of latents we got left. If so, Mailer's the genuine arti- cle, case closed, call in the media people, let the circus begin. If not, we got a major-league con artist here—two of 'em, be- cause Leonard would have to be in on it—and we got enough prima facie evidence to arrest both of 'em on suspicion of conspiracy to defraud and suspicion of conspiracy to commit murder. Police here make the arrests, we have a John Doe fugitive warrant. Found out before I left New York that the U.S. has a small embassy in Port-of-Spain and that an extradi- tion treaty, ratified in nineteen-fifty-eight, is still in effect. So we'd have it made, if it turned out he's a phony and they're both con artists."

Chief thinks on it, glances at Lou and Judy. "Louie?"

"He's got a point, Chief, no question. If there's any doubt at all, prints would be proof positive."

Chief nods. "Judy?"

"Naturally, I agree about the prints. I have two or three questions. One, if this guy's a phony, how can he *look* so much like Mailer? Plastic surgery? Two, if he's an imposter, what happened to the real Dr. Mailer? Three, I'd be curious to know how many shares of stock in ICC are held by Leonard and Mailer right now."

"All good questions," Chief says. "Particularly about how he could resemble Mailer that closely. I mean, I've studied the photos, too. Over years. Mailer's face is branded indelibly into my brain. And after last night, seeing him up close, listening to him, there's just no doubt in my mind. None. It's him. Got to be. Little John, I don't understand, buddy, maybe I'm missing something. You were convinced, too, you made a positive ID. How come, all of a sudden, now you got doubts?"

"Can't really explain it, Chief. Combination of a lot of things. All I know, it just boils down to a strong gut feeling."

"Your fuckin' intuition again, right?"

"Can't help it, Chief. Gotta be honest about it."

Chief frowns, head down, then looks up at me and smiles. "All right, okay, what we got here is an honest difference of opinion, Little John. I don't happen to buy your side of it, that's all, I think Mailer's Mailer, period. But don't get me wrong, I respect your opinion, even if it's a crock of crap, you got a right to it, buddy, you've earned it. So, I gotta call Stegmueller back now, here's what I'm gonna do. I'm gonna ask him to get Mailer's personnel file, including the fingerprints, and bring it down himself on the ten-thirty flight. That way, if we don't come up with good latents at the meeting—and you know how hard it is to get good, clear latents off papers—if we don't get 'em, we'll have an ace up the hole: Stegmueller himself. He worked with Mailer for at least twelve years while the team at ICC was doin' their R and D. Right? So, if Mailer's Mailer, Stegmueller'll know it in ten seconds flat. One question is all it'll take. One highly technical egghead question that only he'd know to ask and Mailer'd know to answer.

Now, is that a double-whammy compromise solution, or what?"

"Excellent," I tell him.

"Huh? Louie?"

"Fail-safe perfect."

"Judy?"

"Super. And what about the media?"

Chief frowns. "Oh, shit, the media. Forgot about the media. Well, look, let's face it. No matter what happens now, one way or the other, we're talkin' fast-breakin' major, major news here. Huh? Now, if we don't tip the media, if we play it safe, if we hide our heads in the sand till six, seven o'clock tonight, what've we got? I'll tell ya what we got. If we gotta wait till tomorrow night before the media can get down here to cover fast-breakin' major news—the boys and girls of the media got a nifty little metaphor for this kinda gag-rule blackout. They say it changes hot shit into cold turd. Huh?"

"Excellent metaphor," I tell him.

"Huh? Judy?"

"Sure sounds like the media."

"Louie?"

"*Daily News* all the way."

"No *way* I'm gonna serve it up cold," Chief says decisively. "This racket, ya gotta slap it on the grill, serve it up steamin'. I'm gettin' Jerry Grady on the horn, tell him to pull all stops, call the top media moguls at home, wake 'em up if need be, tell 'em to drop their cocks and grab their socks. I mean, these clowns are used to fast-breakin' shit, they're weaned on it, they eat it up, they get their rocks off jumpin' jets, half of 'em got perpetual hard-ons anyhow."

"Reminder," I say quietly. "Your ass is on the line."

Chief grabs the phone. "I thrive on this crap, Little John. That's the difference between us."

"Hot shit and cold turd?"

"You said it, buddy-boy, not me."

Nice afternoon, we walk from the hotel to the Trauma Center, take in the colorful parade of steel-band orchestras marching in scaffolds down Queen's Park East, together with thousands of costumed people, all headed downtown for tonight's celebrations in Independence Square. Not that far a walk, get to the Trauma Center early, about 4:50; Kinch is in the lobby, lovely young receptionist in the place of Queen Pit Bull. Calls Dr. Leonard's office, tells him we're here for the meeting, Doc says come right up. Take the elevator to the second floor, stroll down the spotless hall, door to office 227 is wide open.

Leonard's standing behind his desk again, studying X-rays on the big light box. Looks distinguished as ever, tall and lean in the white duds, matching white hair, bald pate, scholarly tortoiseshells. Pleasant British accent: "Please come in, you're the first to arrive."

I introduce Vadney very formally, Louie thanks Leonard again for everything, we all sit down. Must say, our little group looks like a million bucks for the auspicious occasion, Chief's orders, coats and ties, shoes shined, Judy's straight out of *Vogue* in a pale pink outfit with matching jacket, low white heels. I mean, it's not every day you recover stolen property worth maybe a cool hundred million from a gentleman who may or may not have been frozen stiff for nineteen years. Wish Grady was here to take a group picture. Nice thing to show your grandchildren, tell 'em all about it. Naw, they'd never believe shit this wild.

Leonard's desk holds two manuscripts with black covers, each about two inches thick, and a light-blue styrene plastic box that looks like a common food and drink cooler that you take to the beach, the kind with the twin lids that you freeze overnight before using.

"As you know," Leonard says, "the original research documents have been kept in the hospital safe." He indicates the two manuscripts. "There are two volumes, a total of eight hundred thirty-eight pages, representing twelve years of development. Dr. Mailer has the only copy, a 'protection copy,' as he calls it, that he's been using to research his book." Now he touches the plastic box. "The remaining twenty-four vials of artificially constructed virus particles have been refrigerated at a constant temperature for some twenty-three years now, first at my home, later at the hospital. I've taken the liberty of placing them in this cooler for transportation, but I would suggest that you have them refrigerated at your hotel as soon as possible after the meeting."

"At what temperature?" Judy asks.

"As close to thirty-five degrees Fahrenheit as practicable."

Chief clears his throat. "How about transportation back to New York?"

"All air-freight carriers have refrigeration facilities for perishable products. I suggest you use those facilities." His phone rings, he answers it, listens. "Please send the gentlemen up." Hangs up. "Dr. Mailer has arrived with my attorney, Mr. Baden-Smythe."

Couple of minutes later, in they pop, Mailer in a smart blazer and striped tie, carrying a fat attaché case; Baden-Smythe in a dark but lightweight three-piece suit, ultraconservative tie, looks about Leonard's age, mid-seventies, pure white hair, ruddy complexion, medium height and build, scholarly demeanor, carries an ancient fat briefcase. All rise, solemn salutations, firm handshakes.

Turns out Mailer's been in conference with Baden-Smythe most of the afternoon, they really got their act together at this point, looks to me like they rehearsed, they know their lines cold, no pun intended. Baden-Smythe's got the lead role, starts off with a low-key show-and-tell routine. We're all handed copies of an eleven-page document titled simply "Restitution Agreement." That's as simple as it gets. Baden-Smythe proceeds to read all eleven pages aloud. In a British accent that puts Leonard's to shame. Standing. Wearing real pince-nez glasses, yet. Yeah, clipped to his nose by a spring or something. Reads slowly. In a monotone. Frequent pauses for dramatic effect. Shakespearean vaudeville. Legal lingo straight from sixteenth-century England, House of Lords, all he needs is the long white wig. Me, I'm starting to nod off by page seven, I don't have the glimmer of a clue what this clown's into here. Then, very gradually, I become aware that somebody—I'm not pointing any fingers—dropped one. Somebody in that office, as the British would put it, broke wind. Louie and I exchange glances. He shrugs. I shrug. Baden-Smythe keeps reading, pauses momentarily as his nose is assaulted, pince-nez twitch a fraction, clears his throat slowly, as if to indicate he's aware that such behavior is commonplace in the colonies, then continues, stiff upper lip. Chief gives me his best Duke Wayne *True Grit* glance. I shrug. Judy, she's biting her lip, she's about to break up at our innocent expressions. Who, me? Suddenly hits me who did it. Not Mailer, not Leonard, they're both sitting behind the desk, too far away. Not any of our gang, we're sitting too close together, we'd know. That leaves Baden-Smythe, Esq. Got to be. Guilty beyond any reasonable doubt. Sanctimonious old dog. Facial expressions and tone of voice get progressively more indignant by the page. Knows attack is the best defense. Then, by page ten, I'm feeling sorry for the old gent. Yeah. Seventy-five years old, who knows, maybe he's incontinent. Happens. Maybe he dumped. Maybe he's wearing one of those modern Sta-Calm disposable diaper rigs. If so, the poor devil won't be able to sit down, right? Might make a squishing sound. Couldn't risk it. My guess, he'll have to excuse himself from the room, stiff-leg it down the hall to the men's john. Dispose of it discreetly in the trash can. Hate to think of stuff like this. Getting old ain't fun. Step back and smell the roses? Tell me about it.

Finally gets to the last page, reads: "This agreement shall be governed and construed as if entered into and wholly performed within the State of New York and the United States of America. In witness whereof, the parties have signed this agreement by their duly authorized representatives and selves as of the day and year first above written." Stops, peers at us over his pince-nez. "Miss Cooper, gentlemen, do you have any questions?"

We glance at each other anxiously, hoping against hope that one of us picked up on enough of this gibberish to ask an intelligent question. Baden-Smythe waits, blinking, pince-nez twitching. Silence is broken by Dr. Leonard's phone. Notary public just arrived at the reception desk. Says to send him up. Now he punches some buttons, asks Nurse Goody to come in with Nurse Two Shoes or something to witness the signing of a document. Before they arrive, Baden-Smythe removes his pince-nez, quietly informs Leonard that he'll be right back, slips out the door. Does it with nonchalance. Got to hand it to these Brits, they can hold their own.

He's back before the signing, dignified as you please, ready to orchestrate the main event. What happens, Chief and Mailer sit at the desk, sign the original and five copies, followed by the two witnesses, who also write their addresses, and finally signed and sealed by the notary public. Mailer doesn't handle anything but the original and five copies. Baden-Smythe collects them all, gives Mailer the original, two copies to Vadney, one to Leonard, one to Kinch (who wore his best suit and tie for the occasion and didn't get to say boo), and keeps one himself. So our copies have been handled by a minimum of six people. Not good. But now, when Leonard gives the two original manuscripts to Vadney, plus the plastic cooler, Mailer opens his big attaché case, takes out the two volumes of his "protection copy," which has blue covers, and hands them to me, one on top of the other. I accept them palms up, of course, so I only touch the bottom cover.

"Only one copy was ever made," he tells me. "I used it for research on the book, but I have no further need of it."

I place the volumes on my chair, shake his hand. "We appreciate it."

"So that's it," he says. "That's everything."

"Ladies and gentlemen," Baden-Smythe announces, "that concludes these proceedings. As you know, Dr. Leonard has an unusually hectic schedule this time of year, so he has to return to work as soon as possible. Thank you all for coming. Thank you very much indeed."

All rise, solemn salutations, firm handshakes. I pick up my two volumes by the bottom cover, notice Vadney's doing the same; Louie grabs the plastic cooler, away we go. Next stop, headquarters.

Outside in the parking lot, headed for Kinch's car, Chief walks next to me, holding the volumes carefully, glancing up at the clear blue sky. "Meetin' broke up just before five-thirty, Little John. Pan Am flight should be gettin' in about now. Another half hour, that hotel will be crawlin' with cameras."

"What hotel they staying at?" I ask.

"Hilton. Grady's takin' 'em straight to the Hilton."

"Hilton's booked solid, Chief."

He stops dead, closes his eyes. "Oh, shit."

"Every hotel in town is booked solid."

"Holy shit," he says. "Where they gonna *stay*?"

"Good question. I got an even better one."

"What's that, buddy?"

"Where *you* gonna *hide*?"

12

POLICE HEADQUARTERS blows us out of the water, don't know what we expected, this one reminds me of the one in Miami, three graceful floors of reinforced concrete (Miami has five floors), recessed windows shaded by slanted overhanging concrete slabs, high wall surrounding it encloses a bright green courtyard of stately royal palms. Kinch takes us straight to the Forensic Lab, top floor, introduces us to Lieutenant Joe Selogy, commanding officer. Lab's not all that big compared to Louie's shop in NYPD, but it's loaded with all the latest high-tech computerized space-age crap you can imagine. Selogy, he's a no-nonsense-type guy, late forties, about six-one, maybe 205, dark curly hair, dark eyes, wears a trim mustache. Louie and him, they're wired to the same weird wavelength immediately, instant marriage, flying on formaldehyde. Best shot we got for clear latent prints, Louie's opinion, is the front blue cover of the "protection copy" volume that's on top of the other. Selogy whips out two pairs of latex gloves sealed in plastic containers. Louie and him will wear them, the rest of us peons please keep our mitts off everything. Chief says he wants a pair, too; says it like a kid playing chief of detectives. Selogy gives him this look, says it all, tosses him a pair.

Tell you why Selogy isn't exactly thrilled with Vadney in the first place. Normally, lab's only open till five o'clock unless they got an emergency of some kind, okay? It's now about 5:45, Selogy's two staff technicians and his civilian secretary have gone home; in fact, he let them off early because tonight happens to be one of the biggest nights of the whole Carnival. Why's *he* here, commanding officer, on a simple latent prints dust and match deal? You guessed it. This morning, Vadney puts in a call to the chief of police here, explains the situation, requests the lab stay open as late as necessary. Chief of police asks only one question: Is this an emergency, or can it wait till tomorrow morning? Vadney says it's a real emergency, tells him about the planeload of top media people due to arrive at 5:30, tells him about Dr. Stegmueller, president of International Cryogenics Corporation, making the trip himself, rushing the guy's prints straight to the lab, da-da. Next thing, Selogy's called into his chief's office, ordered to keep the lab open as late as necessary. When he finds out it's a dust and match deal, Selogy says he'll do it himself, no need to take it out on his staff, they've all got big plans for tonight, just like him. Exactly when is "late as necessary"? When NYPD Chief of Detectives Walter F. Vadney says so, that's when. So, anyhow, that's why Selogy isn't too thrilled.

Make a long story short, we follow Selogy as he carries the top volume of the "protection copy" from his office out to one of the modern forensic counters in the lab, he's surrounded by high-tech equipment, but he doesn't use any of it. Simply switches on a small high-intensity lamp, inspects the blue cardboard cover with a large magnifying glass, Sherlock Holmes style. Next, he uses a device, resembles a miniature hair dryer, to blow away dust particles. Now he picks up a little glass container, looks like a salt or pepper shaker, sprinkles a fine black powder evenly on areas at the far right side of the cover, upper and lower corners, where your fingers would normally touch the cover to open it. Waits a few seconds, tilts the cover up, lets most of the black powder slide off onto a paper towel. Uses the magnifying glass again, inspects those areas. Lets Louie take a peek. Now the two of them are into their element, talking about stuff like arches, loops, whorls, composites. Next thing, Selogy gets out a box that reads Scotch Magic Plus Removable Transparent Tape 8ıı. Yeah. Looks like you could buy it in the corner office supply store. Pulls out a two-inch strip, looks like it's the standard three-quarter-inch width, places it carefully over one of the areas he dusted, rubs it down flat. Repeats the process with maybe eight to ten two-inch-long strips. Me, I can see with my naked eyes that he's picked up close to a dozen prints, don't know how clear they are. Talk about space-age forensic technology, now he gets out a regular single-edge razor blade, patiently lifts the lower edge of each strip of tape, lifts each strip off the cover with infinite care, places each on a high-gloss individual white card, same size as your standard snapshot photos. Rubs each strip down flat, center of each card.

Turns out he's got ten cards, he lines them up on the counter, lets the peanut gallery take a gander, please don't touch. Majority of the cards have at least two prints, or parts of prints, some of them relatively clear to my eye. Chief, Judy, Kinch, me, we're standing around, bent over these things, hands behind our backs, jockeying for position. Feel like a kid in science class on lab day. Remember lab days in high school? Dissecting frogs, shit like that? Hated it. Felt sorry for the frog. Hated that lab smell. Smells something like that in this place.

What happens next, Selogy picks up his cards, we follow him into a windowless little room that seems like it's full of microscopes. Maybe six or eight, all sizes and shapes, each with its own table and chair. Selogy sits down at one, tells us it's a Leitz fingerprint comparison microscope. Louie explains that this thing performs the same basic functions as a ballistics comparison microscope. Actually, it's two microscopes combined optically. Take a fingerprint, tear it in half, place the left side under the left lens, right side under the right lens, focus both, then turn the knobs to bring the two images together optically. That's essentially what we're doing in print match comparisons.

At this point, all Selogy's attempting to do is find the sharpest, cleanest sets of latent prints to be compared optically with the prints from Mailer's personnel file. And this selection process takes time. If he's unable to find any prints that are sharp and clear enough, in his judgment, to be used in a court of law as positive identification, he'll simply have to start over again, try the back cover of this volume, front cover of the second volume (my prints are all over the back cover of that one), he may even have to dust the glass vials as a last resort. Ordinarily, glass is an excellent surface to find good latent prints, but it has to be a relatively wide glass surface, such as a drinking glass. Narrow, sharply curved glass surfaces, like most vials, rarely produce good latents, because only part of the fingerprint is left.

At 6:o8, the telephone rings. Officer at the security desk downstairs says Dr. Carl Stegmueller and Mr. Frank Vadney are here, claim they have a meeting in the Forensic Lab. Selogy tells him to send them up, give them directions.

"Frank Vadney?" I ask Vadney.

Looks a little sheepish. "Yeah, well, I asked Steg to bring him along, Little John, he's been workin' in BCI's New York office, so he was available. I mean, let's face it, BCI, they deserve to be represented now, at the wrap-up, they've worked this case tenaciously, know what I mean, buddy? Tenaciously, on and off, for twenty-two years."

"Oh, I agree," I tell him. "Chief, something I been meaning

to ask you, is Frank Vadney a distant relative of yours or something?"

Clears his throat, straightens his tie, takes a swipe at his cowlick, takes me aside, speaks just above a whisper. "Yeah, well, he's—he's my kid brother, Little John."

"Yeah? Didn't know you had a brother."

"Yeah. Frank's five years younger than me, but he's the— he's always been the brain of the family. Know what I mean?"

"Bright, huh?"

"Bright? Try brilliant. Graduated from Cornell."

"Cornell, huh?"

"Cornell. Top student. Not only that—get a load of this, Little John—kid played first-string varsity football."

"First string, huh?"

"First string. Three years. He was a tackle, Frank was. They called 'em tackles back then. Kid was a star."

"Rare combination, top student, top athlete."

"Yeah, we used to go see his games. I was always very proud of the kid."

"Bet you were."

"I applied to Cornell five years earlier, couldn't get in."

"No?"

"Naw. I mean, I had good grades and all, but not good enough. Had to settle for Duke. Duke Blue Devils."

"Play football?"

"Naw." Shakes his head, glances away. "I mean, I went out for it, I was big enough, but not good enough. I stunk up the place."

"Well, look at you now. You didn't do too bad."

"Yeah."

"Chief of detectives, NYPD. Not too shabby."

"Yeah. But Frank's always been the star. He has all the brains in the family."

"How come he didn't—? Well, brains aren't everything."

"How come he didn't—what?"

"No, I was just—curious is all. I was just gonna ask how come he didn't join the department."

Chief frowns, glances over at the others, puts his hand on my shoulder, ushers me completely out of the room.

"Sorry, Chief, didn't mean to—"

"Truth is, he wanted to be a cop. Kid always wanted to, that's the—that's the irony. Kid wanted to be a cop like me. Always respected the fact that I was a good cop, that I loved my job. But it just wasn't in the cards."

"No, huh?"

"No. See, the thing is, Mom and Dad didn't want him to. Said he was too bright to start at the bottom and climb the ladder in a huge bureaucracy like NYPD. Said he'd never amount to a hill of beans if he was a cop like me. Imagine that, Little John? My own parents sayin' that about me?"

"That's—I'm sure they didn't mean it that way, Chief."

"Mean it? Know what my dad called me when I joined NYPD?"

"What?"

"Called me Shit Heels. Huh? Shit Heels."

"That's—unfortunate."

"Truth is, they were ashamed of me."

"No."

"Yeah."

"No, I can't believe that, Chief."

"Believe it. You got any brothers?"

"No. Two sisters."

"They got careers or—?"

"Yeah. They're both teachers."

"Teachers. They proud of you?"

"Yeah."

"Frank's proud of me. When we were kids, we always talked about being cops, detectives, working as partners in NYPD. When I joined the department, it was always my dream to work together with Frank, be in the same precinct, maybe get paired off as partners on the same beat, so I could take him under my wing, teach him the ropes and all like that. Don't know why I'm tellin' you all this, buddy, sorry if I'm—"

"Not at all. It's interesting. Never knew much about your family."

"Frank and me, that's all now. Mom and Dad, they're both gone, God rest 'em. So, anyhow, Frank joined BCI right after Cornell. He looked around for a couple of months, interviewed with quite a few firms, asked my advice. Finally decided on BCI, small but well-established firm, all college grads, his starting salary—get this, this was back in the autumn of 'fifty-six—Frank's starting salary was more than I was makin' after five years on the job. Mom and Dad, they were tickled with his decision. So, what I'm gettin' at, bottom line, when the ICC theft took place in 'sixty-six, I'd been chief since 'sixty-two, so I was closely involved in the investigation for about a year. When we came up empty after givin' it our best shot for that first year, Stegmueller came to me and flat-out asked my advice about private investigation firms. Naturally, I told him about BCI, I told him it was one of the few established firms that specialized exclusively in industrial espionage. I also told him—right up front—that my brother Frank worked for 'em. Right up front, Little John. Didn't want to give him or anybody else the impression that I was in any way, shape, or form recommending BCI over any competitor. Why? I'll tell you why. Because, technically, a recommendation like that could be construed in some quarters as conflict of interest. Y'follow me, buddy?"

"Certainly."

"Now. What I *did* do is this. When Stegmueller heard all the proposals from all the competitive firms and finally awarded the contract to BCI, I *did* make a perfectly reasonable, responsible, and legitimate request of him. Again, right up front. I asked if he might consider, whenever possible, takin' a low-key approach to the fact that my brother happens to work for the same firm that was awarded the contract. And he's done exactly that. And I've done exactly that. And, Little John, you and me, we go way back, buddy-boy, I'm asking you to do exactly the same."

"Absolutely. No problem."

"Because you know the power of innuendo in a big bureaucratic jungle like NYPD. Huh? Job like mine, I'm livin' in a glass house, I can't send out for fertilizer without some fuckin' mole sniffin' around, askin' who paid for the shit."

Lab door opens, in strides the fashionably dressed Carl Stegmueller and Frank Vadney, attaché cases in hand. Haven't seen Stegmueller in some time now, but first impressions last, this tall white-haired gent's got the hawklike eyes and beak of Vincent Price, same rich resonant voice, slight British accent: "Walter, John, congratulations, job well done." Take a long look at Frank Vadney as they walk toward us. Early fifties, big frame, obviously stays in shape, vague resemblance to his illustrious brother, but the glasses make him look brighter somehow, almost scholarly.

Handshakes and more salutations, now Judy, Louie, Kinch, and Selogy come out of the scope room, introductions all around.

"Hey, Frank, lookin' good!" Chief says. "How's Pat?"

"Pissed off. Had to stay home and work."

"Media people make it?" Chief asks.

Stegmueller laughs. "Twenty-two of them!"

"Partied all the way down," Frank says.

"Holy shit," Chief says. "Most of the biggies?"

"All three networks plus CNN," Frank says. "*Time*, *Newsweek*, AP, UPI, the *Times*, the *News*, and the *Journal*. All in two-man teams."

Chief flashes a molar-shower. "Twenty-two of 'em on only three hours' notice. Knew it, knew it, *knew* it. Grady probably got a bunch of 'em out of bed. He take 'em to the Hilton, Frank?"

"Right."

"We got a slight problem there." Chief turns to Selogy, gives him a playful slap on the arm. "Joe, tell me somethin', buddy. Y'got any sleepin' quarters here at headquarters?"

Selogy shrugs. "Just the lockup."

"How many beds?"

"Fourteen beds, seven cells."

"Anybody in 'em now?"

"I doubt it. They're just holding cells, drunk tanks."

Chief nods. "They start fillin' up later tonight, right?"

"I doubt it."

"Yeah? Why's that?"

"Practically everybody's drunk during Carnival."

Chief narrows his eyes. "So you just cool it, huh?"

"Exactly. Unless a serious crime is committed."

"Joe, we need your help, buddy. Need it bad. Need it now. Now, see, up at the Hilton right this minute, twenty-two of the top mass-media people in the United States of America don't have a place to sleep. Hilton's booked solid. Wouldn't even give *me* a room, even on official police business. Every hotel's the same, booked solid. Now, what I'm askin', out of professional police courtesy, y'think ya could finagle it to let those ladies and gentlemen of the press have those fourteen beds for just a couple of nights? The other eight, we're—Judy and John and Louie and me—we're givin' up our own beds for 'em, we're sleepin' on the floor, buddy, we're givin' up our whole suite, couches and all. Huh? Think ya could finagle those fourteen empty beds that nobody's gonna need anyhow? I mean, let's face it, you sure got enough clout here, you're a lieutenant, you're commanding officer of the Forensic Lab, right? Think ya could finagle those beds as a personal favor to me personally?"

Selogy gives him a look that says it all again, glances away, nods. "You got it."

"Thanks a million, buddy. Don't need to beep your chief?"

"I wouldn't be that inconsiderate, Chief Vadney. He and his wife are out on the town enjoying Carnival, just like everybody else. Just like my wife and I would like to be doing."

"We'll get this print match squared away in no time flat, Joe. It's just a precautionary measure anyhow. I guarantee I'll put in a good word to your chief."

"That won't be necessary. Can we get on with it now?"

Chief turns to Stegmueller. "Give him the prints, huh, Steg? Judy, listen up. Quick like a bunny, get the Hilton on the horn, tell the operator to page Jerry Grady, tell 'er it's an emergency, turn on the charm. Tell Grady to get the media people together, tell 'em their accommodations are all taken care of, tell 'em there's an important press conference at police headquarters in—say, tell 'em seven sharp. Tell 'em it's in—Joe, y'got press facilities here, y'got a conference room we could use?"

"We have a conference room on the first floor."

"Tell Grady conference room, first floor, seven sharp. We'll all be there, we'll alert the security guard to expect 'em."

Quick like a bunny, Judy's off to Selogy's office.

Stegmueller follows Selogy into the scope room now, so we all go in after them. Selogy takes one look at Mailer's prints from the file, tells us they're definitely in the "whorl" category, and quite a few of the latents fell into that general category, so it narrows the field some. Now he sits at the comparison microscope, begins the job of selecting the best "whorl" latents from the ten cards, discarding the others, then optically comparing the best latents against all ten of Mailer's prints. We watch him in silence for a while. What he does, he places each latent print card under the left lens, gets it in focus, places the big card with Mailer's ten prints under the right lens, focuses on one of the ten prints, then adjusts the knobs to compare each set optically, ten prints to one latent print. Takes time.

Fifteen, twenty minutes later, I'm wandering around the lab with Judy and Louie, we're kibitzing the high-tech equipment,

Louie's explaining, when Stegmueller sticks his head out of the scope room and asks us to come in. Soon as we go in and see Vadney's forehead-flattened, ears-back, all-out left-sided molar-shower, we know my intuition just struck out.

"Right-hand thumbprints," Chief tells me. "Identical match."

"No shit."

"Positive ID, Little John. We've all seen 'em."

"Take a look," Selogy says.

I sit down at the comparison microscope, Selogy shows me how to focus both lenses, I do it carefully. Sharp image of the two thumbprints. Now he shows me how to adjust the knobs to move the images together optically. I do it slowly. Whorls on both thumbprints move together, merge to become one print. I'm not saying the match is absolutely, totally perfect, line for line, because the latent happens to be missing tiny parts of a few lines. Otherwise, it's an identical match. I'm sure it would be accepted in evidence as positive identification in any court of law in the United States. I'm convinced.

"Positive ID," I say, sitting back. "Mailer's Mailer."

For some reason, the room falls silent.

Then Stegmueller speaks quietly. "Christ. Do you all—? Even *I* can't grasp—fully grasp—the enormous implications of what this means. We have absolutely no frame of reference. Nothing. It started out—let me be quite candid. It started out as a theory, a scientific theory, nothing more. It started out as one man's theoretical scientific concept. Professor Robert Erickson. Well, in fairness, Jean Rostand of the Académie française first predicted that this would happen someday. Someday in the distant future. That day, incredibly, is upon us now. The theory is a scientific reality. In the first sudden jolt, shock, to the mind, to the senses, it's almost impossible to accept. But it's true. We've just verified it as a *fact*. It's happened. It can't be denied now. We have proof positive. A man died of heart disease, was perfused at the moment of clinical death, suspended in liquid nitrogen for nineteen years, thawed successfully with the help of virus particles artificially constructed at our labs some twenty-two years ago. He was revived, reanimated, underwent heart-transplant surgery—and survived. Survived, from what you say, for at least fifteen months so far, and is presently enjoying normal health."

Silence again. I glance around at all the faces. Serious expressions say it all. Ever been right on the spot at some event of historical significance, accidental or otherwise? That's what the faces reveal. Must say, I feel it too, I'm affected by it. Can't argue with the evidence.

"Chief," Stegmueller says, "you're going to hold an important press conference in about half an hour. Dr. Mailer really should be present, as well as Dr. Leonard. I mean, they'll have to face the press sooner or later, they'll be hounded, I'm sure they both realize that."

Chief's eyes go wide. "Jesus, I forgot about them in all the rush, Steg. Good thinkin'. Little John, think Leonard might still be at the Trauma Center?"

Glance at my watch: 6:35. "Could be. Tonight's liable to be a biggie over there."

"Get him on the horn, huh? If he's not there, you got his home number, right? Tell him what's goin' on here. Tell him to tell Mailer. I mean, if Mailer's such a fanatic about marketing his book, now's the time to kick off the campaign. Huh? My bet, they'll both be here with bells on. If they're late, they're late. It'll take us at least half an hour to *explain* this whole thing, then another half hour just to answer basic *questions* about it. Get goin', buddy-boy!"

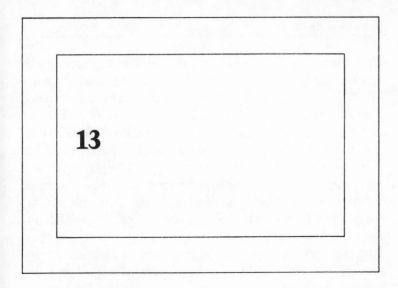

13

PRESS CONFERENCE doesn't start until 8:15, variety of reasons, most important of which is that when I reach Dr. Leonard (at home, via his answering service), he throws a temper tantrum over not being notified at least twenty-four hours in advance, then peevishly agrees to be present, along with Dr. Mailer, only if we agree to three conditions, none of which is subject to negotiation: (1) No matter how long Vadney, Stegmueller, or anyone else speaks, including question and answer sessions, Leonard and Mailer will be granted equal time to present their side of the story; (2) Leonard will be granted permission to screen exactly thirty minutes of highlight footage from his narrated documentary film, which he has already edited in rough-cut form, all on videotape, the videotape facilities with large-screen format to be provided by the Hilton Convention Department, at our expense, set up, tested, and ready to use before the conference begins; (3) Mailer will be granted permission to distribute copies of a 157-page copyrighted outline of his almost-completed book,

The Man Who Survived Death, the number of copies to be determined by media demand, all copies to be duplicated and collated at headquarters and distributed before the conference begins.

I'm taking copious notes on all this shit, I feel like a combination TV producer and literary agent. Tell Leonard I'll get right back to him, put him on hold to avoid the answering service, go take a meeting with Vadney. He throws a temper tantrum over not being notified in advance (logic's not his forte), then peevishly agrees, but only if Leonard and Mailer agree to one condition, which is not subject to negotiation: "Tell the fuckers to get their asses in here no later than seven-thirty!" Yes, sir, I go back, pick up, punch Leonard off hold, relay the message in the language of an altar boy. Deal done.

By the time Jerry Grady and his twenty-two media boys and girls descend on headquarters in taxis at about 6:55, we're all carrying out Chief's orders in an effort to make this circus open as soon as possible with a minimum amount of screw-up, following Vadney's department-famed psychology of effective press relations: Maximum utilization of time and space within given parameters of minimum lead times necessary for meeting deadlines in both broadcast and print journalism. Louie and Kinch, they pull the toughest duty, they're up at the Hilton meeting with the assistant manager, trying to rent the Convention Department's videotape projection equipment in the absence of anybody from that department. Selogy, he's going totally nuts by now, he's getting calls from his wife every ten minutes, he's with me in the Duplicating Room, second floor, testing the Xerox 3450. Quite a machine, feeds itself special three-hole-punched paper, copies come out clearer than the original, also collates up to twenty copies simultaneously. Our major problem, the reams of special paper are locked in one of the steel filing cabinets and he can't find the key. We figure, if each of the two-man media teams ask for one copy of the 157-page outline, that's ten copies, 1,570 pages.

Since one ream is 500 pages, we'll need three reams in addition to the half ream that's loaded in the machine right now. Selogy looks up the home phone of the officer in charge of duplicating, calls, gets no answer. Doesn't surprise him; nobody's home tonight. Now we go down the hall to the guy's cubicle, he searches the guy's desk. Bingo. Bunch of keys, all labeled. Back we go, find the right key, we got our extra reams at the ready.

Not a minute too soon. Exactly 7:05, Jerry Grady strides in, shows us his NYPD Press Package, created, produced, written, and neatly typed on the long flight down. Grady, he still reminds me of a young Jack Lemmon, can't shake the impression, when I introduce him to Selogy, I slip, call him Jack, but recover quickly. He wants an initial twenty-five copies, that's to include the local newspapers, TV and radio stations, they got wind of it, they're setting up with the others in the conference room right now. He's even brought along twenty-five blue Duo-Tang 5-3558 presentation folders with the NYPD insignia on the front; didn't go into the office for them, keeps a supply at home for emergencies. Not as comprehensive a package as usual, didn't have the time and/or enough of the nitty-gritty current details from Vadney on the phone early this morning, but get a load of his opening-page hard-news release:

POLICE DEPARTMENT
NEW YORK, N Y 10013

Contact: Det. Jerry Grady   For Immediate Release

Press Relations

'Dead Man' Returns $100-Million in Trinidad

PORT-OF-SPAIN, Feb. 15--Chief of Detectives Walter Vadney, 59, led a team of four undercover detectives in the recovery of classified documents and vials stolen in 1966 from the New York-based International Cryogenics Corporation (ICC), estimated today to be worth in excess of $100-million.

The confessed thief, Dr. James Mailer, 76, former supervisor of ICC's Chemical Research Division, could not be apprehended because the New York State statute of limitations for this category of grand larceny (industrial espionage) expired in 1971.

The 1966 theft gained international attention when it was published in the Guinness Book of World Records as "the greatest robbery on record attributed to industrial espionage."

Chief Vadney, a 36-year veteran of NYPD, called a press conference today in this capital city of Trinidad, now in the midst of its annual Carnival, to explain the more bizarre aspects of the case.

"We have documented evidence that Dr. Mailer, who suffered from incurable heart disease, was pronounced legally dead here in 1967," Vadney said. "His body was then cryonically suspended in liquid nitrogen by Dr. Derek Leonard, chief of staff at the Port-of-Spain General Hospital Trauma Center."

According to cryobiological research dating from 1965, a human body suspended in liquid nitrogen ($-320°F$.) sustains virtually no cellular deterioration indefinitely.

In October 1986, when a suitable heart-transplant donor was located, Vadney said, Dr. Mailer's body was thawed and reanimated in a process never before attempted, using 12 of 36 stolen vials of virus particles manufactured by ICC and representing 12 years of research and development.

Successful heart-transplant surgery was then performed by Dr. Leonard and a team of heart surgeons at the Trauma Center. Dr. Mailer survived and is now in relatively stable condition, according to Vadney, who talked with the man at length and convinced him to make restitution to ICC.

Although there are known to be at least 20 human beings in the U.S. whose bodies are presently in cryonic suspension, Dr. Mailer is the first person known to have been frozen, thawed, and brought back to life, Vadney said.

"Obviously, this must be considered one of the most significant scientific news events in history," Vadney stated.

Principal documentation to verify the event to the satisfaction of the worldwide scientific community, as well as to the public, is alleged to be an 11-hour film, narrated by Dr. Leonard, detailing every major aspect over a period of 19 years, from Dr. Mailer's clinical death, perfusion, and

liquid nitrogen suspension in 1967, to his thawing,
reanimation, heart-transplant surgery, and recovery in
1986.

According to Vadney, Dr. Mailer is now completing a lengthy
scientific book, titled The Man Who Survived Death, to
further document this unprecedented experience.

#

Press Package also includes background intelligence on case
development and brief biographical sketches on Mailer and
Vadney; the usual 8 × 10 B/W glossy photos of the main
characters are missing because Grady just didn't have time to
stop in the office. No sweat, the conference room is now crawl-
ing with cameras. Selogy runs the package through, then we
all pitch in to get the three-hole-punched collated pages into
the twenty-five Duo-Tang presentation folders.

Down we go to the conference room, each carrying our fair
share. Just as I expected, the joint's already a mob scene, noise
level rising by the minute. First off, room's too small to accom-
modate these polite boys and girls, probably close to thirty-five
of them now, counting the local media and—oh, yeah—even a
few *paparazzi*. It's around 7:20, no sign of the Frankenstein
boys yet, but TV teams from ABC, CBS, CNN, NBC are
jockeying in slightly inebriated conditions with stone-sober-
stubborn local crews for prime locations, to say nothing of
shout-and-shove skirmishes between the hometown folks and
half-bombed reporter-photographer teams from such distinguished establishments as the *Times*, the *Journal*, the *News*,
Time, *Newsweek*, UPI, and AP.

Chief, Steg, Frank, and Judy, their job was to circulate,
glad-hand, and orchestrate this happy gathering, but they've
retreated to the relative safety of the small stage behind the
lectern. Fools walk in where mad dogs fear to tread, so Grady,
Selogy, and me, we waltz around, blithely distributing the
Press Package to anybody without a camera, thereby captur-

ing only the intellectual element. Quite a few left over, so we go up on stage, give the orchestrators a peek.

Sweating Kinch and Louie stagger in at 7:24 with the Hilton's giant-screen videotape console, mission accomplished; they roll it in on a dolly, Grady and I help lift it up on stage, heavy mother, then plug it in. Now I sit back, light a cigar, wait for the curtain to rise on history in the making: "This Is Your Death." Wonder what the Nielsen ratings would be? No business like show business, what can I tell you, where's the popcorn machine?

True to their promise, the Frankenstein boys make their grand entrance almost on the dot of 7:30, both conservatively dressed in dark suits and ties, Mailer carrying a box that's sure to contain his 157-page outline, Leonard carrying an attaché case that's sure to contain his thirty-minute videotape cassette. Practically nobody on the floor notices them, they weave their way through to the stage, experiencing their final moments of anonymity. Chief greets them warmly, befitting the stars of his show.

"What'd ya do, come by way of Barbados? Let's get started here."

"No," Leonard says.

"No!" Mailer says.

"What's wrong *now*?"

Mailer holds up his box. "Keep your end of the bargain. You agreed to have my outline duplicated, collated, and distributed to the media *before* the conference began."

"Lieutenant Selogy," Chief calls.

Selogy ambles over. "Yes, sir."

"How long you figure it'll take to duplicate this here—"

"And *collate*," Mailer reminds.

"Yeah, right, and collate this here outline?"

Selogy takes the box, removes the lid, checks on the number of pages. "How many copies?"

Chief shrugs. "Oh, say, ten."

"*No!*" Mailer snaps. "At least twenty."

"Twenty?" Chief whines. "Half of these clowns are shutter-bugs!"

Mailer shakes his head. "Twenty copies. I insist."

"Twenty," Chief tells Selogy. "How long ya figure?"

"We have a self-feeding machine that also collates, but I'd estimate fifteen, twenty minutes, minimum."

"Twenty minutes?!" Chief says. "That's—ridiculous!"

"Ridiculous?" Selogy snaps. "I have to keep refilling the *paper* tray! One-fifty-seven times twenty, we're talking over *three thousand pages*! That's over *six reams*! The tray only holds *half* a ream!"

"Okay, okay," Chief says. "Don't get—don't get *touchy*, huh? Twenty minutes, you got it, buddy, no problem."

"I could use some *help*," Selogy says. "Help with the paper changing, help with—we'll have to put each copy in a manila folder or an envelope. And I'll need help just carrying them down here."

"Judy," Chief calls.

Judy bounces over. "Yes, sir."

"Honey, go help Lieutenant Selogy here, huh? Off you go, quick like a bunny."

If looks could kill, he'd be frozen dogmeat.

Chief checks his watch, turns to Mailer. "Twenty minutes, figure another five to pass 'em all out, shit. We won't be—we won't be gettin' under way here till eight. Eight-fuckin'-o'-clock."

Leonard points to the giant-screen TV console. "I assume you tested the VCR?"

"Huh? No. Why?"

"Murphy's Law," Leonard tells him. "Keep your end of the bargain. You agreed to have it tested and ready to use *before* the conference began."

Chief takes a deep breath. "Louie?"

Louie staggers over. "Yes, sir."

"Did ya test the tape deck over there?"

"No, sir. We had enough trouble just gettin' it."

"Any way ya can get a VHS cassette?"

Louie thinks on it; still looks like he's been in a fifteen-rounder. "Not unless I go back to the Hilton. That'd take time. Dr. Leonard, could I make a suggestion?"

"Surely."

"Why not test it with your own cassette?"

Leonard glances down and away, towering over Louie, adjusts his tortoiseshells, smooths back his white hair. Leans forward, speaks just above a whisper. "Because I don't want them to see anything yet. I have to set the stage, I have to build up to it in my introduction."

"Oh," Louie says.

"Mr. Diaz, please keep one thing in mind: I'll be showing highlights of what may very well become one of the most important scientific films ever made."

"Tell you what," Louie says. "How about this? Chief Vadney, Rawlings, and me, we stand shoulder-to-shoulder in front of the screen. You pop your cassette in, run it for maybe fifteen seconds, check out the color, all that, then just stop it, rewind, eject. None of 'em'll see a thing."

"They'll hear it."

"Turn the volume all the way down before you begin."

"Sounds good to me," Chief says.

Leonard glances at the big screen, then at the media people, busy setting up lights. "Well, all right then, but please stand as close together as possible."

First time I've ever been invited to an advance screening, a rough cut at that, film destined for immortality, standing room only, Chief tall on my right, Louie short on my left, here we go. Must say, the old geezer's not a bad home movie-maker, he's got a leader and all, big numbers flashing from ten to one; fade to black, then fade into color that's faded a bit with time and the transfer from film to videotape. Starts off with a medium shot of Mailer, same as he looks today, holding the front page of a newspaper over his chest, Port-of-Spain *Guardian*. Now the camera zooms in slowly to focus on the date of the paper, fills the screen: Saturday, July 27, 1967. That's all we get to see, maybe fifteen seconds. Leonard hits the "stop" button, waits for the click, hits the "rewind" button, listens to the short buzz, waits for the click, hits the "eject" button, out pops the cassette.

"Satisfied?" Chief asks.

"Yes, thank you very much."

I turn to Mailer, smile. "You haven't changed much."

He nods, returns a brief smile, takes me aside. "I must say, I like you, Rawlings. I don't care for your Chief Vadney, but for some reason, you interest me. You don't seem to be intimidated by any of this."

"Maybe I don't know enough to be intimidated."

"Oh, yes, you do. I'm sure you do. But somehow you manage to keep a sense of perspective about it, even a sense of humor. Most people, even the scientists, when they examine the evidence, when they hold all of the evidence up to the so-called scientific method, and discover for themselves that it's all in fact true, I know what their reaction will be. Shock. Dismay. Confusion about the long-term implications. I think many people—no, *most* people, most at the start—won't *want* to believe it. Despite all the evidence."

"Why?"

He adjusts his glasses. "Because it disturbs the established order. Disturbs it profoundly. This isn't the time or place to talk about it, but if you're really interested, I'd be glad to discuss it with you. I mean, even *I*—every time I see that film, especially the oldest segments, it gives me a very, very strange feeling. I see my face, I see that date, and it's so—it's difficult even for *me* to believe. It's—unreal. It's frightening."

"You started filming on that date?"

"Yes, July twenty-seventh. I made an opening statement,

introducing myself and Derek, explaining what we were attempting to do, that it was intended to be a very carefully
controlled experiment. Well, you'll hear for yourself when you
see the film tonight. Forty-five days later, on September tenth,
I was dead. Clinically dead. Legally dead. As I say, this isn't
the time or place to discuss it on a personal level."

"Let's have a drink before I leave town."

"I think I'd enjoy that, yes."

"You name the time and place, I'll be there."

Turns out Selogy underestimated the time he'd need. When
he comes back in the room with Judy at 8:10, both doing bal-
ancing acts with ten thick manila envelopes each, noise level is
unbelievable, TV lights have turned the joint into an oven,
cigarette smoke makes you gag, and the party people from
New York are starting to sober up fast. Louie and I grab a
bunch of outlines from Selogy and Judy, we walk around,
hand a copy to each non-camera-carrying member of the
gang; most toss the envelope aside and purr pleasantries like:
"When the fuck we gonna *start*?"

Chief's only too glad to call the happy hour to order at 8:15.
Stands tall behind the tangle of microphones taped to the lectern, shirt-sleeves rolled up, tie yanked down, sky-blues narrowed in the bright glare of celebrity. No-nonsense attitude as
he clears his throat and leans toward the blur of shoulder-
mounted video cameras and glistening zoom lenses. "Ladies
and gentlemen, I've got a brief—"

Strobes flash like Uzi fire, shutters click, motor drives
whine. "Speed!" "Rolling!" "Start over!" "Down in front!"

"Ladies and gentlemen, I've got a very brief opening statement here, then I'm gonna let Dr. Carl Stegmueller take over,
he's president of the International Cryogenics Corporation,
he's here to accept restitution of the hundred million dollars'
worth of classified—"

"*Chief Vadney!*" leather-lunged lady's voice yells out from
the back. "Excuse me, sir, but we all know about the robbery

and restitution from the *press* release! I think I speak for all of us when I say that the big—"

"Madam," Chief says, "will ya please—"

"—when I say that the *big* story heah, the *major* news, obviously, is that a man's been *frozen* and brought back from the *dead*! Would ya please address that question, sir? And I want a follow-up."

"Madam," Chief barks. "I'm *gettin'* to that!"

"Well, hurry up awready!" man's husky voice booms from the side of a TV camera. "We awready missed *network* news, now we gotta get this shit together for the eleven o'clock *locals*!"

"Ladies and gentlemen, if you'll please have the courtesy—"

"Take a fuckin' *hike*!" another gentleman suggests. "Whaddaya, *nuts*? We didn't schlepp down heah to listen to no schlock about no robbery resti-*tu*-tion schmaltz! We wanna heah from Dr. *Mailer*, not you, ya headline-happy schmuck ya!"

"What'd ya call me?"

"Get the fuck off the stage, ya schnook ya!"

First time I remember seeing Vadney at a loss for words. Stands there blinking, squinting, trying to see who just called him a schmuck and a schnook in public. Now he steps back uncertainly.

"We want Dr. *Mailer*!"

"Somebody give this clown the *hook*, will ya?"

Chief knows when he's not welcome. Turns, looks at Mailer, jerks a thumb toward the lectern, walks slowly to his chair, sits down. But he holds his head high, Chief does. Embarrassing in front of his kid brother, but you can't win 'em all, right?

Talk about a change of pace? Boom, here we go from cold turd to hot shit, five seconds microwave fast. Dr. Mailer stands up, lean and distinguished in a banker's gray three-piece suit, blue shirt, red-and-blue striped tie, steps forward from the cold winter of anonymity into the sudden hot mid-summer sunshine of mass-media superstar. Boredom becomes bedlam as the whole room stands simultaneously and lurches forward, strobes explode like Roman candles, Macy's Fourth of July finale, everybody's shouting something: *Doc-tah! — Over heah! — Speed! — Down in front! — Rolling! — DOC! — Heah! — Downinfront! — May-lah! — Ohvaheah! — DOC! — Getoutamaface! — Doctah Maylah! — DOWN-INFRONT! — Stickitinyaeah! — Doctah! — Getouttamy-fuckinwaywillya! — Doctahmaylahovaheah!*

Ever wonder how it'd feel to be an instant megastar? Christ. I mean, a mob scene like this, it's got to scare the crap out of you, right? Got to. Not Mailer. No way. Me, I stand up fast, jump off the stage, jog to the back of the room where it's empty now, take a gander at this geek. Sorry to use that word, but that's what he is to these veteran media people, nothing more, nothing less. Geek of nature. Positively fantastic news event, breakthrough blockbuster, front-page shoo-in worldwide, shoot thirty-six quick as your motor drive can grind 'em out, change film fast, change cameras, push, shove, elbow, get him from every angle, go for broke. Mailer stands tall, motions for them to quiet down, hands as steady as a surgeon's, voice calm: "All right, okay, fine, appreciate it, thank you." Action is character—move, gesture, point, smile, give 'em what they want, they have a job to do, make it easy for 'em, make it boil, make it pour, how sweet it is. Where'd he learn to do that? Watching Reagan on TV? No, I'm serious now. Gives me pause, can't help it. Me, I'd have to pop a Valium one full hour before I faced mass-media hysterics like this. And he knew he'd have to face it. Knew it for certain. Maybe he did pop a Valium, what do I know? But somehow I doubt it. Stands there, straightens his tie, takes a swipe at his dark hair, gray-white at the temples, adjusts his thin black steel-framed glasses; tan makes his teeth seem very white when he smiles.

Looks and acts like a politician, takes it all in stride.

Quiet comes gradually. When they're finally all seated, except for the TV cameramen, he waits until he has almost total silence.

"Ladies and gentlemen," he says softly, "I have no opening statement, because I want to make this as spontaneous as possible, but I think you'll agree with me that we'll have to handle the question and answer session in an orderly fashion for the mutual benefit of all. Therefore, I'll accept questions from the networks first, in alphabetical order, followed by the newspapers, wire services, and newsmagazines, in that order. Each correspondent will have an automatic follow-up question. I'll attempt to answer every question as thoroughly as possible, within reason, so please cooperate by not asking multiple questions. After the question and answer session, Dr. Derek Leonard, chief of staff at the Port-of-Spain General Hospital Trauma Center, will introduce and screen a thirty-minute videotape of the highlights of his documentary film that's mentioned in the press release. Immediately after the film—and not before or during the film—Dr. Leonard and I will be available to give private interviews to each news organization, in the same alphabetical order as the question and answer session, maximum fifteen minutes, which I think is more than adequate for the first night. The envelope you received is a detailed outline of my book, *The Man Who Survived Death,* which will supply all the facts, figures, dates, times, and other basic research you'll need for your stories. Please note that the outline carries a copyright under my name and is fully protected under the International and Pan-American Copyright Conventions. Now, I'll accept the opening question from ABC News. Will you please stand? Yes, sir, good evening."

The Man Who Survived Death.

Is this geek for real?

Fingerprints don't lie, right?

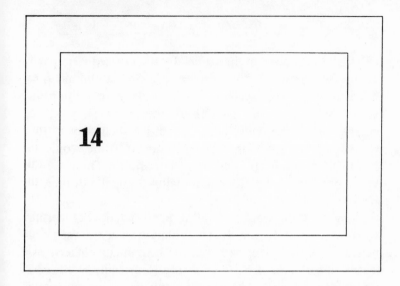

14

FINGERPRINTS DON'T LIE, but as the evening rolls on, I pick up on something that intrigues me no end. When Dr. Leonard finally gets around to screening his thirty-minute videotape, after a lengthy introduction, I get a chance to hear Dr. Mailer's remarks of July 27, 1967, in addition to three other segments (all "slated" by newspaper dates), in which he spoke at some length before his clinical death, September 10, 1967. Now, the final segment of these film highlights was an interview of Mailer by Leonard, slated November 15, 1986, twelve days after the heart-transplant operation. In that segment, Mailer explained why he stole the documents and vials: He knew he was dying of cardiomyopathy; he made an educated assumption that, based on the work of Dr. Christian Barnard, heart-transplant surgery would probably be commonplace within a few decades; he wanted to be the first "guinea pig" subject in a carefully controlled experiment performed by Leonard and documented on film to determine: (a) whether or not the thawing process would be rendered viable

with the introduction of the artificially constructed virus particles; (b) whether or not the process of reanimation, aided by
futuristic life-support systems, would render his condition stable enough to endure such heart-transplant surgery; (c)
whether or not he could actually survive such surgery; (d)
whether or not the length of such survival time would be
scientifically significant; and, most important to him, (e) the
day-to-day physical and mental quality of his life during the
survival period.

Thing that intrigues me is his pronunciation of certain
words, before and after. In particular, during the 1967 segments, he seemed to my ear to retain the remnants of a British
accent on the endings of certain words, especially words end-
ing with the letter "t." In 1967, it seems to me he enunciated
the "t" in those word endings, as so many Brits do; in 1986,
and even today, in person, he seems to my ear to have subtly
softened that letter, among other, less obvious letters in word
endings.

So, after the film, when Leonard and Mailer are set to begin
their private interviews with the various news organizations, I
go over to Louie. Wish you could see this kid's face. Mike
Tyson's sparring partner.

"Enjoy the film?" I ask.

"Yeah, except it bored the shit out of me."

"Scientist like you?"

"After the first five, ten minutes, I knew what was coming
next. Bor-ing. Besides, I'm tired, John. Past my bedtime."

"Question: When we were doing our little tour of the lab,
you happen to notice if they had a voice-comparison machine?"

"A *voice*-comparison machine?

"Yeah."

"John, I think maybe you're talking about a sound spectrograph."

"Whatever. What's it do?"

"Produces a sound spectrogram. That's a graphic representation of the frequency—let's see, the frequency, intensity, duration, and variation of the resonance of a sound. Or a series of sounds. It's also called a sonogram."

"Happen to notice if they had one?"

"Yeah, they have one. I mean, they got a very modern lab here, John, I was surprised. Question: What the hell you want with a sound spectrograph?"

"Can it actually compare one voice with another?"

"Sure, that's one of its capabilities. What y'got in mind?"

"Humor me. I want to play a hunch."

"John, we talkin' intuition again?"

"You got it."

"After positive-match *fingerprints*?"

"You got it."

Chief comes over with his brother Frank and Dr. Stegmueller. "Little John, Louie, we're gonna have dinner up at the Hilton. You guys don't mind sleepin' in the lockup tonight, do ya? I mean, Frank and Steg, they got no place to sleep, it's my fault, so I invited 'em to share the suite with me. It's just for one night, we're all goin' home tomorrow anyway, huh?"

I shrug. "Chief, you got four beds and a couch up there."

"Yeah, but I *snore*, Little John. *Loud.* I mean, I wouldn't subject man or beast to that. Even my *wife* can't stand to sleep in the same room with me, she says I ain't *human.* Her words, not mine, okay? She says, 'Walter,' she says, 'you ain't *human.*' She says, 'When you snore, the doors shake, the windows shake, it sounds like some sex-crazed orangutan pullin' his pud all night.' No, that's what she said, that's no exaggeration. Imagine that, Frank, Steg? My own *wife* sayin' shit like that to me? Anyhow, that's why I gotta have a room all to myself."

"Where's Judy gonna sleep?" Louie asks.

"Oh, yeah, Judy, forgot about Judy. Well, okay, she's welcome to the couch. Tell 'er we'll set it all up for her, make her up a bed and all."

"What about Grady?" I ask. "What about the eight media people that were supposed to—"

"Fuck 'em," he says softly. "Huh? After the way those ignorant slimebags treated *me* tonight? Let all twenty-two of 'em sack out in the *cells*! Let the scumbags sleep on the *floor* where they belong!"

"Jerry Grady, too?" Louie asks.

"Yeah, well, he's gotta pretend to be one of the *gang,* know what I mean? He can't get preferential treatment, he'd lose their *confidence,* he knows that. I've already told him, he understands perfectly. Also, he's the one's gonna have to break it to 'em. About their—hah!—accommodations. They don't know yet. They don't know squat. Like to get a look at their pigfucker pusses when he tells 'em. Huh? *Hah*! Keep Selogy around to do the honors, tell Kinch he can split now. Okay, look, you guys can grab your pajamas and shavin' gear from the suite anytime you like. Anything happens you can't handle, let Selogy take charge, he's got the clout. Take care now."

Louie and I go over to Selogy, who's sitting there glancing at his watch. It's now about 10:20.

"Joe," I say, "I know you want to get out of here, but would you do us one last favor?"

"Can I go after that?"

"Yeah," I tell him. "We'll take full responsibility for the lockup, all like that."

"Okay, name it."

"Just open up the lab again and let Louie use your sound spectrograph."

"That's it?"

"Yeah," Louie says. "We'll lock up for you."

"Done. Let's go."

Take the elevator to the top floor, Selogy opens the lab,

turns on the lights, goes to the sound spectrograph, turns it on. Big green terminal screen lights up.

"Know how to operate it?" he asks Louie.

"Yeah. It's like the one we got."

"Last thing," I say. "Can we borrow a tape recorder and a blank cassette—preferably a new cassette?"

"Sure thing."

Follow him to his office, he gets out a Sony TCM-600, opens a new cassette, clicks it in, hands it to me. "Just push the red button to record." Grabs the phone, dials fast: "Honey, I'm out of here! Meet me in the—Dawn? Come on, honey, come on, don't cry. I know, I know, honey. Dawn, listen, I know, but we can stay up *late*. Screw it, we can stay up all *night*. Okay, meet me in the lobby, I'll change to costume in the men's room. Right. See you." Hangs up, pulls out the key chain on his belt, maneuvers two keys off the ring, holds them up: "This is the lab; the big one's to the outside door of the lockup. The officer at the front desk is there all night. If you need anything else, ask him, he's got all the keys."

I take the keys and the tape recorder. "We'll go down with you."

Out we go, leave the lights on, door locks automatically, take the elevator down. Bunch of media people are milling around the lobby, waiting their turns for the private interview. Leonard and Mailer are in a small office near the conference room, door shut, giving the first interview to ABC News. I figure they've been in there at least seven or eight minutes, maximum is fifteen, so we'll wait for the break. I tuck the tape recorder in the inside pocket of my blazer, light up a cigar.

"Tell me what you got in mind," Louie says.

"We wait for the break, go in, tell Leonard we missed the first ten minutes of the film; could we please see it? He doesn't know, the lights were off. He's got no reason to refuse. Take the cassette, play it, record the first segment, fast-forward the film, record the last segment. Rewind it, return it quickly, thanks very much. Back to the lab, compare the two voices, see what we got."

"John, voice comparisons won't hold up in a court of law. Inadmissible evidence. You know that, right?"

"I know. Humor me."

Selogy's waiting near the front door, talking to Gordon Kinch. Forgot to tell Kinch he can take off, so we go over there.

"Chief said it's okay to go," I tell him.

"Yeah?"

"He's all heart," Louie says.

Kinch smiles. "Actually, I enjoyed the circus atmosphere here. More laughs than Carnival. You two have to stay?"

"Yeah," I say. "We're sleeping in the lockup."

"No. What happened to your suite?"

"Vadney and his VIPs."

"You're welcome to stay at my place."

"Thanks, Gordon," I tell him, "but we'll be fine."

"See you tomorrow?"

"Absolutely," Louie says. "Thanks for everything."

Couple of minutes after he leaves, door opens, I can't believe what I'm seeing: Tall kid in the uniform of the Miami Dolphins—helmet, full pads, aquamarine jersey with the big white number 13, he's even wearing cleats. Lady with him, she's dressed as a bellydancer, silver-spangled bra, matching long skirt worn very low on the hips; bracelets, beads, bangles, anklets, little cymbals on her thumbs and forefingers. Kid's got the figure for it, what can I tell you?

"John, Lou," Selogy says, "like you to meet my wife, Dawn, and my son, Joey."

Handshakes, greetings, then Joey tosses his dad a duffel bag with his costume. Off they go to the men's room, Joey's cleats clacking, media people smiling.

"Sorry we had to keep him so long," I tell Dawn. "Chief Vadney's orders."

She nods, shrugs, beautiful kid, five-six, maybe 120, short blond hair, hazel eyes. "That's the price you pay for being married to a cop."

"Nice uniform Joey's got," Louie says. "Why the Dolphins?"

"We have family in Miami, so we go up there whenever we can. Tonight, Joey wants to play Dan Marino, that's all. I feel like playing a bellydancer tonight; tomorrow night, we'll play somebody else. That's what Carnival is all about, to play what we call 'mask,' to play at fantasies, whatever you feel like being, the wilder the better."

"What's Joe's costume?" I ask.

She smiles. "You'll see in a minute."

Short time later, here they come down the hall, Dan Marino flanked by—it's so good I have to laugh—Tom Selleck as Magnum P.I. Yeah! Fantastic rubber mask pulled over his head, perfect likeness, you'd swear it was him from a distance. Detroit Tigers baseball cap, wild aloha shirt, cutoff jeans, all he needs is the red Ferrari.

We joke around, Dawn gives us a quick teaser sample of undulating hips and tinkling cymbals, then announces "*J'ouvert!*" and they're off into the long night of Carnival, three million people playing mask, drinking rum, street-dancing to steel-band calypso, doing anything they want, wearing anything they want, being anything they want. Nice tradition, must admit. Wish we could join them. Really do. Who would I play? Robert Redford? Paul Newman? Marlon Brando? Naw. Me, I'd buy a rubber mask of Duke Wayne and play Chief Vadney for a night. Yeah! Tonight. Get bombed out of my skull, stumble up to the Hilton, sneak into his room in the wee hours, listen to the wall-shaking snorts of a sex-crazed orang-utan pullin' his pud, then snap on the light and yell: "Asshole, you ain't *human*!" Huh? Scare the living, breathing, bubbling black bile out of this sucker. Man might never snore again. Man might never *sleep* again.

Back to reality as we know it. First private interview is over about 10:35, door opens, ABC News boys exit, CBS News boys enter, Louie and me on their heels. Go through the whole innocent routine with Leonard: Had to work, missed the first ten minutes of the film, heard it was the best. Please, Dr. Leonard, we'll guard it with our lives, we'll have it back before the interview's over. Snaps open his attaché, hands me the VHS cassette. Now that he's flying on fame, he can afford to toss peanuts to the peons; good time to catch him.

Conference room's completely deserted now, air's still pee-you with cigarette smoke, but it's cooler now in the absence of TV lights. I take out my Sony tape recorder, turn on the TV, slide in the VHS cassette, push the "play" button on the VCR, wait for the leader to cue, push the red "record" button on the Sony, and we're in business. Giant screen fades to black, then fades into the faded color of the opening shot: Mailer holding the newspaper over his chest. Camera slowly zooms to the date—Saturday, July 27, 1967—holds for a few seconds, then pulls back to a medium shot of Mailer, who puts down the paper, talks directly to the viewer in a normal tone of voice: "My name is Dr. James Mailer. I am fifty-four years old at present and reside here in Trinidad, West Indies. For the past several years, I have been suffering from an incurable heart disease called cardiomyopathy. My physician and longtime friend, Dr. Derek Leonard, who is shooting this film, believes that I have now reached the start of the terminal stage of this illness. His prognosis is that I have a very short time to live, perhaps as little as another month." Camera begins to move in slowly on his face. "Some time ago, Dr. Leonard and I made a joint decision to conduct a scientific experiment that, to the very best of our knowledge, has never before been attempted."

I push the "stop" button on the VCR, wait for the click,

push the "fast-forward" button, and turn off my tape recorder. Now I turn down the volume on the TV console. Louie and I watch the blurred image of Mailer as the videotape advances rapidly.

Voice behind us: "Mr. Rawlings, may I ask what you're doing?"

Startles us. We turn fast. It's Mailer. I realize instantly that bluffing is out of the question: I'm holding the tape recorder in my hand; the giant screen is running his image on fast-forward. Nothing left to do but tell the truth, see what happens.

"I'm tape recording your voice."

"Obviously. For what reason?"

"Voice comparison. First segment with last."

He smiles, shakes his head. "Did it ever occur to you— y'know, you disappoint me, Mr. Rawlings, somehow I expected better logic from you. Did it ever occur to you that our voices change over the years? It's a medical fact. Just like our eyesight, hearing, sense of smell, sense of taste, you name it. More than nineteen years had passed between the first and last segments of that film. So that a voice comparison is less than useless, it's odious, in my judgment."

"But you weren't alive during those years," I tell him quietly. "You didn't change physically like the rest of us. Why did your voice?"

"It didn't."

"It did."

Adjusts his glasses. "In what way?"

"You lost the remnants of a British accent. Hardly audible, I'll give you that, but we can prove it on a sound spectrogram."

"Then please go ahead. Get on with it. Frankly, I welcome such a comparison. I have absolutely nothing to hide and I think I've proved that here tonight to the satisfaction of everyone present."

"Except one." I smile to distract, turn on the tape recorder.

"Yes, quite, and I must say that—baffles me. Of all the people gathered here, seeing the evidence, hearing the evidence, you alone—and perhaps Mr. Diaz, although I doubt it—remain stubbornly unconvinced that I'm telling the truth."

I shrug. "There's one in every group."

"Why must you be so cynical?"

"I'm not. I'm just realistic."

"Realistic? In the face of such overwhelming evidence?"

"What evidence is that?"

"Don't play games with me, Rawlings. Don't insult my intelligence. I'm talking about the fingerprint comparison. If you won't accept that as positive identification, then what *will* you accept?"

Click-click. Videotape reaches the end, stops. Louie steps over, turns off the TV screen.

I wait a beat, then: "Dental records."

"Dental records?"

"Yeah. They're accepted as positive identification in any court of law in the United States. In fact, as I'm sure you know, they're the *only* means of positive identification in the case of disaster—plane crashes, explosions, fires—when fingerprints are—"

"Then go ahead," he snaps. "By all means. Check my dental records. Anything to get you off my back. I'll cooperate fully, I'll give you the name, address, and telephone number of my dentist in New York. I went to the same man for many years, twenty-five years."

"Who's your dentist here?"

"I don't have a dentist here, I've had no need of one. But I'll submit to a complete set of X-rays, of course, if that will satisfy you."

"It would. When?"

"Whenever you like."

"How about tomorrow morning?"

"Rawlings, I suppose you don't realize this, but the Monday and Tuesday of Carnival are national holidays in Trinidad. Virtually every business is closed, except those directly related to Carnival. I'm certain that no dentist in the entire city will be working tomorrow. The next day is Ash Wednesday, of course, which is also a national holiday. So the earliest I could get an appointment—"

"By tomorrow, the wire services will have your lies spread all over the world."

"*Lies*? Did you say *lies*?"

"Lies."

"Rawlings, you disappoint me. For some reason I thought you might be a bit more sophisticated than the average New York cop, but obviously I was mistaken. You're arrogant, obnoxious, and cynical, just like all the rest. Why? Because, on a day-to-day basis, year after year, you deal with the very worst elements of society, from petty thieves to serial killers. I suppose your attitude is predictable. I suppose a job like yours would make almost anyone a cynic. In any event, I'm withdrawing my cooperation. I refuse to give you dental records. And there's no way you can force me to do it, as you know only too well." Glances at his watch. "I've kept the gentlemen from CBS waiting long enough. Give me the film, please."

Louie hits the "eject" button. *Click-click.* Cassette slides out, he hands it over.

Click. I turn off the tape recorder.

Mailer glances at the machine, frowns, then looks in my eyes. "Rawlings, you disgust me."

"The feeling's mutual."

About 10:55, I go up to the Hilton alone to collect our shaving stuff; Louie decided to grab a bed in one of the cells. Big lobby's total bedlam, blur of costumes, steady roar of voices over steel-band calypso. Decide to have a drink before I go up. Need one. Carnival Bar's not as crowded as I expected. Cool, dark, relatively quiet, huge windows overlooking the lighted mountainsides. Manage to find an empty stool, order a Beefeater martini on the rocks with a twist, light up a cigar. Nice. Nice place to unwind. First drink goes down cool, quick, easy. I'm working on the second, more relaxed, enjoying the view, when a hand touches my shoulder. Look up, it's Frank Vadney.

"Hey, Frank, nice to see you."

"Where's Louis?"

"Sacked out in a cell. Judy get here yet?"

"About half an hour ago. She's asleep by now."

"On the couch, right?"

"Yeah. Anything new?"

"Yeah." I turn, glance around the room, looking for an empty table. Spot one in the far right corner. "Let's get that table."

"I'll grab it. Pay your tab."

Sign for my drinks, include a generous tip, what the hell, all expenses paid. By the time I get over to the corner table, the waitress is there taking Frank's order, so I order another Beefeater. I figure I deserve it, I got something to celebrate.

"So what's happening?" he asks.

"Found out something important tonight, Frank. Haven't told anybody yet. Don't know if I should, at least not yet. It's gonna blow everybody out of the water. But one part of the puzzle's still missing."

Frank's eyes go wide behind the tortoiseshell glasses, he leans forward, broad-shouldered guy, trim hair gray at the temples, face flickering in the glow of the candle lamp. Deep voice, but soft-spoken: "Whatever you say stops with me. Until you're ready. You have my word on that."

I take a deep breath, look at the candle. "Had an altercation with Dr. Mailer tonight. Louie and me, we were trying to tape-record his voice from the film, first and last segments. Occurred to me that his accent sounded slightly different in those two segments. He came in and caught us at it. I told him the truth, I told him exactly what we were doing. Also, I baited him a little, I admit it, I figured I had nothing to lose at that point, I wanted to see how he'd handle it. Bottom line, he asked me why I was so cynical about him, cynical in the face of such overwhelming evidence. I asked him, I said, 'What evidence is that?' He lost his temper, said not to play games with him, said not to insult his intelligence, then he said, 'I'm talking about the fingerprint comparison.' His exact words. I tape-recorded them.''

Frank nods, blinks, lets it sink in. "Holy—shit."

"Okay? How could he possibly know?"

"He couldn't, John. There's just no way. He couldn't possibly know unless he was told by . . . Dr. Stegmueller."

"That's right. Outside of our little group here, *nobody* else knew. Nobody except Stegmueller. You realize what that means?"

He sits back now, keeps looking at me, nods slowly. "Jesus Christ. Conspiracy."

"Conspiracy. Stegmueller, Mailer, and Leonard. And it had to be from the *start,* nineteen-sixty-six. A planned robbery. Planned down to the smallest detail. Reason? My guess, strictly a guess, after twelve years and twenty-four million dollars, ICC came up empty. Product was useless. Happens. Happens in chemical research labs all over the world, large and small, it's nothing unusual. Trying to develop a new virus, a new wonder drug, it's always a crap shoot. Millions down the drain. Insurance doesn't even begin to cover the losses. So they came up with another plan, Stegmueller, Mailer, and Leonard."

"Dr. Mailer *was* dying. We established that fact beyond any doubt. I interviewed the cardiologist in Boston myself, I read his diagnostic report, I saw the independent lab reports."

"Of course he was dying, Frank. That's what must've made the plan so enticing. The fortuitous factor was present. God, it must've made the whole scheme seem almost irresistible. Quality control all the way. He could be cryonically suspended by Leonard with every major step documented on film. That film leaves no doubt in my mind that the same man, the real Dr. Mailer, was perfused at clinical death, suspended in liquid nitrogen, and thawed nineteen years later. Obviously, Stegmueller and Leonard didn't figure they'd have to wait nineteen years for heart-transplant surgery to become an accepted procedure. That's the one factor over which they had absolutely no control. They just had to wait it out and hope they'd live long enough to see the plan work. And to finally reap the benefits. Tomorrow morning, when the story hits the headlines, TV, radio, worldwide—and it will, there's no stopping it now—when that happens, when it's digested, when the shock and novelty wear off, ICC's stock will go through the ceiling. That virus will be worth a fortune. To say nothing about the rights, the worldwide rights, to the book and the film."

Waitress comes back with our drinks. Glad to see Frank's a martini man (vodka martini on the rocks with a twist), gives me a good feeling. Like his style. We clink glasses.

"Congratulations," he says. "Please go ahead, you got up to the thawing process."

I take a sip, stare at the candle again. "Yeah. So I have no problem with the perfusion, suspension, and thawing; I think that part of it was all genuine. Obviously, he was injected with the virus particles during the thawing process, we saw that at length during the time-lapse sequences."

"Right. I mean, I could even read the labels on the vials."

"So could I. But now, think about this next part, Frank. Maybe I'm wrong, but I don't think we ever actually saw the body reanimated, brought back to at least some semblance of life, before the hospital scenes."

He thinks about it, candlelight reflected in his glasses. "I remember a gradual—when he was placed on the heart-lung machine, just before the glycerol was drained and the blood was pumped in—I remember a gradual change in his coloring, his skin tone, as the blood began to circulate. But that's about it. He certainly wasn't breathing on his own."

"Not even when we saw him on the life-support system at the hospital. But consider this: His physical condition was stable enough to endure five hours of heart-transplant surgery—and survive."

"So you believe the man we saw in the hospital was somebody else?"

"Right. That's my theory. I know it's full of holes right now, it leads to more questions than it answers, but that's my theory."

"Okay, I'm just playing the devil's advocate, John, but remember the man's heart? We saw his original heart just minutes before the actual transplant. Remember that close-up shot? Now, I don't know what cardiomyopathy looks like, I don't know what any diseased heart looks like, but I know damn well that wasn't a healthy heart. It was flabby and enlarged, remember?"

"No question. Frank, you worked this case from the beginning, right?"

"Right. Christ, I was only thirty-four when we actually got the contract in 'sixty-seven. I was just a kid, I still had energy to burn."

"Refresh my memory on Mailer, on his background, his personal life, his family."

He sips his drink, stares into space. "Well, okay, I know the basics by heart. He was born in London in nineteen-twelve. Graduated from Magdalin College, Oxford, nineteen-thirty-three, majored in chemistry. Married that same year, July, I think. Wife's name was Mary. They moved to the U.S. in September, same year, and he attended Columbia-Presbyterian in New York. Graduated in nineteen-thirty-seven. Joined ICC as a research chemist in nineteen—"

"Children?"

"Yeah, two sons and a daughter."

"Tell me about the sons."

"I don't know that much about them, John."

"Basics? Birth dates?"

"I know the approximate dates. Let's see, the first son, James Jr., was born during his first year in med school, that'd be nineteen-thirty-four. Daughter came next, I believe it was two years later, 'thirty-six. Second son was born in nineteen-forty-one, named Edward. Mailer's wife passed away—"

"Frank?"

"—about nine years ago. Yeah?"

"Now I know why your big brother says you got all the brains in the family."

"Yeah? Why's that?"

"Remember I said one part of the puzzle's still missing?"

"Yeah."

"You just found it."

"I did?"

"You just solved the case."

He smiles. "I *did*?"

"Yeah."

"How'd I do *that*?"

"With your memory."

"My memory?"

"Yeah. James Mailer Jr. is fifty-four years old."

15

Now that we know who's who and what's what, I get this sinking feeling in my stomach because something tells me we're too late. Tell you why. Most con artists, major and minor league, pro and am, have at least one instinct in common: They know when the game's lost; they know when to split. When Frank and I get to the suite, Judy's asleep on the couch, Chief's having a nightcap out on the terrace, and Stegmueller's gone. Chief says his buddy Steg got a phone call less than half an hour ago from Dr. Leonard, asking if he'd come back to headquarters for a private interview with NBC News. My guess, Mailer Jr.'s alerted both of them that we're just too close, that it's simply a matter of time, that as soon as we get down to the methodical grunt work we'll collar all three of them on suspicion of conspiracy to murder. Check it out by calling headquarters immediately, talk to the officer at the desk, ask to speak to Dr. Leonard. Not there. Interviews were temporarily interrupted at 10:55 when Leonard and Mailer took a break for a late dinner, said they'd be back in an hour.

It's now 11:20, so they have around a half-hour head start on us. Anyhow, first things first, Frank and I sit down with the Duke, explain the cast of characters and scenario as calmly and quickly as we can. Chief goes through three clear-cut emotional stages: Astonishment, disbelief, then total euphoria when he finds out his kid brother provided the key that cracked the case.

Next order of business, try to put ourselves in their places. Major consideration: They don't know for sure if we know for sure, but they're not going to do anything that's obvious. What's obvious? My opinion, they'll stay away from Piarco Airport altogether; they'll stay away form charter boats in the downtown dock area along South Quay. Me, I'd opt for a small private airstrip somewhere on the island, there must be a few, then start calling small charter outfits, flying buffs who own planes; I'm sure Leonard knows at least a few. I get out our big map of Trinidad, look for the airport symbol (silhouette of an airplane), find Piarco easily, big plane with a circle around it. Now I find two very small "airports," symbols so tiny they must represent private airstrips. One down near San Fernando, second largest city on the island, about fifty miles south of Port-of-Spain, the other up at Chupara Point, northeast of La Cuevas Bay, on a continuation of North Coast Road, a narrow red line that the map key identifies as a third-class road. I look at the scale of kilometers and miles, measure with my forefinger, find out Chupara Point is only about fifteen or twenty miles northeast of La Vache Bay, where Leonard and Mailer live. Obviously, they wouldn't drive fifty miles south to the airstrip there; this one's made to order. They'd drive home immediately, pack whatever valuables they wanted, including all the cash they have, then Leonard would start making his phone calls. Granted, it's a tough night to catch people home, but that's what I'd do. Tell 'em it's an emergency, offer 'em a good chunk of money, arrange to be picked up at the airstrip, then they have their choice of destinations, depending on the size of the aircraft: Tobago is too close, but they could probably make Grenada easily, Barbados, St. Lucia, Martinique, even as far north as Dominica or Guadeloupe.

Chupara Point airstrip's my recommendation to the Vadney boys. If I'm wrong, we've blown it, of course, they'll be long gone; if I'm right, at least we have a shot, but they've got a half-hour lead already, there's no time to get Kinch or another local cop to go with us, we'll have to leave immediately. Chief and Frank talk it over briefly, agree it's probably the most logical plan. We decide to let Judy sleep; it's exactly 11:29 when we leave the suite.

Chief wants no part of my Mini Minor, he strides up to the Hertz counter in the lobby, plunks down his gold American Express card. "Honey, I want the most powerful sports car y'got, money's no object."

Young lady nods. "The most powerful we have is the Probe LX; factory air, electronic climate control, electronic instrumentation cluster—"

"*Probe*? Never heard of it."

"It's the latest from Ford, sir."

"*Ford*? Honey, I'm talkin' Lamborghini, Maserati, Jaguar here."

"Budget rents the expensive ones, sir, next counter."

"*Budget*?" Steps to the next counter, plunks down his American gold. "Honey, I want the most powerful—"

"Yes, sir, I heard," honey says. "We have an 'eighty-eight Maserati Spyder convertible available tonight; factory air, electronic—"

"I'll take it." Slaps down his driver's license.

She slaps down the rental form, picks up the phone, asks for the car, zaps the Duke's card, asks him to sign. "In U.S. currency, that's ninety-nine ninety-nine per day, Mr. Vadney."

Chief signs. "What color is it?"

"Red."

"Red? Good. Like red."

"I'm glad, Mr. Vadney." She waits till he signs the rental
agreement, tears off his copy, hands it over with his license and
card. "Your Maserati should be at the front entrance soon.
Happy motoring."

Out we go into the throng of costumed revelers waiting for
their tin lizzies. Freshly washed and waxed red Maserati Spyder convertible booms into the bright lights, sparkles like fire.
Costumed revelers: "Aaahhh!" Chief struts to the driver's
side, tells the kid jockey to put the top down. *Snap-snap, buzz-
buzz, whiiirrr,* down it goes. Costumed revelers: "Ooohhh!"
Chief slaps a buck into the kid's waiting mitt, strips off his blue
blazer, chucks it in back, slides in with an all-out left-sided
molar-shower, slams the door with a sweet-sounding *thunk.*
Frank jumps in front, I jump in back (thank God). Seat belts
on, hand brake off, headlights on, factory air off. Chief gives
'er three quick revs, sounds like a hungry tiger in our tank.
Me, I don't know the horsepower of this sucker, but when the
Duke turns 'er loose, it's like booming out of a pit stop at the
Indy 500: Engine goes *Buuurrr-eeeooo-rrraaa-koooooo,* tires
squeal, I'm slammed back into top-grain Italian cowhide as we
blast off into the warm Caribbean night, oblivious to the peons
playing fantasy. Tom Selleck, eat your mustache, Paul Newman, suck our smoke. We got an appointment with destiny.

Of course, the Duke of Paducah doesn't have a clue where
the fuck he's going, so I have to be the shouting navigator with
my wind-whipped map in moonlight glow. Right turn into
Circular Road, not a car in sight, Queen's Park Savannah's
deserted, everybody's downtown. Hang a right into Saddle
Road, now we got a straight stretch northeast all the way to
Maraval, brights up, turbo kicking, broken white center line
coming at us like tracer bullets, we must be doing ninety-five
easy. Me, I wouldn't know; by this time I'm crouched way
down in back, head against Frank's seat, gale-force winds rip-
ping in on both sides, if it wasn't for my seat belt, I'd be

history. Vadney boys can't feel a thing up there. But they can hear. We can all hear as that peculiar sound behind us seems to be getting louder: *Wheeeeee!—Burk-burk!—Wheeeeee!* Glance back, I can see the red-and-blue revolving lights above the headlights now.

"Hot damn!" Chief shouts. "Smokey *Bear*! Hot-fuckin'-diddly-*damn*! We got us an *escort*!" He slows down gradually, pulls over to the side. Whipping winds become a gentle breeze.

Squad car stops behind us, siren fades, red-and-blue flashes continue, we can hear a voice on his radio squawking through static. Driver's door swings open, out steps a uniformed officer, tall, heavyset, muscular, trooper type. Walks slowly with the swagger of authority, stands with hands on hips. Name plate over his left breast pocket reads: T. DAMIAN.

"Evenin', Officer Damian," Chief says brightly.

"Good evening, gentlemen."

"You're a sight for sore eyes," Chief tells him.

"May I see your license and registration?"

"Sure thing." Turns, grabs his blazer from the back seat, pulls out his license together with his ID holder and gold shield, hands them over. "Chief of Detectives Walter Vadney, New York Police Department. This here's my brother, Frank, and Detective John Rawlings, also NYPD. We're on official police business."

Damian inspects the ID and license carefully. "Chief Vadney, allow me to remind you of what you already know. You're not on official police business in this country unless you're accompanied by a police officer here."

"We *are*. We're working with—what's his name, Little John?"

"Detective Gordon Kinch."

"I know Kinch." He hands back the ID holder and license. "So where is he?"

"Where?" Chief asks. "I don't know. Probably at Carnival."

"In that case, Chief Vadney, you're not on official police business. Do you have any idea of how fast you were going?"

"Officer Damian, listen, this is an emergency."

"What kind of emergency?" He takes out his pad and pen.

"We're headed for—what's the airstrip, Little John?"

"Chupara Point," Frank answers.

"We're headed for Chupara Point airstrip to stop three men in an unlawful flight to avoid prosecution."

"What's the charge?"

"Suspicion of conspiracy to *murder*! They killed one of our detectives!"

Damian's jotting it all down. "Who are the three men?"

"Dr. Leonard, Dr. Mailer, and Dr. Stegmueller. That's S-t-e-g-m-u-e-l-l-e-r." Chief glances at his watch. "They've got a half-hour head start on us. We've gotta get there before their plane arrives or we've lost 'em for good. Officer Damian, wouldya help us out here? Wouldya please be our escort up there?"

"Certainly." He finishes writing, snaps his pad shut. "I assume you don't want the siren and lights."

"Well, yeah, we'd like 'em on the way up, might be helpful, know what I mean? But then, when we get close to the airstrip, shut 'em off. Huh? Don't want to scare 'em off."

"All right, please follow me. One word of caution. When we get up into the mountains just beyond here, the road is narrow, winding, and has no guardrails. Drive with extreme caution."

"Will do, buddy. Appreciate it."

Damian gives a smart salute, goes back, uses the radio to report what he's up to. Pulls ahead, emergency lights flashing, now he turns on the siren as he picks up speed. Three, four minutes later, we turn left into North Coast Road and start climbing gradually.

I'm crouched down in back, listening to the distant whine of the siren, looking at the stars—they're really bright—hoping we're going to the right place, knowing it's a crap shoot based on experience, and I'm thinking about these guys now, concentrating on them, wondering if I'll ever understand exactly what their motivations were. More complex the people, more complicated the motivations. Thirty-two years on the job and I don't think I've ever been involved in a case even remotely like this one. Money? Fame? Sure. Absolutely. But it's got to go far, far beyond that. With the information I put together tonight, I realize now that they weren't merely waiting those nineteen years for heart-transplant surgery to become an accepted medical procedure; that was part of it, of course, they had to wait for that, but they were clearly waiting for something else to happen: They were waiting for James Mailer Jr. to reach his mid-fifties. No question. The plan was that calculated, that meticulous. He had to be as close to his father's age at death as possible, thereby creating one more unbreakable link in the long chain of events that would attempt to present irrefutable documentation to the scientific community, as well as to the public. Got to give them credit, right? Hell of a plan. Took a lot of patience. Then, finally, fifteen months after the operation, they got their chessmen all set up, they got their game plan down cold, nothing left to pure chance, they're ready for the first move. Stegmueller leaks the intelligence that Mailer was undergoing confidential treatment by a prominent Boston cardiologist back in 1965. Boston office of BCI checks it out. True. Frank Vadney goes to Boston fast, interviews the cardiologist himself, reads the diagnostic report, reads the independent lab reports. All true. Cardiomyopathy. Fatal disease. Next move, Stegmueller leaks the information that during the summer of 1966 Mailer went to Oak Park, Michigan, to visit an old friend, Professor Robert Erickson, founder of the cryonics movement, longtime consultant to ICC. No way for BCI to check it out without detection, so Stegmueller's ready for his third move: Contacts old buddy Chief Vadney, tells him what's happening, says he needs an

investigator who isn't known in the movement, who's had absolutely no connection with the case, but has extensive undercover experience, to infiltrate the movement under the guise of
wanting to arrange for his own cryonic suspension. Chief
thinks on it. Thinks of his scrapbooks. Enter me. Another
pawn. Looking back, I'm certain now that Bob Erickson and
Ed Cerabino weren't involved in the scheme. They were un-
knowing pawns, like me, capable of moving only one step forward at a time.

Ingenious strategy, must admit. Seen in retrospect, it's totally Machiavellian. Vincent Price, patient chess master with
the hawklike eyes. Sends a chill up my ass. I had absolutely no
suspicion that I was being manipulated at any time. I was
plodding, like always, one clue at a time, using logic and experience as well as intuition. Leonard's a consummate actor,
never a false move. Ditto Mailer Jr. Full points. Only chink in
the chain of events that made no sense to me at the time, that I
interpreted as panic on Mailer Jr.'s part, was the murder. Now
I know better.

Stegmueller reasoned that we'd find Mailer down here
sooner or later, helped by a few subtle moves by Leonard, but
then, when we found him, the rest of the story would be quite
predictable. We couldn't collar him, of course, all we could
really do is convince him, through harassment or otherwise, to
make restitution. Is that a big deal after twenty-two years? Is it
a major news event? Would it be a significant enough achieve-
ment, from a media point of view, for Chief Vadney to make
the trip all the way down here, just to accept some research
documents and vials? No. No, Stegmueller understood Vadney's preoccupation with media coverage far too well to risk
his nonappearance for a non-event. He also understood the
potentially more important psychological problem: That Vadney's interest in cryonics, like most laymen's, was marginal at
best. The fact that a human being was frozen for nineteen
years and then brought back to life, by whatever scientific

means, would strike Vadney as morbid, initially, like most laymen, then it might serve as fodder for a variety of earthy jokes, then it would quickly fall back into the realm of the morbid and depressing. However, the same fact, if presented to the media boys and girls in the right way, under the right circumstances, with a dependable clown like Duke Vadney leading the circus and putting his ass on the line, moons up, could trigger that special competitive chemistry that characterizes an exciting, fast-breaking, hard-news story with a decidedly bizarre mass appeal. *National Enquirer* stuff, but with a granite mountain of hard facts to back it up. Which was the atmosphere that Stegmueller not only wanted, but needed. Needed desperately to attract the degree of media attention that would snowball to ensure the eventual success of the whole complex plan. Something would have to happen down here that would guarantee Vadney's appearance, which would in turn guarantee mass-media coverage—but for altogether different reasons.

Namely—and it disgusts me to say this, but it's the truth—the plan obviously called for Louie and me to be killed. If that happened, or if any of the four of us were killed, Vadney would have no choice whatsoever; his appearance on the scene would be a departmental necessity, as it always has been when any cop is killed in the line of duty. This being the case, and given his personality, the Duke would be alert and amenable to any coincidental media event that Grady could milk for what it was worth as an enticing preliminary to the main event (as the headline and lead paragraph of the press release demonstrated only to clearly). So Vadney was slated to be a double pawn in the overall strategy, his emotional reactions anticipated far in advance by a man who thoroughly understood today's real mass-media mentality and priorities—namely, an event's entertainment value (as the media takeover of the press conference demonstrated only too clearly). Of course, Stegmueller had the added advantage of "working" the media people during the long flight down, so that what happened at the start of the press conference wasn't spontaneous in any sense of the term.

But the incredibly cold, clinical, premeditated aspect of the murder is what hits me hard. When that realization dawns on me, then finally sinks in, I'm appalled, disgusted, and really angered. Those three words are the only ones that come close to describing the way I feel. And all three emotions are extremely rare for me on the job. A lovely, bright, talented young lady died because of these monsters, and I'm sure they didn't really give a damn who it was, as long as the killing served its purpose. It did. Terri McBride just happened to be at the wheel.

It's almost midnight when we reach Maracas Bay, clouds have obscured the moonlight and stars, it's become very humid, and we can smell the oncoming rain. Up ahead, Damian's siren continues its monotonous whine. I lean forward, tell Frank that we'd better stop and put the top up while we still have time, that Damian will stop when he sees we're far behind. Wind makes it difficult to hear, so Frank relays the message, Chief pulls over and stops. *Whiiirrr, buzz-buzz, snap-snap,* up it goes. Chief starts up again as we press buttons to close the windows. Now Frank turns on the factory air, full blast at first. Big difference. Damian didn't stop, but we catch up to him quickly. Less than five minutes later, rain begins to sprinkle the windshield, drum on the convertible top. Chief turns on the wipers. About two or three miles beyond Las Cuevas Bay, the two-lane blacktop of North Coast Road ends, to become a narrow dirt road. Damian slows, shuts off his siren and emergency lights. We continue through a field of tall sugarcane that seems almost ready for harvest. Real tall stalks in the headlights, maybe eight to ten feet. Rain sprays in sheets now. Dirt road is full of ruts with puddles, so we slow way down as we bounce through them; couple of times, mud kicks up and splashes our windows.

About five minutes later, Damian switches to his fog lights; means we're probably getting close to the airstrip. Chief does the same. Very little visibility up ahead in the rain. Chief, he's leaning over the steering wheel, squinting, his forehead's almost touching the windshield. Drive along like that for another couple of minutes, then Damian stops, turns off his fog lights. Chief waits until he's right up behind him, stops, kills the engine and fog lights. We sit there in darkness, waiting for our eyes to adjust. Finally, we see what Damian obviously saw. Looks like a clearing just twenty-five, thirty feet ahead. Not as dark up there. Can't see anything more because the sugarcane on both sides of the road blocks our view.

Lights inside the squad car come on as Damian opens the door, steps out, wearing a black poncho, no cap. Lights go off as he closes the door quietly and walks back to us in the rain. Chief lowers his window.

"Can you see the strip?" Damian asks.

"Yeah," Chief says.

"Want to go up and take a look?"

"Yeah."

Rain bounces off Damian's bald pate. "I suggest we go up together, then spread out. Chief Vadney, you and I will go to the right, the others to the left. Keep off the asphalt, stay as close to the cane as you can. We'll each walk toward one end of the runway."

"You have a flashlight?" Frank asks.

"On my belt, yes, but I'd rather not use it until we know what's going on. There's an old lighthouse at the tip of the point, you can't see it from here, it's still in use for the commercial fishermen. As I remember it, the spotlight moves around in a slow circle every minute or so. We might be able to see some of the runway every once in a while when the spot comes around, I'm not sure. All set?"

Frank and I take off our blazers, we all get out, close the doors quietly. Rain is heavy. But cool, nice and cool. Air is like a stimulant. We follow Damian's silhouette, poncho glistening, along the muddy road toward the clearing. As we get closer, we can hear the rain hitting the asphalt; sounds like a hard, steady hissing. Now we get to the end, we pair off, Frank and I to the left. There's a small space to walk between the asphalt and the tall sugarcane.

I spot the lighthouse immediately, we're walking toward it. Spotlight's moving slowly out over the sea, clockwise. There's a wide open space around it. My guess, aircraft probably come in over the sea, heading south, pass over it before landing, then take off over it, heading north. We stand still for a while, wait till the spotlight sweeps around toward the runway. Around it comes, rain flashing through the long, wide shaft of white. Doesn't hit the runway itself, but it illuminates the end of the runway to the south, a big field of sugarcane. Whole landing strip is flanked by cane, except the north tip. And in those few seconds, as I take one sweeping look around, I know we struck out. No aircraft in sight, no car, nothing. It looks to be a fairly short runway, maybe only a couple of hundred yards. Overwhelming emotion I feel is anger. Just pure, frustrated anger. I'm thinking: Shit, we come all this way, we bust our asses, we finally get a break, we get this close, and we blow it. But Frank and I start walking again, drenched to the skin; he had to remove his glasses, he probably can't see too far. I look back a couple of times, try to spot Chief and Damian. Can't see any movement against the dark border of cane.

When we're nearing the open space at the end of the asphalt, I freeze. Squat down fast, grab Frank's arm, pull him down. I think I can see a dark object on the other side of the runway, up near the open end, but back off the asphalt, against the cane. Very, very hard to see it because of the rain. Frank pulls his glasses from his shirt pocket, wipes them off, puts them on, shields the rain with his hands against his forehead. I point. He moves his head behind my hand, squints. I'm breathing fast now, my heart's pumping like crazy. I shield my eyes like him, take another long look. Rain hisses on the asphalt.

He glances at me, nods. "It's a car."

"Yeah. Question is: Is anybody in it? If not, they're long gone. If so, they're waiting."

Spotlight comes around again, ever so slowly, illuminates the field of cane at the far end of the strip; I keep watching the car. Just enough light to see the dark shape: Classic lines of the old Jaguar XKE sports coupe, black, top up, windows closed. Impossible to tell if they're in it. If they are, they might be armed. If we just crouch here and wait for something to happen, Chief and Damian will eventually reach that area. What if they don't see the car in time? Damian isn't armed, of course, so they could be in serious danger. Only thing I can think to do, I pick up a small rock, stand up, throw it high and hard toward the field of cane behind the car, crouch as it falls through the tall stalks; I couldn't hear it hit, but I'm on the other side of the runway. Wait, look, listen. Nothing. Total silence except for the hard spatter of rain on asphalt. Occasional sound of a bird.

"Nobody home," Frank says softly.

"Maybe not. But keep in mind, rain's pouring on the convertible top, on the hood, all over. Also, if they're in there, they're probably talking. Maybe listening to the radio."

Before I finish speaking, we both hear something that's music to our ears: Distant sound of an airplane engine. Definitely not a jet sound, must be a propeller engine. Can't see anything because of the cloud cover. Sound seems to be coming from the southeast. Wait, look, listen. Seems to be moving north, toward the sea. We turn, watch the open area around the lighthouse. Spotlight appears narrow as it swings slowly out to sea. Around it comes, east now, finally south toward us, rain blowing at an angle through the shaft.

Now we see the plane's lights as it banks around, heads south, starts to lose altitude, approaching the runway. Two bright beams in front, small colored lights on the wing tips. Lights are bouncing in the wind and rain; must be a very light craft.

Suddenly, the Jaguar's headlights snap on, high beams, pointing directly down the runway, we can see the broken white center line clearly. Spotlight flashes over the cane field at the far end. Off to our left, here comes the plane, looks like a single-engine Piper Cub from this distance, wing lights bobbing up and down, pilot must be having a shit hemorrhage up there. So what the hell're we gonna do? I know that as soon as the plane touches down, the Jag will race out, follow it to the end, where it'll turn around, board 'em fast, take off immediately. So, I figure, we got just one chance: All three men are sure to be watching the plane as it streaks past them and lands; they won't move until that happens. That's our chance.

I grab Frank's arm. "We'll rush 'em. Follow my lead."

One more look at this light little plane bouncing crazily as it approaches, seems to me it's coming in too high for this short strip, but what do I know? Frank and me, we're standing now, set to run, I'm already breathing hard, adrenaline pumping, heart going nineteen to the dozen. Thought occurs to me, I'm too old for this crap, I could have a coronary halfway across the runway. Frank, he's in shape, first-string tackle at Cornell, you kidding? Now I notice his glasses are back in his shirt pocket, he's squinting, he probably can't even see the car.

SWOOOOOOSH! Plane flashes past us, we're off instantly, sixty-yard dash across the asphalt in the dark, rain stinging our faces, eyes half closed, sprinting toward the side of the Jag, I can see somebody's profile in the glow of the dashboard, he's looking straight ahead at the plane. We're still fifty feet away, I go into a speed gear I didn't know I had, a dozen high-kicking strides, then I *dive* at the hood, last second, *dive,* flat-out, land up on the windshield—*splaaat! KA-BOOM!*—Frank leaps on the convertible top and goes straight through it. *Vaaarrrooom!* Jag's engine ignites, tires squeal, off we blast down the runway. Shatterproof windshield is splintered so badly, they can't see out, I can't see in; soon as we pick up speed, I'm slammed against it, I feel it give, I know I'm sinking into it. *Reeeooow!* Jolt of second gear does it—*crrrackle-pop!* —in it goes intact, in I go on their laps. Tangle of arms and legs, shatterproof glass, rain pouring in, we're still speeding, zigzagging around now, completely out of control, nobody steering. Nobody steering because Frank's throwing punches at all three of them, shots to the backs and sides of their heads, they're ducking, scrambling, screaming.

"Brake it, John!" he shouts. *"Hand brake!"*

Me, I'm squirming around, trying to find it, Frank's big mitt reaches over my head, pulls the ignition key, then reaches under my back, grabs the hand brake, yanks it toward him. *Eeee-keee-rrreee!* Tires burning, smoking, stinking, first we fishtail, then we skid sideways, now we spin completely around. *BOOM!* Tire blows, sounds like a bomb, scares the crap out of me. But we're stopped. My head's still spinning, but we're stopped. Everybody's coughing, bleeding, groaning, swearing. Doors open, we all stumble out in the rain. Where are we? Almost at the end of the runway. Where's the plane? No plane in sight. My guess, he aborted the landing, he was coming in way too high. Now he's probably circled north, he'll give it another try.

Chief and Damian run toward us, pass through the Jag's headlight shafts. Astonished expressions. Stegmueller, Leonard, Mailer are sitting on the asphalt in the rain, out of breath, exhausted, bleeding from small cuts to their faces and hands, picking glass fragments from their clothes. Frank, he's leaning casually against the car, arms folded, legs crossed, smiling at his big brother.

"Frank, John," Chief says. "What—what the fuck happened?"

Kid brother shrugs. "Maybe they gave us an argument."

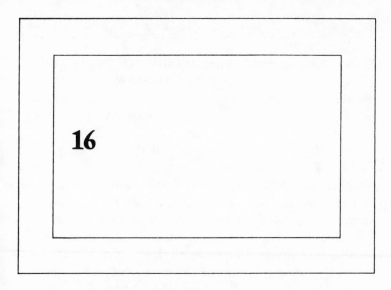

16

W*HEEEEEE!—BURK-BURK!—WHEEEEEEE!*
Squeal into headquarters about 1:25, me in the squad car with
Damian, Frankenstein boys locked in back, Vadney boys hot
on our tail in the magnificent Maz, tear around back, stop at
the door to the lockup. Siren fades into the patter of rain as we
escort our handcuffed gentlemen through the flashing red-
and-blue glare, lockup door's unlocked, in we go. Total darkness. Silence broken by contented snores. Breakthrough
blockbuster news stories filed, presses printing even as they
sleep, media boys and girls are all tucked in for a long winter's
nap. Ho-lee shit. When what to their wondering eyes will appear, but headline-happy schmuck Vadney and Doctahmaylahovaheah. Me, I go hide as soon as the lights go on.
Fluorescent overheads. Daylight white. Twenty-odd pairs of
bloodshot peepers peer from behind the clean white bars of
seven jam-packed coed open-toilet ladies-first cells: *Turndem-*
fuckinlightsoffwillya! — Yafuckinassholes! — Takeafuckin-
hikewillya! — Vadneywhatdafuckyadoinwithdoctahmaylah?

Rude awakening remarks to that effect.

Damian's clearly confused by all this; looks at these strange people, looks at the open cell doors, looks at couples coupled, he can't even pick up on what language they're speaking. Chief takes him aside, explains briefly, tells him to simply follow routine, take the suspects to the front desk to be booked. Dr. Leonard wants to call his attorney, Baden-Smythe, he has that right, he can do it from the desk. Next, first aid for their cuts and bruises, if they need a physician, have Leonard call the Trauma Center, get somebody to come over here. Then it's upstairs for processing until their attorney arrives, fingerprints, mug shots, all standard operating procedures. Damian looks relieved, takes one last look at the foreigners in the cells, hustles the good con men off to the front desk.

"Vadney, whaddaya, *nuts*?" lady's musical voice asks.

"Whatcha got dem *doctahs* cuffed for?"

"What da fuck's goin' *on* heah?"

"*Gee-*zus, we awready filed our fuckin' *stow-*rees!"

"Then *un*file 'em." Chief struts with Frank down the line of cells, looking for Jerry Grady. I come out of hiding to join them, I figure the worst I can get is spit on. Grady's in the corner cell, bunk bed above Louie Diaz; they're both awake now, sitting up. One male reporter's asleep on the floor, wrapped in a brown blanket.

"Jerry, better get dressed," Chief says. "We got a ton of work to do here."

Grady jumps down. "What's happening?"

Chief speaks loudly enough for the reporters in the next cell to hear: "Mailer's an imposter, a con artist, he's actually the *son* of the real Dr. Mailer, the guy who was frozen. It was an ingenious conspiracy—Stegmueller, Leonard, and Mailer— we were all duped, all of us except my brother Frank. Frank found out who Mailer really is, cracked the case, then—"

"Walt, I didn't—" Frank starts.

"—captured 'em on—don't be modest, Frank, this is no time for modesty. Then he captured 'em on an airstrip north of here tonight. Beat the shit out of 'em as they—"

"Walt, that's not—" Frank tries again.

"—were tryin' to escape, that's why they're all bleedin' like that. Kicked the piss out of 'em. They're bein' booked right now, suspicion of conspiracy to murder, suspicion of conspiracy to defraud. They're callin' their attorney, he'll be here shortly. They'll be held over till the arraignment later on this morning, then we'll start extradition proceedings at the embassy."

Two men and a woman in the next cell got their faces pressed against the bars, eyes wide, listening. Instant Chief finishes, they bolt out of the cell in their underwear, yelling: "It's a *con*! Call your editors, it's a *con*!"

Starts a stampede, twenty-odd boys and girls sprint down the hall in various stages of undress, looking for telephones. All except one. Newsman on the floor of our cell, he's got the blanket pulled over his head, he's dreaming sugarplums. Me, I feel sorry for the guy, wouldn't want him to lose his job, I kneel down, reach out to touch his shoulder.

"Don't do it," Louie tells me.

"Why not?"

"He's the guy called Chief Vadney a schmuck."

"Yeah?" Chief says, then lowers his voice: "Him, huh? Ya sure about that?"

"Positive."

"Who's he work for?" Chief whispers.

"*Daily News,*" Grady whispers. "Name's Leo Lipschatz."

Chief puts a finger to his lips, motions all of us out of the cell. Louie and Jerry grab their clothes and shoes, give Leo Lipschatz a wide berth as they leave. Chief closes the cell door very slowly and quietly, then motions for us to follow him down the hall. Off we go.

"Where they keep the cell keys?" he asks Grady.

"I think it's the office just up the hall here."

"Cells numbered?"

"Yeah. We were in number seven."

Chief grins like a naughty kid. "Get the key to number seven. Lock the schmuck in. Then *hide* it."

"Chief, I—I can't do a thing like that."

"That's a direct order, buddy-boy."

"A direct—*why*?"

"Vinnie C., that's why."

"Vinnie C.?"

"Casandra, managing editor of the *News.* "

Grady shuts his eyes in horror. "Oh, shit."

"Sadistic little ratfucker. I been waitin' for a chance to nail that slimebag scrote since—since 'eighty-*one*! Remember that? When he started that fuckin' cartoon series about me and Ed Koch? What was the title? Oh, yeah, 'How'm I doin'?' Makin' us look like dipshits while I was workin' that big hotel heist. Then—then he started that other cartoon series, 'Rambo Bambo,' back in 'eighty-five, remember that one? Day after motherfuckin' day, turnin' the screws, while we were workin' that Great Pyramid gig. Now he's just layin' in wait for me like the slimy, sneaky, shithouse snake that he is, coiled for a biggie legit excuse to fang me in the butt again. Not this time. Now's my chance to catch the pigfucker with his pants down."

"How?" Grady asks.

"How? By keepin' sleepin' Joe Schmuck locked up, that's how. Incommunicado, buddy-boy, unable to call the night city editor, unable to kill the front-page story that's gotta be one of the most embarrassing con jobs the *News* ever fell for. That's gotta leave venomous Vinnie Casandra whistlin' 'Who's Sorry Now?' with his head up his dunghole."

Grady clears his throat, chooses his words with care. "Chief, as you know, all these media people came down here in two-man teams. All the print people came with a reporter and a photographer. Leo Lipschatz is a reporter, but his photographer is probably calling the *News* right now, telling the night city editor to kill the story." Glances at his watch. "We're an hour ahead of New York, so it's only twelve-thirty-five there now, they won't start the first-edition print run for—probably close to another half hour."

"That mean he'd have time to—for the later editions, I mean—he'd have time to write another story, the true story, so we don't look like we fell for all this weird shit?"

"Sure. I'm sure he could dictate one in time for the final."

"Okay, tell you what, Jerry. Go back and wake the man up. Now, listen up, I want you to be very diplomatic about this. Get him up to speed, tell him it's an exclusive for him and him alone, tell him it's my orders, because I happen to like his style, huh? I mean, turn on the charm, know what I mean? And don't forget about Frank, how he cracked the case with his memory, how he captured 'em and all."

"Walt," Frank says, "come *on,* knock it *off.* If anybody deserves credit for cracking this case, it's Rawlings. I mean, I appreciate the thought and all, but let's tell the truth, okay?"

Chief shakes his head, water still dripping from his hair, looks at Grady. "Modesty. Kid was always like that. Always. Still insists on a low profile, Jerry, imagine that? Works this case, on and off, for twenty-one years. Twenty-one *years.* Now he cracks it with his *brains,* he captures 'em with his *fists,* and what's he do? Stands back, wants to give all the credit to an old plodding grunt like Rawlings here. Not that I'm taking anything away from you, Little John, don't get me wrong, buddy, you're gonna get a commendation for this, just like always, you made a contribution too. Jerry, go back there, wake up Leo Schmuck—very gently now, you're his pal, okay?—and tell him the straight shit like I told ya. Frank gets the credit whether he wants it or not. He's earned it in spades. *Daily News,* that's got the biggest daily circulation of any newspaper in the fuckin' *world*! Huh? Who knows, by the time that final edition hits the streets this morning', Frank's gonna be *famous*! Long overdue, Frank. Long, long overdue, buddy-boy. It's high time ya quit being a tackle and start streakin' down that great field of life for some game-winnin' Super Bowl *touchdowns*! Huh? Think of your family! Think of Pat! She picks up that paper this mornin', reads all about your exploits down here, that lovely lady's gonna feel drunk as a fiddler's bitch!''

Even Frank has to smile, wish you could see his face, his eyes, as he studies his brother. Wearing his tortoiseshells again, wiped clean, trim hair wet, white shirt soaked, spattered with blood here and there. Imagine being a kid brother to a guy like Duke Vadney? Imagine the Duke as a teenager? Take away the wrinkles, he still *is*. That's what Frank's eyes tell me: Somehow, Walt's never made the mental transition. He's still a kid. Happens. Looney Tunes all the way, but it's a refreshing change of pace, he's not just an empty suit.

Five, ten minutes later, we're up in the detective squad-room, second floor. Damian's fingerprinted all three men, he's taken their mug shots, I'm impressed. He says arresting officers do basic stuff like this routinely at headquarters, they're trained to, for the simple reason that the department is very understaffed, they just don't have the budget to hire more officers. Stegmueller, Leonard, and Mailer are uncuffed, they're sitting in the corner drinking coffee, waiting for the attorney. Don't know why, but it gives me a strange feeling to see them like this, soaking wet, disheveled, blood-stained shirts, bandages on their faces and hands: Two white-haired old men, mid-seventies, and one my age, who nearly got away with one of the most bizarre cons I ever heard of. Question crosses my mind: What if they'd succeeded? What if they'd eventually convinced the scientific community as well as the public that it was possible, right now, to extend human life almost indefinitely? What would've happened out there? Mass hysteria? Mad rush to buy freezers? Me, I don't think so, but what do I know? My guess, a small number of people would've sunk a large amount of money into the idea, but most of us wouldn't have done anything. Just a guess, but that's the intriguing thing to me: Most of us would've read about it and turned to the next page.

Chief tells Louie and me to go back to the hotel, grab some sleep, he and Frank will meet with Baden-Smythe, wade through all the legal bullshit, schedule the arraignment, all like that. I'm glad to go, I haven't even had dinner, I'm bushed. Louie, he's fully dressed now, but his face still looks like Brando's in the last scene of *Waterfront*. Kid's gotten his taste of what it's like to be a street cop these days. Wouldn't surprise me if he wants to get back to his desk.

We go out into the warm night, it's not quite two o'clock, the rain's finally let up, we can see the stars again. Manage to get a "drop taxi" along Charlotte Street, no other passengers, driver says everybody's still downtown, they'll be celebrating till dawn. Get up to the Hilton about 2:10, lobby's practically deserted, we decide to go out to the pool bar for a nightcap.

Just a few people at the grass-thatched circular bar. Lighted pool looks beautiful, changing colors slowly. Air smells fresh from the rain. Both of us order a double brandy, we figure we've earned it. Now we clink glasses, toast to the good memories of Terri McBride. Only the happy memories, because that's all we have, that's all we'll ever have.

Terri would've wanted it that way.

About the Author

John Minahan is the author of seventeen books, including the Doubleday Award-winning novel *A Sudden Silence,* the million-copy best-seller *Jeremy,* and the six thrillers in this series. An alumnus of Cornell, Harvard, and Columbia, he is a former staff writer for *Time* magazine, and has taught novel writing at Harvard. Minahan and his wife Verity live in Miami.